THE NEGLECTED MOUNTAIN

MALCOLM SAVILLE

Girls Gone By Publishers

COMPLETE AND UNABRIDGED

Published by

Girls Gone By Publishers
4 Rock Terrace
Coleford
Bath
Somerset
BA3 5NF

First published by George Newnes Ltd 1953
This edition published 2009
Text © the estate of Malcolm Saville
Introduction © Mary Cadogan 2009
Malcolm Saville © Mark O'Hanlon 2006
Further Information © Laura Hicks 2005
Lone Pine Shropshire © John Allsup 2009
Map and photographs on pp11–23 © John Allsup 2009
Publishing History © John Allsup 2009
Note on the Text © Sarah Woodall 2009
Appendix I © Sarah Woodall 2009
Design and Layout © Girls Gone By Publishers 2009

Typeset in England by Little Pink Cloud Limited
Printed in England by CPI Antony Rowe

ISBN 978-1-84745-065-4

CONTENTS

INTRODUCTION

In this seventh book of the Lone Pine series the setting is once again, as Malcolm Saville's foreword says, 'the wild and lonely border country between Wales and Shropshire'. As always, Malcolm's descriptions of the natural scene are compelling, but in *The Neglected Mountain* he frequently focuses on the sombre and dramatic quality of the landscape rather than its sunnier aspects. Nevertheless, the overall golden glow which we associate with the stories is still there:

> 'The summer holidays came at last and the Lone Piners converged on Witchend with that wonderful feeling that these were the longest holidays of all and that it was almost impossible to see the end of them.'

The book was first published in 1953. By this time, with the series so well established, the author had to respond to the challenge of keeping the relationships between his main characters fresh and believable. He must have realised that the saga was set to continue for several more books although he could hardly have predicted that almost two-thirds of the Lone Pine stories were still to come!

In *The Neglected Mountain* we see clearly that the Lone Piners are now older than they were when we first met them in 1943 in the first book, *Mystery at Witchend*. David and Petronella ('Peter'), the founders of the Club, are now 16 and so is Tom. Jenny is 15 and the Morton twins, Mary and Dickie, have advanced to being 10 year olds. They—Mary in particular—are shown as being more mature than in the previous books—more discerning, and less inclined to precocity and 'cuteness' than before.

A satisfying element of the story is the strengthening of Peter and Mary's friendship which, like many of the celebrated relationships in school stories, shows Peter as the older girl being very protective of her young friend. Peter, rather than David who is the Captain of the Club, now takes the lead on several occasions, and she blossoms into an extremely engaging personality—so engaging that even the down-to-earth David begins to see her in a new and (slightly) romantic light:

> David … suddenly realized that one day, and very soon now perhaps, other people would look at Peter and see that she was a very beautiful girl.

The Neglected Mountain brings back some popular adult characters who have appeared in previous books. However, the colourful gipsies, Reuben and Miranda, Peter's previously long-lost grown-up cousin Charles Sterling, and Mr Cantor, the professional detective, play only small parts. The main thrust of the action is, as we would expect it to be, with the Club members.

The Lone Piners are always in search of adventure and this book provides plenty of it. There is also a strong sense of mystery. Who is the strange man with no memory who suddenly appears in Peter's home? Does the light which David and Peter, on a late-night walk, see in the distance, come from a crashed aeroplane? Are there strange goings-on in the decrepit, Grimms'-fairy-tale-like house in the forest? And, most puzzling and threatening of all, what is happening to the local canine population?

It soon becomes evident that dogs of all shapes and sizes are being abducted for some mysterious purpose—and the Lone Piners' main task in *The Neglected Mountain* is to rescue and restore them to their owners. Matters come chillingly to a head when the Mortons' Scottish terrier, Mackie, disappears. Mary's selfless devotion to her pet is touchingly conveyed, and all readers who are, or ever have been, dog-owners will empathise with her.

The Club members have to face some of their greatest challenges in this story and, of course, they rise splendidly to these. Peter especially shows enormous courage in jeopardising her own safety when Mary's life seems to be in danger. It is in that dark moment that David becomes very aware of what Peter means to him:

> "Peter! Say something, Peter. Say you're all right, Peter ... Nothing matters if you're all right. You've got to know that, Peter ..."

Yes, delicate hints of romance are in the air, and the Lone Piners are definitely growing up. (At one point in the story they even acknowledge that they are getting a bit too old for simplistic adventure-seeking.)

However, we know that their long literary future is in safe hands! As *The Neglected Mountain* shows, Malcolm Saville knows how to tailor childhood and teenage ambitions to suit the growing maturity of his attractive and extremely resilient leading characters.

Mary Cadogan
2009

7

MALCOLM SAVILLE

Malcolm Saville was born in 1901. His first book, which was written under a pseudonym, was published in 1937, and his career as an author really began to gather momentum from 1943 when *Mystery at Witchend*, which was his first children's book as well as the first title in the Lone Pine series, was published. From that moment onwards writing became a passion that was to dominate his life.

It often comes as a surprise to readers to learn that, despite his prolific output of over ninety books between 1937 and his death in 1982, Malcolm Saville was actually a part-time author insomuch as writing stories for children was not his main profession.

Saville believed strongly that potential authors were more likely to flourish at writing if they also had other careers. Apart from the financial security of having a more reliable income, he believed that it was important to gain experience of life and of people in general before it was possible to write with any authority. It was his belief that this experience was not something that could be gained by sitting with pen and paper poised behind a desk, and this was why he was always so meticulous in researching areas by visiting them in person and reading around the storyline topics that he went on to use in his fiction. It was this accuracy that set his work apart from that of many other authors.

For his own part, with the exception of a 'short break' from the industry during the war years, Malcolm Saville spent his entire adult working life within the publishing arena, in a combination of roles ranging from sales promotion to editorship. No doubt his working-life experiences were an influential source of introductions to a colourful range and variety of real-life characters to whom he could make reference in creating his own fiction.

Having left school when he was 16, Saville carved a career for himself by moving between the larger publishing houses of the day until, in his heyday, he was editing general books published by George Newnes Ltd. It was during this period, while his own secondary career as a writer was flourishing, that he edited the books of some of his more widely remembered contemporaries such as Richmal Crompton, who became a respected friend. Even when he officially retired in 1966 he went on to devote his leisure time to writing and corresponding with his readers, many of whom had now had children of their own and introduced his books to a completely new generation.

Throughout his writing career Saville was more than once faced with the prospect of having to reinvent himself as an author while still maintaining the momentum of his series fiction, an occurrence caused by his lengthy writing career stretching over five decades. This was perhaps most obvious in his non-fiction writing, with, for example, the metamorphosis of his *Country Scrap-Book for Boys and Girls* of the 1940s, through *Malcolm Saville's Country Book* in the 1960s, to a shortened *Country Book* and *The Countryside Quiz* of the 1970s. Far from being a criticism, this shows how Saville constantly adapted to keep up with modern times and the changing demands of his young audience—an approach he also adopted in his fictional storylines. Saville's stories were also characterised by their real geographical settings, and this was evident from the very first in the Shropshire setting of *Mystery at Witchend*.

Mark O'Hanlon
2006

FURTHER INFORMATION

The Malcom Saville Society, formed in 1994, publishes four magazines a year, has a lending library and also organises Saville events. It can be contacted at 19 Strachan Close, Mountsorrel, Leicestershire LE12 7FJ, or via its website www.witchend.com/

The Malcolm Saville Centenary website, at www.malcolmsaville.co.uk/ , created and maintained by John Allsup, contains a wealth of material on Saville and his books, with links to other useful sites.

Mark O'Hanlon has written *Beyond the Lone Pine: a Biography of Malcolm Saville* and *The Complete Lone Pine*; full details of the latter can be found on page 288.

Laura Hicks
2005

Malcolm Saville

LONE PINE SHROPSHIRE

Malcolm Saville set his Lone Pine adventures in real places all over England, and often gave information about these places in the books' forewords. These, although helpful, are naturally very brief, so this slightly extended guide to the locations in *The Neglected Mountain* might be of assistance to readers of the series, especially as the journeys made by the youngsters in the course of this story—the fifth adventure set in Shropshire—involve revisiting the locations of the previous books.

Although the adventures were penned more than fifty years ago, the rural nature of the area means that the landscape and towns have changed very little over the intervening years.

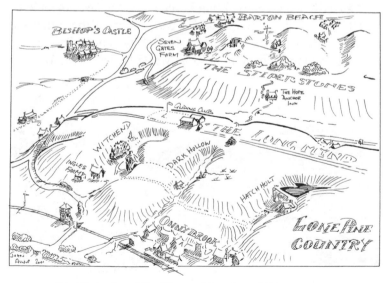

Saville's simplified Long Mynd and Stiperstones

Lone Pine Shropshire is bordered on the north by the county town of Shrewsbury and to the south by the lovely castle-crowned town of Ludlow. The Welsh border hills and Offa's Dyke form the western edge, and the hills on the other side of Church Stretton are the eastern boundary.

Near the centre of this region is the little town of Church Stretton, which became established and gained popularity in Victorian times as a health resort. The town is tucked in against the eastern slope of the Long Mynd. Towards the southern end of this mountain lies the village of Marshbrook, and it was to the house Cwm Head, near here, that Malcolm Saville moved his family away from the bombing of London in the early 1940s. The house looks across to the southern slopes of the flat-topped Long Mynd. In its garden are large mature pine trees, around which the children played.

The eastern side of the Long Mynd is cut into several valleys, locally known as 'gutters', and it was in one of these that the author sited the old house he called 'Witchend'. This house features in the first of the books he wrote for children, *Mystery*

The garage at 'Onnybrook'

at Witchend, the book that started the whole Lone Pine series.

In the book Saville describes the Morton family's journey to the house—leaving the train from Shrewsbury at 'Onnybrook' station, getting a taxi from the local garage, and being driven

*Hamperley farm, the original 'Ingles': the crossroads (above)
and the farmhouse (below)*

13

up the valley past 'Ingles Farm' to their new home, 'Witchend'. The station was in fact at Marshbrook and is no longer there, but the level crossing and the garage where they obtained the taxi can still be found (see p12), as can the lane leading up to the crossroads by Hamperley Farm, the original of 'Ingles'.

The farm spreads over both sides of the turning (see previous page), its barn on the corner of the road up to 'Witchend'. The lane then narrows further—walking here is recommended if you are exploring—and it curves up and ends at the house known as Prior's Holt. This is 'Witchend'.

The Savilles were friendly with the family living in Prior's Holt, and the author adopted the house's location for his first story. The location, if not the description of the building, is exact. A stream runs across in front of the house and on the opposite slope there is a larch wood. The track that runs by it leads on up the valley past the site of the original Lone Pine, and eventually appears on the top of the Mynd.

Prior's Holt, the original 'Witchend'

A glider over the Portway on the top of the Long Mynd (above), and the view down to the reservoir in Carding Mill valley from the top of the Mynd (below)

On the top is the Portway—the track runs the length of the Mynd—and nearby is the gliding station where, in *The Neglected Mountain*, Peter's father finds the 'Doctor' looking for his friend on the mountaintop.

Readers of *Mystery at Witchend* will recall the children's meeting with Peter by the waterfall in 'Dark Hollow'. In reality this is Callow Hollow, a valley a little to the north of Prior's Holt. 'Hatchholt' reservoir, beside which Peter and her father live, is in Carding Mill Valley, still further north, and sadly lacking any cottage.

The Long Mynd is aligned approximately south-west to north-east. More or less parallel to it but further west is the ominous mountain ridge known as the Stiperstones. From the top of the Mynd this can be seen as a crest crowned with high rocky outcrops, the most significant of which is the one known as the Devil's Chair.

In *The Neglected Mountain* David and Peter repeat the hike that he made with the twins in *Seven White Gates*, taking a break at 'The Hope Anchor'. This inn, which also appears in the earlier book, is really The Bridges Inn, about halfway between the mountains. Its fictional name comes from Rye. If you look for the 'Gay Dolphin Hotel' at the end of Watchbell Street ('Trader's Street' in the books) in Rye, you will find the inn's namesake.

Beyond the inn a stony track leads up to the Stiperstones. The author condensed the journey for dramatic purposes, but kept true to the locations.

Of all the Lone Pine locations, the one that has the strongest presence is the Stiperstones. There is an ominous feel about the place that suffuses the stories set hereabouts—so much so that, years after reading the books, I still feel unease here.

Surprisingly, Malcolm Saville had not visited the Stiperstones area when he wrote *Seven White Gates*. He seems to have gained

The track leading up to the Stiperstones ridge

his knowledge of the geography and its sombre atmosphere from the works of Mary Webb, and also from an excellent book, first published in 1935, called *Through the Highlands of Shropshire on Horseback* by Magdalene Weale. This author had explored all of the area around the mountain on horseback, and recounts her travels entertainingly and with insight. She paints a telling picture of the countryside and the characters she meets along the way. Saville made good use of her experience and knowledge.

That Saville could absorb and regenerate the atmosphere of the area is remarkable; however, the detail of his Stiperstones differs somewhat from that on the ground. He introduces the area in *Seven White Gates* by describing Peter's cycle ride from her school at Shrewsbury. After an important meeting with some travelling gipsies she eventually arrives at the village of 'Barton Beach'. This village, the home of Jenny, might well be a very modified Stiperstones village, and the two valleys cutting into the western slopes, 'Black Dingle' and 'Greystone Dingle', may well be based on Perkins Dingle and Crowsnest Dingle respectively—but few recognisable landmarks are to be found.

*One of the rocky outcrops on the Stiperstones ridge (above),
and an abandoned mine on the same mountain (below)*

However, the land is littered with abandoned mine-workings and ruined buildings, just as described in the books. Even now, when many have recently been tidied and stabilised, Magdalene Weale's label of 'Land of Dereliction' and Jenny's 'neglected mountain' seem to fit the landscape perfectly. Above these abandoned workings and dark dingles the massive rocky outcrops crown the skyline.

Although the Devil's Chair itself exists, the farm below it, the oddly named 'Seven White Gates', is an invention. Some of its features are adopted from West End Farm near Harpenden, where Saville lived, but the farm is essentially a figment of the author's imagination.

On the western edge of Lone Pine Shropshire are the towns of Bishop's Castle and Clun. The former appears in

Looking down into one of the Stiperstones dingles

The King's Head, Bishop's Castle

Lone Pine Five: it is the market town where Jenny and Tom meet up, and you will find the yard where sales were held each market day through the arch behind the King's Head (named the 'Rose and Crown' in *Lone Pine Five*). Here Tom bids for a spoon …

On market days Bishop's Castle's steep main street resounds still with the atmosphere of a busy country town. This town is also where Charles Sterling's fiancée grew up and where her father has his vet's practice, crucial to the plot of *The Neglected Mountain*—as is the fair on the town's show field.

A handful of miles to the south of Bishop's Castle lies the little town of Clun. Here the author gathered all eight Lone Piners for the fourth adventure in the series, *The Secret of Grey Walls*. Clun is beautifully described. Its ruined castle, which became HQ3 in that adventure, stands on its own hill just to the north of the river. It was here that the swearing-in of Jon and Penny to the Club was carried out in great secrecy.

Clun: looking down to the valley, with town and church to the left and castle to the right

Clun castle

Another view of Clun castle

The Buffalo Inn, Clun, which features in
The Neglected Mountain

The Buffalo Inn and the ancient bridge across the River Clun are still to be found in this little town exactly as described in the books. Crossing the bridge and turning to the west you can find the farm Buryfield. Alan Denton's farm, 'Bury Fields', is shown on the maps in Malcolm Saville's books as being to the north of Clun. However, according to the story it is across the river to the south (see p26 for more about this anomaly). Beyond Buryfield, Offa's Dyke curves south across the hills. One of the walks in Robert Smart's book (see p25) leads this way and passes Garbett Hall, possibly the inspiration for the mysterious house 'Grey Walls'.

Clun bridge

Ludlow, visited by the twins in *The Neglected Mountain*, is crowned by its castle and edged by the River Teme. The town is a delight to visit and has many attractions for the explorer. Not the least of these is the café that the twins use in this book, which is at the top of Broad Street, just below the town's Buttercross. It is in fact the famous De Grey's Café, with its timbered front and long, dark-timbered interior. All of its traditional fittings

23

would have been there when the book was written, and it is easily recognisable from the description in the story. Broad Street runs steeply downhill from here to Ludford Bridge: here, as the Teme rushes by below, the twins meet to talk privately with the enigmatic Mr Cantor.

Shropshire has had many fictional visitors: Ellis Peters's Brother Cadfael tramped this country from Shrewsbury Abbey; in Wodehouse's Shropshire the delightful Lord Emsworth exhibited his beloved Empress of Blandings at the local agricultural shows; and Mary Webb's characters lived here in superstition and wild emotion. It was, however, Malcolm Saville who brought the young folk to Shropshire. The Mortons steamed north during the early years of the Second World War and teamed up with others to form friendships that in their turn influenced thousands of readers to share the lasting values of friendship and trust which have kept his stories alive for more than half a century—all amidst some of the most beautiful scenery in England.

If you have never visited Lone Pine Shropshire, do. You won't regret it.

John Allsup
2009

Further reading

O'Hanlon, Mark. *The Complete Lone Pine*, Revised edition, Ludlow, Mark O'Hanlon, 2005, ISBN 0 9528059-4-4
A detailed analysis of all things Lone Pine. See page 288 for more information.

Saville, Malcolm and O'Hanlon, Mark. *The Silent Hills of Shropshire*, Ludlow, Mark O'Hanlon, 1998, ISBN 0-9528059-1-X (paperback).

A book that Saville never completed, which has been finished by Mark O'Hanlon.

Smart, Robert. *Church Stretton & South Shropshire Walks*, ISBN 0-9529539-0-0

An inexpensive but excellent guide to walks in the area, with notes on Lone Pine locations: an essential guide to exploring the area on foot. For more information, availability, current price etc, contact Robert Smart, Church Stretton, Shropshire SY6 6DS.

PUBLISHING HISTORY

The Neglected Mountain was first published in September 1953. An advertisement (see right) from the back page of the glossy *Young Elizabethan* Magazine describes it as 'Another thrilling adventure set in the wild and lonely border country between Wales and Shropshire', and the story is indeed set throughout the Shropshire border country, which is the spiritual home of the Lone Piners.

Maps have always attracted me, and *The Neglected Mountain* is a veritable atlas of Lone

Advertisement from the Collins Young Elizabethan *Magazine, October 1953, back page*

Pine Shropshire. The story uses three journeys made by pairs of characters to link the locations of the previous Shropshire books. A map of the route accompanies each of these journeys. These maps are in addition to the usual endpaper map. That for Tom and Jenny's journey has an error, probably deriving from the map oddity that I described in the publishing history for the GGBP edition of *The Secret of Grey Walls*: north and south are reversed in Clun. The castle and the Buffalo Inn are shown on the south bank of the river and Denton's farm, Bury Fields, appears incorrectly to the north.

The first edition, which was published at 8s 6d, has tan cloth boards with the pine tree logo on the front board, and lettering there and on the spine in red. It consists of 248 pages with map endpapers (see pp36–7), and has a title-page vignette of Mackie and eight full-page illustrations, all by Bertram Prance. All of the original illustrations are reproduced in this GGBP edition.

Bertram Prance's atmospheric picture for the dustwrapper, reproduced on the cover of this GGBP edition, shows Peter and David on their night climb to the Devil's Chair. They are accompanied, for the picture only (according to the text he did not join them on the climb), by Mackie.

Newnes reprinted the book in 1959 and again in 1965. Both these impressions are bound in blue cloth but are otherwise as the first edition. The six-year gap before the first edition was reprinted may be the result of a large print run, or perhaps of the choice of this book as the first of the Lone Pine series to be published by Foyle's Children's Book Club. Their edition is not dated, but it would have appeared a year or more after the first, and was probably produced in large numbers. It was priced at 3/6, less than half the price of the first edition. It has all the original text, maps and illustrations but is more cheaply bound in plain, light-green cloth with no logo on the front board. The dustwrapper shows the twins approaching two gipsy caravans (see overleaf). This artwork is not credited.

In the 1950s and 1960s paperbacks had not really taken off for children's books. Various publishers did produce them— Collins and Blackie both had books at 2/- each and Penguin Books launched Puffins—but it was not until May Fair Books produced the Armada series in 1962 that the scene changed.

Armada books were cheaply produced but had a bright, cheerful appearance, and the prices were low enough for children to buy their own copies. And they had very popular authors. The

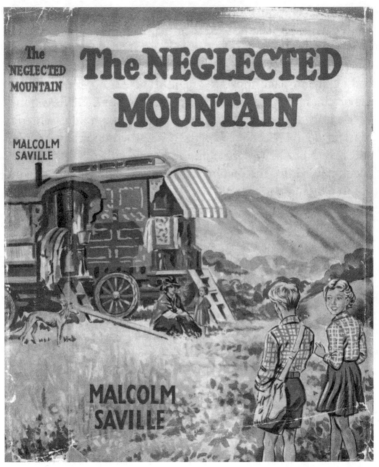

The Children's Book Club edition—cover artist not credited

first books in the series included titles by Enid Blyton and W E Johns, Monica Edwards and Malcolm Saville. They were soon found in displays in local corner shops. Newsagents as well as bookshops stocked them—and they sold.

The books were mostly of a standard size and so were edited and abridged to fit a length of about 190 pages. The earlier ones had some, at least, of the books' illustrations, but those selected for publication later on had their illustrations removed. They were printed on cheap paper and poorly bound, but these disadvantages were outweighed by their easy availability.

Five other Malcolm Saville titles had already been published by Armada when *The Neglected Mountain* appeared in 1964 as number C78—the first of the Lone Pine series to appear in paperback in Britain. Peter Archer's lively front cover design (see below) shows Tom and Jenny meeting with Reuben and his family, and the rear depicts David and Peter looking at the air crash on the Long Mynd. The book has all the maps and

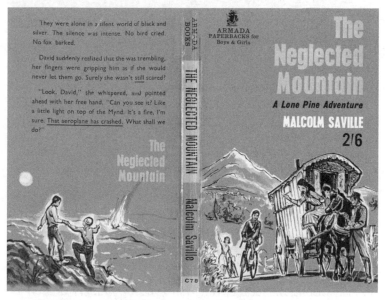

The first Armada edition, 1964—cover by Peter Archer

illustrations of the original, the foreword—here titled 'Older than the Ice Age'—and the usual short introduction to the characters under the heading 'The Lone Pine Club' (but without the paragraph about Jon and Penny Warrender).

The Armada edition of *The Neglected Mountain* was reprinted several times, I'm sure, before reappearing in 1969 as number C295. Armada reprints can normally only be recognised by price changes, but as inflation was negligible in the 1960s the price remained constant until this new edition was produced. The major change at that time was to the cover (see below), which shows David and Peter being confronted by a loose guard dog on the front, and Peter's dramatic fall on the

The second Armada cover from 1969—again credited to
Peter Archer

back. The cover artwork is credited to Peter Archer, although the style differs from that of his earlier work. The vignette of Mackie, present on the half-title page of number C78, is missing from number C295; the foreword has lost its new title and is slightly expanded; and the 'Lone Pine Club' piece is rewritten (See Appendix II). In their text, maps and illustrations the books are otherwise identical. Decimalisation was under way: hence the dual cover price of '2/6 12½p'. This book was reprinted regularly, appearing at five different prices in the subsequent decade; the final impression in 1978 cost 50p.

Collins took over the Armada imprint at the end of the 1960s and not only continued to issue Malcolm Saville's books in the Armada guise, but also reprinted some as hardbacks with dustwrappers or as cheaper 'Budget' hardbacks with pictorial boards. Most of the Lone Pine series appeared in one or the other, or indeed both, of these hardback formats; but *The Neglected Mountain* did not. No reason for this omission is known.

The dominance of paperbacks within the children's book market by the 1980s might well have been one of the reasons why John Goodchild launched his new hardback editions. This was a brave and a welcome move, and did provide an outlet for authors whose work was considered 'dated' by the mainstream press of the time. Unfortunately, however, the books were edited, abridged and modified. The illustrations were not used, and the text was chopped and changed in an attempt to update it. Fortunately the main lines of the plot remained and in *The Neglected Mountain* the maps are there, all reproduced from the Newnes originals.

With all their faults these Goodchild editions are attractive books, and Gordon King's splendid wraparound dustwrappers set them off beautifully. For *The Neglected Mountain* he painted David, Peter and Mary with Mackie tumbling down

The Goodchild edition, 1986—artwork by Gordon King

the rockslide into the darkness, backlit by the light from a mysterious stranger's torch (see above). The horror of the episode's description in the book is, however, somewhat at odds with the cheerful appearance of the characters on the cover.

There are no other editions in English, and only one foreign edition has come to light. It will be no surprise to the avid collector of Lone Pine Books that this is from the Spanish publisher Molino, who published their translated edition of the book in hardback in 1965 as *La Montaña Abandonada*, with a dustwrapper (see opposite) by Pablo Ramirez. The book is 208 pages in length and contains seven of the original Bertram Prance illustrations; the fairground picture from chapter VII is missing. Also missing are the vignette of Mackie, the endpaper map and the map of the twins' journey. However, the other two journey maps are included—redrawn and with text in Spanish. These maps are neither signed nor credited.

The Spanish edition, published by Molino in 1965 with artwork by Pablo Ramirez

The advertisement mentioned at the beginning of this article stated that *The Neglected Mountain* was 'a new book in the famous Lone Pine series, the first, and still the most popular books, by Malcolm Saville'. That statement is still true, as shown by the continuing success of the series in its republication by Girls Gone By. The author would be surprised and, I'm sure, delighted to see this new edition more than 55 years after its first appearance.

John Allsup
2009

NOTE ON THE TEXT

For this Girls Gone By edition we have used the text of the first edition; it contained some typographical errors, and in Appendix I we explain what we have done about them. We hope we have not introduced any new ones.

We have reproduced the illustration captions and the text of the List of Illustrations exactly as they were in the original (some of the wording differs slightly between the captions themselves and the versions in the list).

There is an error in one of the hand-drawn labels in the map on page 133—'had' is obviously missing in 'Here they an ice cream'—but we have not attempted to correct this.

Sarah Woodall
2009

COMPLETE NUMERICAL LIST OF LONE PINE TITLES

1. *Mystery at Witchend*, London, Newnes (1943)
2. *Seven White Gates*, London, Newnes (1944)
3. *The Gay Dolphin Adventure*, London, Newnes (1945)
4. *The Secret of Grey Walls*, London, Newnes (1947)
5. *Lone Pine Five*, London, Newnes (1949)
6. *The Elusive Grasshopper*, London, Newnes (1951)
7. *The Neglected Mountain,* London, Newnes (1953)
8. *Saucers Over The Moor*, London, Newnes (1955)
9. *Wings Over Witchend,* London, Newnes (1956)
10. *Lone Pine London,* London, Newnes (1957)
11. *The Secret of the Gorge,* London, Newnes (1958)
12. *Mystery Mine,* London, Newnes (1959)
13. *Sea Witch Comes Home*, London, Newnes (1960)
14. *Not Scarlet But Gold*, London, Newnes (1962)
15. *Treasure at Amorys*, London, Newnes (1964)
16. *Man With Three Fingers*, London, Newnes (1966)
17. *Rye Royal*, London, Collins (1969)
18. *Strangers at Witchend*, London, Collins (1970)
19. *Where's My Girl?*, London, Collins (1972)
20. *Home to Witchend*, London, Armada (1978)
[21. *The Flower-show Hat* in *The Guide Gift Book* (1950), Worcester, Malcolm Saville Society (2000)]

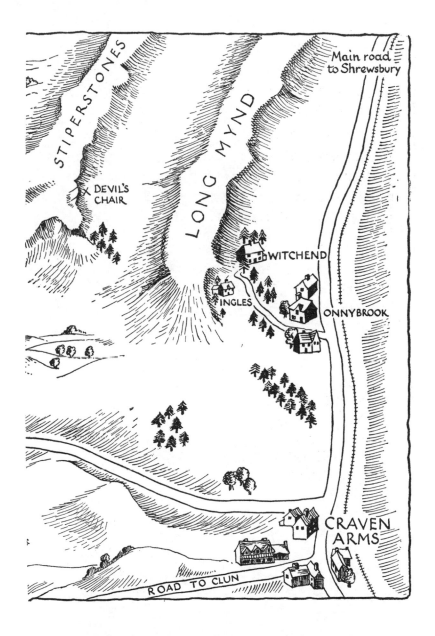

THE NEGLECTED MOUNTAIN

A LONE PINE STORY

BY
MALCOLM SAVILLE

Illustrated by
BERTRAM PRANCE

FOREWORD

THE scene of this story is in the wild and lonely border country between Wales and Shropshire, hard by a mountain known as the Stiperstones. It is said that the curious outcrop of black quartzite rocks on the summit, known as the Devil's Chair, is one of the oldest parts of England—older even than the ice age—and it is little wonder that this desolate, neglected country is rich in folk-lore and legend.

You will find the Stiperstones and the Long Mynd with its Gliding Station on the map and you can go to Shrewsbury, to Clun and Craven Arms and Bishop's Castle and explore them for yourself. But you will not find Black Dingle or Greystone Dingle or Barton Beach, for these places are as imaginary as are all the characters in this story.

M. S.

CONTENTS

LIST OF ILLUSTRATIONS

THE LONE PINE CLUB

IF this is the first story you have read about the Lone Pine Club and its members you will probably enjoy it more if you know something about them both before you begin.

The Club was started by some boys and girls at a lonely farmhouse called Witchend, in the heart of the Shropshire hills. Readers who have known the members for some time have asked that they should not grow up from book to book, and so they will continue to have adventures at their present ages.

The Club rules, which were originally signed in the members' blood and are kept hidden under the solitary pine tree in their first secret camp, are very simple and are set out in full in "Mystery at Witchend." The most important rule is "To be true to each other whatever happens," and this, as most of us would agree, is a good start to any Club. There are other rules about being kind to animals, and one very honest statement that the Club was for "exploring, watching birds and trailing strangers." So far the Lone Piners have trailed strangers with more enthusiasm than they have watched birds, and it is true that they seem to have a happy knack of finding adventures.

As the members live many miles apart and go to different schools—all, that is, except Tom Ingles, who works on his uncle's Shropshire farm—they can meet only in the holidays.

The original headquarters of the Club is still the old camp, with its sentinel pine tree, at Witchend, but others have been established as necessity arose—one in the barn at a lonely farmhouse called Seven Gates, which is described in this story, and another at the ruined castle of Clun, some miles to the south, near the Welsh border.

The Lone Piners' secret signal to each other is a whistled imitation of the peewit's plaintive call.

The Members

DAVID MORTON. The captain of the Club. Aged sixteen and sometimes, to his more impetuous friends, rather infuriatingly steady. He is a good leader, has never let down any of his friends and can be relied upon in any crisis. The Mortons live near London, but some of the family come to Witchend whenever they can in the holidays.

RICHARD ("DICKIE") MORTON and MARY MORTON. These two are ten-year-old twins and although they have recently been sent to separate boarding schools, they are inseparable at all other times. They are alike in looks and speech and occasionally in thought. Mary, the elder by an hour, is the more level-headed. They are often extremely irritating to their friends, and particularly to grown-ups, but they will tackle anything and have the outstanding qualities of courage and of loyalty to each other and to their friends.

PETRONELLA ("PETER") STERLING. Peter is sixteen, and this is really her book. She has no mother, but lives in the holidays with her old father, who is in charge of a reservoir called Hatchholt, not very far from Witchend. Her father has made great sacrifices to send her to boarding school in Shrewsbury, but she is only really happy when she is roaming her beloved Shropshire highlands on her Welsh pony, Sally. Perhaps it is because she is so independent that she still persists in wearing her hair in two fair plaits. Her fearless eyes are as blue as forget-me-nots and her skin always clear and brown. She looks nice in anything, but most comfortable in jodhpurs and a blue shirt. She knows the stars better than most of us know a map of our own county. She loves animals and everything in the open air and can swim faster than most boys of her age, and ride ten times better.

Peter has never been afraid of solitude and does not make friends easily, but her life was changed when the Mortons came to Witchend, for then she realized how lonely she had been. She is the Vice-Captain of the Club and David is her special friend.

TOM INGLES. Nearly sixteen, a Londoner who now lives and works on his uncle's farm only about half a mile from Witchend. There is no nonsense about Tom, who has a quick wit and an even quicker tongue, and is liked by everyone who meets him. At times he pretends that the Club "is only fit for kids," but he is exceedingly proud of his membership.

JENNY HARMAN. Was born in Shropshire and lives in a lonely village called Barton Beach, not far from Seven Gates. She is fifteen and small for her age. Her father keeps the local newspaper shop and post office, but she does not get on particularly well with her step-mother. Peter befriended her when she was lonely and miserable and badly needed a friend, and although the others all tease her, anybody can say anything so long as Tom will stand by her. And he always does.

There are two other members of the Club who do not appear in this book—JONATHAN and PENELOPE ("PENNY") WARRENDER. These two are cousins and firm friends, but they live at Rye, in Sussex, and cannot often meet the others.

There is one more member of the Morton family who thinks the Club belongs to him. He is MACBETH—a black Scottie dog—who loves them all, but especially Mary, who has nearly wrecked many an adventure because she will carry him when his short legs tire. Mackie plays a very important part in this story.

CHAPTER I

FORCED LANDING

IT was the last evening of the Easter holidays and six children and one black Scottie dog were sitting round a trestle table set in the open doors of a huge barn. A chilly wind was sighing through the tops of the dark pine trees in the wood below the lonely farmhouse and a few bats were fluttering crazily in the dusk. The clouds over the great bulk of the mountain towering over the house were touched with crimson as the sun went down behind the wood.

The eldest boy, David Morton, looked down the table with disapproval at his twin brother and sister as the latter picked up the Scottie from the floor, put him on her lap and allowed him to lick the plate which, a few minutes ago, had been piled with bacon and baked beans.

"Why do you spoil him so, Mary?" he said. "You teach him the most disgusting manners. I've thought once or twice lately that he's getting out of hand. He's disobedient."

"Oh, no, he's not. He's wonderful. Acksherly, Dickie and me have noticed lately that really he only obeys people he likes and respecks … Anyway, this isn't spoiling him. It's just teaching him tidy habits and nice manners, like never leaving anything on his plate … You're not spoiled, are you, my darling?"

Her twin guffawed loudly as Mackie's pink tongue scooped up the last taste of bacon fat and then licked Mary's face in love and appreciation.

Then, "If everybody's finished," he said, "we may as well do something else, as it's gettin' dark. Mary and me thought we'd just have a last stroll an'—"

Tom Ingles, sitting next to him, forced him back on to the bench with a heavy hand.

"Oh, no, you don't, my lad. We've all heard that story before. It's your turn to wash-up and no excuses. Jenny and Peter got the meal and you wash it up. I reckon Mackie will help you if you speak to him nicely."

Jenny Harman, the red-headed girl with freckles sitting opposite, leaned across the table.

"Don't let any of us do anything special yet, please. Let's just sit here as it gets darker and tell stories and talk about the things we've done and maybe what we'll do next holidays, which are the best of all 'cos they're the longest. You don't know how I hate it when you all go away and the Club has to break up. There's just nothing but going in to school every day and helping Dad a bit in the shop on Saturdays. I wish some of you would write to me sometimes. Why don't you?"

"I will," Mary said promptly. "I don't seem to have much time at school because they all bully us smaller ones round so much that there isn't time even for the things we want to do most. But I'll write to you, Jenny, if you'll write me one of your really thrilling letters back."

"Of course, I will, Mary. I should have thought there would have been some others here who could spare a few minutes sometimes for someone like me who's lonely all the time," and here she looked meaningly at Tom, who only stuffed his hands in his pockets and grinned at her.

"No good looking at me like that, Jen. I'm a working man as you know. Uncle Alf keeps me jolly busy and I never was much of a hand at letters … He said the other day that he has so many forms to fill up every week that there'll be a job for a smart girl at Ingles soon … Maybe you'd better apply for it."

Jenny put out her tongue at him and turned to the slim, fair girl sitting near the door.

"What about you, Peter? You'll write to me, won't you? Don't you *hate* going off to school every term and leaving your darling old father all alone at Hatchholt?"

Petronella Sterling, who had been sitting with her elbows on the table and her chin on her brown hands, got up and leaned against the doorpost and looked out across the farmyard.

"Of course I don't like leaving him, but it's to please him that I go. He's not one of those people who get lonely, Jenny. You know what he is. He knows every inch of the Long Mynd and our valley, and in the evenings, when it's light enough, he potters in the garden and keeps an eye on Sally for me. Then he likes some of the programmes on the radio and he's crazy on his books, most of which he knows by heart ... And then Uncle Micah and Aunt Carol go over from here to see him sometimes on Sundays, and once or twice a term he comes to Shrewsbury on a Saturday and takes me out, and that's grand ... I always do write to you, Jenny, anyway, so why are you making such a fuss to-night?"

"I don't know, except that I hate the end of nice things and specially the end of holidays. I'm sure I'm going to be lonely because, you see, there's only Tom near me in term-time and, as he said just now, he's a working man and is much too busy for his friends. I expect I shall do a lot of reading."

They laughed at this because Jenny's reading habits were familiar to them all. Try as they would, they could never cure her of her taste for romantic novelettes, and although she was teased unmercifully she just said that she knew what she liked and that they didn't know what they were missing.

"You can laugh," she went on good humouredly, "but I believe there's the most wonderful romance going on in this very house, right under our very noses this very minute. Did *you* notice anything, Peter? I mean when Charles drove up before supper with that girl from Bishop's Castle. I forget her name."

"Yes, Jenny, I know what you mean. They looked thrilled and excited. I did notice. Her name is Trudie. Trudie Whittington, and her father is the vet. in Bishop's Castle. Wouldn't it be thrilling if they're going to get married?"

"I s'pose it would for them," David said as he got up and went over to the open doorway with her. "But I can't see what it's got to do with anybody else and why it's so thrilling and exciting for us."

"Don't try and be grown-up, David," Peter said. "Anyway, Charles is my cousin and the most wonderfully handsome man I've ever met. I agree with Jenny, that maybe there's a romance brewing. How can we find out without being too nosey?"

"Send these cheeky twins over to the house to wash-up. They'll nose out anything," Tom suggested. "It's getting dark. Shall I light up and put some more wood on the stove? Perhaps we'll want to sit up late to-night and it's getting colder."

The barn in which the Lone Piners were camping belonged to the farm known as Seven Gates, which was owned by Peter's uncle, Micah Sterling. Mr. Sterling's son, Charles, who just before the war had quarrelled with his father and gone to America, came home not long ago, shared an adventure with the Lone Piners, made up the old, foolish squabble and was now running the farm for his father. They all liked and admired Charles.

Uncle Micah, who had never forgotten how the Lone Piners had helped him to find his son again, gave them the great barn for their own use and they knew they were always welcome at Seven Gates. They called the barn HQ2 because it was their second headquarters. It was pillared and vaulted like a church and above it, under the roof, was another little room which the girls used as their dormitory. Below, along one side, were six divisions which once had been used for storing grain and now made bedrooms for the boys. At the far end was an old iron stove with a chimney, on which they did their cooking. HQ2 was a fine, roomy indoor camp and they knew how lucky they were to have it when they wanted it.

But Seven Gates was not otherwise a cheerful place. It was over a mile uphill from the village of Barton Beach, where Jenny lived, and was built in the shadow of a lonely mountain called the Stiperstones. Once the Romans had mined these solitary hills for lead, and it was not so very many years ago that mining on a large scale was finally abandoned, although it is still possible to see traces of the old workings and some parts of the hills are still honeycombed with galleries and caves.

For some reason which is difficult to explain, the Stiperstones country has a bad reputation. It has always been lonely and most of the cottages used by the miners in the dingles are now deserted ruins. Many people living in Barton Beach, including Jenny, will not venture out on the mountain at night, or, indeed, at any time when the piled, black rocks known as the Devil's Chair on the summit are hidden by the mists which so often come sweeping over the hills from Wales. At such times, when the Chair is hidden, the natives say, "He's on his throne," and go into their houses and bolt the doors. Superstitions in remote country districts die hard; but many strangers who come for the first time to this wild and lonely country feel something of the strange spell which it seems to cast over all those who live in the shadow of the mountain.

Peter turned from the door and with a quick change of mood, laughed when she saw the expression on the faces of the twins.

"You heard what Tom said, twins. Your turn to wash-up. Aunt

Carol won't mind you using the scullery and perhaps you'll be able to pick up a little gossip about Charles and Trudie."

"Wash-up?" Dickie said in shocked surprise. "You really want us to wash-up? On our last night here? You just can't ask us to do that, Peter. Why, we're *guests* here. You know we are. Old Uncle Micah is *your* uncle and you practically live here and we're quite sure guests are never asked to wash-up ... It just isn't done, Peter."

"Yes, it is," David said firmly as he yanked the twins to their feet by the collars of their wind-cheaters. "No arguing. Remember the Club rules."

"Club rules?" Mary squeaked. "There's nothin' in the rules about washing-up ... If there was we wouldn't have joined, would we, twin? ... Let us go, David, you beastly bully."

David laughed. "We'll help you carry the crocks over and if you don't fall asleep when you come back you can sit up with us until you do."

While the twins were away Tom threw some more wood on the stove and pulled up a bench, while David fetched two of their straw mattresses.

"It will be too cold to sit outside, but the moon will soon be up. Let's do as Jenny says for our last night and sit round here until we fall asleep ... You can curdle our blood with Stiperstones stories, Jen. Tell us the ghostliest ones you know."

"It's all very well for you to laugh, David. You don't live up here. Really, you're only a visitor. Even Peter, who's lived all her life at Hatchholt, doesn't quite know how the Stiperstones people feel. Don't you remember how scared I used to be about this very place? I wouldn't come up to Seven Gates alone through what we still call the whispering wood for anything— not even now I wouldn't ... And there's the Dingle, too. I still hate that. It's difficult to explain, but I do."

Tom sat down on the bench and stretched his legs out towards the stove.

"You're a silly kid, Jen. I don't rightly see how you can be scared of *places*, but I'll believe you if you say you are. I've never been scared of a place, but I have of people … Trouble with you is that you read too many silly books."

"I never thought you'd turn against me, Tom," she said as she sat on the mattress at his feet. "If you don't understand me, I'm sure Peter does. I know she understood me the very first time we met when I was terrified of the wood and the Dingle and of Uncle Micah, too, before he changed and shaved off his beard. You know what I mean, don't you, Peter?"

"Of course I do. Sometimes I get the most peculiar feelings about *people* when I first meet them, but not so often about places, like Jenny does. I don't care what anybody says, but I know that I wouldn't go alone up to the Devil's Chair at night. I don't like Black Dingle either, but now that people are happy here, at Seven Gates, I'm sure we all feel differently about it. I know it's a hideous house and I know it's lonely. Once, when I first came here by myself, I was terrified of it, but we found Charles for them and Uncle Micah stopped rumbling in his beard like a prophet in the Bible and walking about the hills at night, and everything seemed to change and it's been different ever since."

"Maybe it's because the people changed," David said shrewdly. "I don't really think there's anything frightening about one place more than another. If you feel scared of the Chair at night, Peter, the thing to do is to go up there and see if there's a reason for it. I'll come with you."

"Don't be so superior," Peter replied. "I just know that at Hatchholt I'm not scared of anything. Often I've walked up to the head of our valley and along the top of the Mynd at night.

I've done it in winter when there's no moon and I've only had the stars to tell me which way I'm going. I've never felt frightened of the Long Mynd and that's lonely enough. You can walk or ride ten miles along the top and never see anybody."

"It's lonely in a different way," Jenny tried to explain. "The top of the Mynd is wide and smooth, and although it's lonely it's not cruel ... If you won't laugh at me I'll tell you what I think about this country here and the Stiperstones. Dad told me once that people have often come here to try and make money in the old mines and to see what they can find inside the mountain. Some of them, he said, have stayed quite a bit, but in the end they go away. The mountain beats them. It's—it's too clever for them. It's too *cruel* for them. It wants to be left alone and maybe when it is left alone everything is all right round here ... And maybe it's because those of us who live here know that's what the mountain wants that we try to keep away from it. I thought of a name for it the other day. It isn't that all this country is lonely like the Long Mynd. It's *neglected*. I call it the neglected mountain ..."

It was most unusual for Jenny to make so long a speech, but none of them laughed when her voice tailed off into silence and a flickering flame from the stove lit up her red curls.

Peter spoke first. "The neglected mountain. What a wonderful title for a story, Jenny. I think it's a very good name for it, anyway."

Before anyone else could say anything, there came a yell from the farmyard and then Mackie, as a vanguard, came trotting into the barn.

"You haven't been eating anything here, have you?" Dickie said suspiciously as he saw them all round the stove. "Has anyone found any sweets that we don't know anything about, or baked chestnuts?"

"What's happening indoors, Mary?" Peter said as the little girl clutched Mackie and flopped down on the straw mattress. "What are they all doing?"

"We don't know exactly, but nobody came out to greet us. They're all in the dining-room—I s'pose that's 'cos they've got this visitor, Trudie—and Uncle Micah is acksherly laughing like anything and booming in his biggest voice, an' we thought we heard corks poppin' and everybody sounds very happy. We thought maybe we'd go in and ask if they'd forgotten us, but Dickie and me always know just when we're wanted and when we're not an' so—"

Dickie rolled over on to his stomach and looked up at Tom.

"D'you know what, Tom? I wish we lived up at Witchend always. I don't want to go back to-morrow. It all seems such a waste o' time when there's so much we could do together ... Besides," he added unexpectedly, "I miss Mackie."

Tom had never really got used to the twins. Sometimes they made him so angry with their cheeky self-assurance that physical action was the only way in which he could express his feelings, but as it was never possible to attack one without the other he did not always get the best of such encounters. All the same, although he would have found it difficult to put into words, he admired their courage and loyalty—loyalty, not only to each other, but to all the Lone Piners. During these holidays, while the Mortons had been at Witchend, he had noticed that Dickie had seemed to be interested in his work on his uncle's farm and had once actually come down without Mary and sought him out. But before he could find a suitable reply to him this time they heard a cheerful shout from the farmyard.

"Hi, kids! Where are you? We've got some news for you."

Peter and Jenny glanced at each other and smiled as David called:

"We're here, Charles. Round the stove. Come in and see us and we'll make you some coffee."

The open doors of the big barn were now in deep shadow, for the light had faded from the evening sky. Tom had already lit the oil lantern and hung it on the iron hook over their heads, so that when Charles Sterling and his companion stepped over the threshold their faces could not be seen. Just for a few seconds there was a curious feeling of tension in the barn. Nobody spoke as the two grown-ups—it was Jenny who noticed first that Trudie was holding Charles' hand—stepped forward into the circle of orange light.

Charles Sterling was the most handsome man Peter had ever known. There was nothing about him which she did not think wonderful. He was strong and kind. He had been wonderful to his father, to Peter's old father and to his step-mother, Aunt Carol. He had changed everything at Seven Gates and made it look like a prosperous farm again and—most important of all, perhaps—he had never been too busy to take notice of her and her friends, and had never treated her as if she was a child. As the light from the lamp lit up his brown, smiling face, she noticed how he looked down at the slim, lovely girl at his side and her heart began to thump and unexpected tears pricked her eyes.

Trudie Whittington was not much taller than Peter herself, who, although she had seen her several times before, had really only noticed her because she had been in Charles' company. She remembered that she was dark, had a pretty figure, that her eyes were wide and grey and her nose tip-tilted, but when she looked at her now Peter realized that she was radiant.

"This is what being happy does to you," Peter thought as Charles began to speak in a voice which sounded a little chokey.

"We heard this was your last night, kids," he was saying, "and so, before you all break up, we wanted you to know our news ... This is Trudie. She's just promised to marry me—I can't see why—and Dad says you're all to come indoors and drink our health in cider and wish us luck—"

But he never finished. Mary launched herself at him and flung her arms round his legs.

"Charles, you beast! I've always wanted to marry you. Why didn't you wait a bit for me? This doesn't mean that you're going out of our lives, does it?"

They all crowded round them then with whoops and cheers, and Peter suddenly found herself kissed by Charles and then by Trudie, who was saying, "You're all so sweet to me and I do want to know you all better," to which Tom was heard to say, "I expect you jolly well will if you're marrying Charles. You won't be able to help it."

Then they all went in to the dining-room, where Uncle Micah beamed at them and gave each of them a glass of cider and made a booming, rather rambling speech, which was well-meant but embarrassed them all because not even Aunt Carol was able to stop him for ten minutes. Then, quite suddenly, Jenny giggled loudly and unexpectedly and said, "This is the most wonderful romance of my life and the most wonderful, exciting evening of my life and—"

"And I think it's time you went to bed, Jenny," Aunt Carol said. "You must all be tired and it's been an exciting evening."

"Off you go," Charles said. "I'm going to take Trudie home now and make my peace with Mr. Whittington. I'll see you in the morning before you go, and thanks for all your good wishes."

The Lone Piners strolled out into the farmyard. The moon was just showing over the tree-tops and, before long, the farmyard would be patterned in black and silver.

"Let's see them off," David said as he went over and opened the white gate across the track leading down through the wood. Charles came out whistling cheerfully and backed the estate van out of the barn he used as a garage. Mr. and Mrs. Sterling came to the front door and waved "Good-bye" to Trudie. Charles stopped the van at the gate and the girl leaned forward and spoke through the open window.

"You'll all come and see me as soon as you can, won't you? I mean, you'll come over to Bishop's Castle and meet Father and we'll have a terrific party. I do want you to come—specially you, Peter."

The red tail-lights disappeared as the track turned in the darkness of the wood.

"I'm glad for him," Jenny sighed sentimentally. "I expect he's sometimes lonely up here. I wonder where they'll live? Oh, well. There doesn't seem much else to say, does there? Let's go to bed."

The twins went first.

"*All right*," Dickie said. "We're not making a fuss. We're goin'. All we ask is that when you come in to bed you just keep quiet. I just want to ask David and Tom not to go blundering about and drop their shoes and whisper so that it's worse than a shout, an' you, Mary—just you see the other two don't do any silly giggling and whispering."

The four elder ones stayed by the gate for another ten minutes. There wasn't much more to say and they were all too shy to talk about breaking camp to-morrow. It was very quiet except for the murmur of the wind in the trees and the far-off cry of an owl.

"Like Witchend," Peter whispered. "I never hear an owl without remembering when we first met at Witchend and had our first adventure. We're too late now for one this hols and I s'pose it will be twelve weeks before we meet again. You'll write and let us know if you're coming as soon as you break up, won't you, David?"

David nodded. "Yes, I'll write. Not much time in the summer term, though, because of cricket."

He turned and smiled at Peter, but it was too dark for them to see each other.

"Funny about Charles and Trudie," he went on. "We never knew a thing, did we?"

"Funny?" Peter and Jenny cried indignantly, and then the former went on, "Don't be so ridiculous, David. There's nothing funny about it—it's wonderful. I've never seen two people look so happy. Come on, Jenny. If the boys can't say anything more sensible than that, let's go to bed … Good night."

Mary was already asleep when they crept up the ladder into their loft and Jenny was too tired to talk as they undressed. But Peter could not sleep. For a quarter of an hour she heard the monotonous murmur of the boys' voices below and the easy breathing of Jenny and Mary beside her. She wriggled round in her bag and looked through the little window only two feet from her head. The moon was just above the tree-tops now and the roofs of the barns on the opposite side of the yard were glistening in its silver radiance.

She thought a lot about Charles and Trudie and wondered how different life would be at Seven Gates in future and whether Uncle Micah would now retire and go somewhere else to live with Aunt Carol. And then she thought of her own father who, so often, she seemed to desert when she went off with the others, and who, she supposed, would have to leave Hatchholt one day. But she didn't want to leave Hatchholt—ever. But perhaps she wouldn't mind leaving if she got married? If she ever did? And then, of course, she couldn't leave Daddy, who had sacrificed so much for her, and it all seemed to be very difficult.

There was no sound now but the girls' breathing. The boys had stopped talking; the owl was silent. Uncle Micah and Aunt Carol had probably gone to bed. Charles was at Bishop's Castle with Trudie and it might be hours before he came back. Something had happened to-night which was going to alter everything … Seven Gates would never be quite the same again. Nothing was ever the same again … Next hols would be different and they were twelve weeks away …

At last she slept and did not even hear the van come back and Charles' steps across the farmyard.

She woke suddenly with the feeling that something was wrong. The moon was high now and shining right through the little window. She turned over and raised herself on one elbow. Mary and Jenny were still sleeping soundly. Why was she awake?

Then she knew. Quite clearly, and getting louder every second, she heard the sound of an aeroplane engine—but surely not an ordinary engine? There was something very odd about it, for every now and then it stopped for a few seconds, spluttered and then started again with a roar. It was coming nearer. The engines cut out again, and Peter sat up with the horrible feeling that it was hurtling, out of control, down through the night right on to the roofs of Seven Gates.

Just before the engines re-started so loudly that even Mary and Jenny stirred, she thought she heard somebody whispering her name. She sat up, and in the moonlight from the window saw David's tousled head just above the level of the trap door.

"You awake, Peter? Good. Hoped you would be. There's something wrong with that plane. Get some clothes on and we'll go out and have a look."

His head disappeared before she could answer, and "Why does he think I'll come just because he asks me?" she thought to herself as she pulled on jodhpurs and sweater over her pyjamas, grabbed her shoes and stepped over the other two girls and climbed down the ladder.

David was already fumbling with the big white door of the barn and hardly looked over his shoulder as she tiptoed up behind him and whispered, "Wait while I put my shoes on."

He swung back the doors and they went out into the yard together. The aeroplane was circling. Coming back.

"There's something wrong with that plane, Peter. It's trying to find a place to land … Look! There it is."

She followed his pointing finger and saw briefly in the moonlight a small aeroplane against a shifting background of cloud. It was swooping low in silence, but soon rose sharply as the engines roared again, and disappeared over the tree-tops in the direction of the mountain.

"But it can't land on the Stiperstones," Peter said. "It's too rough up there. It would turn over at once."

"I don't suppose the pilot knows that," David replied, "but he could land on the Mynd. We know all about that, don't we, Peter, and how the spies were dropped there by parachute in the war. Anyway, it's smooth enough on the top for gliders, so if he's in trouble and can see in the moonlight he can come down there easily enough."

They stood in silence while the sound of the plane's engines died away and then he said:

"What shall we do now?"

"Do?" she said a little shakily. "What do you mean? Go back and get some sleep, I s'pose … Why did you call me, anyway? I'm not keen on aeroplanes and I daresay Tom is."

"I don't really know," David said, "except that I'm feeling particularly crazy to-night. Are you game for an adventure, Peter?"

"What do you mean?"

"I told you. I feel crazy … Let's climb up Black Dingle to the Devil's Chair. I can't sleep now and it's our last night and we'll scare away your bogy about the Chair for ever by going there at night."

"We can't take the twins and I doubt if Jenny would come, even if Tom did," she began before he interrupted her.

"Don't be so dumb, Peter. I'm not suggesting the others. I mean you and me. Let's do something on our own for once. I'll leave a note on Tom's sleeping-bag just in case they wake up and wonder what's happened to us, but we can be back in an hour. Where's Mackie? Up with Mary?"

Peter nodded feebly. She didn't see any sense in dragging up through gloomy Black Dingle to the Devil's Chair in the middle of the night. She hated the place even more than she had tried to explain earlier in the evening, but David seemed suddenly very determined, and as she couldn't remember ever refusing anything he asked her—although, no doubt, he had never even noticed such a thing—she just nodded and said,

"All right. I'm not properly dressed, but I s'pose it'll do. This sweater will keep me warm. You go and scribble that note to Tom and I'll wait here. Don't wake them."

A few minutes later they crossed the farmyard and opened, very quietly, a white wicket gate, and then went down a narrow track between the pine trees. This track was rarely used, for it was only a short cut to Black Dingle, which would lead them right up to the Devil's Chair on the summit.

They were walking in single file with David a few paces ahead, when Peter said, "Why are we doing this, David? What's the real idea?"

"Just an idea," he said. "I was worried about that plane and if it has come down on the top here we ought to see if there's anything we can do ... Anyway, I couldn't sleep and I thought it might be an experience to go up there in the moonlight."

"I see," Peter said quietly. "I don't know anything about aeroplanes. Why didn't you ask Tom?"

David waited for her to catch up.

"Don't ask so many silly questions. It's all right now we're here, isn't it?"

"Yes. But why didn't you ask Tom? I don't see why I shouldn't know."

"I thought of it," David admitted. "But he'd have started arguing and wakened everybody up. I knew you wouldn't argue and I thought you'd like to come. If you're riding Sally back to Witchend to-morrow we shan't have much chance for another talk."

He stuffed his hands in the pockets of his corduroys and looked straight ahead.

"I see, David," she said quietly. "I'm glad you asked me," and that was all until they came to a little rocky plateau where three paths met. Here an old signpost pointed a weather-beaten finger up to the black rocks of the Chair now showing clear and sinister in the moonlight.

"We've been here before, anyway," David said. "Let's get up to the top as quickly as we can. I can't hear that plane now ... You know, Peter, there really *is* something about this place. Jenny gets worked up about it, doesn't she? All the same, 'The Neglected Mountain' was rather bright of her."

"Don't you be patronizing about Jenny," Peter said as she hurried ahead up the track. "I think she's grand. She's sensitive, and when we're not all here she's lonely. She doesn't seem to make friends at school, and, anyway, I know almost exactly how she feels about this place. It doesn't matter what you say, David, *I hate it* ... And I'm afraid of it, but nothing you could say or do would make me go back now, so let's hurry."

He had the sense not to attempt an answer to this outburst, but looked very puzzled as he followed her up the dingle. He didn't suppose he ever would understand girls, who were the most curious creatures. Anyway, Peter was the most sensible he'd ever known.

But Peter herself, stalking on ahead with a straight back and her chin up, was feeling very unhappy. On a few occasions in her short life she had experienced the horrible sense of foreboding which possessed her now. It might, of course, be a natural feeling of fear and sympathy for the passengers in the struggling aeroplane. It couldn't have anything to do with going back to school, although she always hated leaving home and her father and the others. There didn't really seem anything to be afraid of and it was silly to pretend that there was any truth in all the stories and legends about the Stiperstones which Jenny so often related—stories of the black riders who were seen to ride along the skylines before a great disaster, or of the phantom hounds of Wild Edric. She caught her breath as she looked up at the Devil's Chair—very much nearer now, for she was walking fast.

The dingle narrowed as they climbed and became very wild. A few stunted hawthorn trees struggled for existence among the rocks. The path was narrow and a little stream, running more strongly now and never far from the track, whispered over its rocky bed. The moonlight gleamed on the black rocks of the Chair, but here in the dingle they were both in shadow.

David was whistling behind her and Peter, realizing she was not behaving very well, turned and smiled at him.

"Am I going too fast for you?" she asked.

He grinned cheerfully. "You can run if you like. I was getting worried about you, though. Thought you'd forgotten how to speak … Another five minutes and we'll be up. Like me to go ahead?"

She stood aside and let him pass, and when they began to climb the loose rocks at the base of the Chair she took the hand he held out to her and did not let it go as they scrambled up out of the shadows into the ghostly moonlight. They were alone in a silent and eerie world of black and silver. The silence was intense. No bird cried. No fox barked, and only one little alien breeze blew chill on their hot faces as he pulled her up to a ledge of rock from where they could look east over a wide valley to the long, broad bull-backed ridge of the Long Mynd—their own mountain.

David suddenly realized that she was trembling and that her fingers were gripping him as if she would never let them go. Surely she wasn't *still* scared? He had never known her to be really frightened of anything.

"Look, David," she whispered, and pointed ahead with her free hand. "Can you see it? Like a little light on the top of the Mynd. It's a fire, I'm sure. That aeroplane has crashed. That's what's happened. What shall we do?" and she turned away from him, covered her face with her hands and burst into tears.

Then he saw it, too, and knew she was right. A tiny flickering point of red light.

"If only we were at Witchend or Hatchholt we might be able to do something. There's only one thing we can do now, Peter, and that's to run back to Seven Gates, wake up Charles and telephone the police from there. Sorry I dragged you up here for this ... Buck up, Peter. It's not our fault."

She gulped, sniffed and wiped her eyes indignantly with the back of her hand.

"Sorry to be such an idiot, David. I don't know what's wrong with me to-night. I told you I hated this place, and so I do, but I've had the most horrible feeling ever since we started off that something awful was going to happen ... Now it *has* happened, and I don't like it. Let's get away from here quickly ... You can say what you like, David, but something always seems to go wrong when any of us come up to the Chair. It always has and I believe it always will."

They scrambled down the way they had come and were running down the dingle before David puffed, "The fire looked nearer to Witchend than Hatchholt. Dad will have heard the plane, and there's not much he doesn't know about aero engines. He'll be doing something, Pete. I'm sure he will."

"He'll want to, David, but there isn't a 'phone at Witchend or at Ingles. He'd have to get the car and go down to the 'phone-box at Onnybrook."

"That's what he'll do, then ... I wonder what Charles will say when we wake him up? Do you know his window?"

Peter nodded and ran on, and ten minutes later they had reached the old signpost and turned to the left into the little wood.

Considering everything, Charles was very good-tempered, although they had to throw a lot of gravel and several clods of earth through the open window of his bedroom before he put his head out.

He let them in at the back door and tried not to look astonished when he saw they were dressed.

"Come in, and don't make a row," he said. "Why do we want the police? What's happened?"

Peter seemed to have more breath left than David, so she told their story, and almost before she had finished Charles was at the telephone.

Feeling rather deflated and suddenly very tired, David and Peter sat down on two hard chairs in the hall while Charles was speaking.

"Right ... Thanks ... Oh! Good ... Two kids—friends of ours—camping up here heard it and went up to the top and saw fire on the Mynd ... Nothing we can do, then? ... That's all right ... 'Bye."

Then he turned, beckoned them into the kitchen and closed the door.

"No need to wake everybody up," he whispered. "What about a cup of tea? It doesn't look as if anything could keep you two awake, but we might as well risk it ... No. There's nothing we can do. Somebody gave the alarm and a rescue party is on the way ... It's an odd thing, but you know I thought I heard a plane soon after I got into bed."

David and Peter looked at each other and grinned feebly.

"It made a *lot* of noise, Charles," Peter said, "but we'll forgive you for not doing anything about it because you've had an exciting day ... I think tea is a wonderful idea."

Then she found herself nodding over the kitchen table and David's friendly face kept dissolving in a mist. The tea revived them, and then Charles came to the back door and put his arm round her shoulders.

"I won't ask too many questions about what you have been up to, but you'd better get a few hours' sleep now. You've got to be away in good time in the morning ... And don't worry too much about that smash. Maybe the pilot made a forced landing and it burst into flames after the passengers got out ... Good night, both."

"All the same," David whispered as they crossed the farmyard, "it's odd that a plane got lost over here. I'm sure there's no regular passenger route over this way."

He closed the barn doors gently behind them and they stood listening for a long minute. Tom was snoring gently and there was no sound from upstairs. At the foot of the ladder David whispered:

"Sorry if I dragged you out, Peter. Maybe it wasn't very

clever of me, but all the same I'm glad I didn't wake Tom, and I felt I had to go."

"I'll be glad too," she replied, "if we can hear to-morrow that nobody was hurt … 'Night!"

Breakfast took a long time because they had to confess to the others what they had done.

"Traitors," Dickie said tersely as he emptied a packet of cornflakes on to his plate. "Traitors to the Club … That's what you both are."

"It's terrible to think that the worst of them is our brother and the captain of the Club," Mary went on, "and it's awful when we remember that the vice-captain went with him. We ought to have a special meeting and expel them and if Tom and Jenny realized just how serious it was we'd jolly well do it now—an' if you haven't guzzled all the marmalade, David, we'd be *very much obliged* if you'd kindly pass it over."

Before the uproar had died down Charles came in.

"I've 'phoned the police again. So far as they know, nobody was badly hurt. It was a hired plane on the way to Ireland. They've found the pilot, but not the two passengers, who seem to have wandered off—or bolted. The fire didn't begin until they were all out, so there's nothing more to worry about, Peter."

Then came the horrible job of packing up, taking the sleeping bags and crockery into the house and sweeping and tidying the barn. They all had bicycles except Peter, who was riding her pony, Sally, and Jenny, who had only got to walk down through the wood to the village.

The twins, with Mackie in a basket on the back of Mary's cycle, went off first after touching farewells to Uncle Micah, Aunt Carol, Charles and Jenny.

"You may never see us again, Uncle Micah," Dickie said as he solemnly shook hands. "They make us work so hard at school that sometimes I wonder if I'll ever last the term out."

The others walked down through the wood with Jenny and said "Good-bye" to her outside Mr. Harman's shop in Barton Beach. They all hated these "good-byes" and pretended not to see her tears as she turned from them and ran inside. Tom was very quiet for the next half hour.

Their pace was rather slow because Peter could not hurry Sally until the road had a grass verge. She could have taken a short cut up to the top of the Mynd, but decided to go with the others to Witchend so that she could say good-bye to Mr. and Mrs. Morton, who had always been so kind to her.

The twins had been home some time when the main party arrived, and although they pressed her to stay for a little while, Peter said she must get on to see her father.

"You may not find him at home," Mr. Morton said. "He's probably helping to look for these two missing men."

"I think I must go, all the same, thank you. I've got some packing and lots of other things to do, and I'd like to be there when Daddy does come back. Good-bye—and thank you again for such a wonderful holiday."

Mrs. Morton kissed her and so did Mr. Morton. Mary hugged her and said she was forgiven and Dickie, very cheekily, asked her to write to him. Tom and David came over with her to the gate.

This was the moment she hated. They all felt shy and said ridiculous things at the same time.

"I'll be seeing you, Pete," Tom said as he jumped on his bike and wobbled off down the lane to Ingles Farm, and "Cheerio, then," David said. "It's been grand."

"Yes, it has," she replied, and this wasn't what she meant to say at all, and then, both together, "Only twelve weeks," and then she nudged Sally and rode off down the familiar track to

Dark Hollow and Hatchholt, which was the beginning and end of so many adventures. She turned once and saw David still standing at the gate. She waved. He raised his arm, and then the path turned and she was alone in the hills.

Sally knew that she was on her way home and Peter did not even have to guide her. Soon they were riding up her own valley by the pipe-line from the Hatchholt reservoir at the top, and a few minutes later she could see the cottage.

She jumped off Sally to unfasten the five-barred gate and "cooeed" loud and clear. This signal always brought Mr. Sterling to the door, but there was no sign of life now about Hatchholt. The sun had gone in and the sky was grey and suddenly Peter shivered with the foreboding she had felt last night in Black Dingle.

She hitched Sally to the gate-post, slipped off her knapsack and ran up to the house.

The front door—it was, indeed, the only door—was open.

"Daddy!" she called with an edge of fear to her voice. "Where are you? I'm home again!"

She ran up the little flagged path where her father's neatly arranged wallflowers were nearly in bloom, and stopped short on the threshold.

A strange man was sitting at the table in their tiny sitting-room facing the door which opened directly into it.

He could hardly be more than thirty, although he wore a brown beard and his hair was long and unkempt. His face was pale and he peered at Peter short-sightedly with brown eyes which somehow looked both puzzled and wary. He was wearing an untidy light fawn overcoat over a shabby blue suit. A bulging brief-case was on the table beside him. His face was scratched and his right hand tucked into his jacket as if it was hurt.

"WHO ARE YOU?" GASPED PETER, STARING AT THE STRANGER. "WHAT
ARE YOU DOING HERE? WHERE'S MY FATHER?"

There was no sign of Mr. Sterling.

The stranger stared, but did not speak.

"Who are you?" Peter gasped with a horrid catch in her throat. "What are you doing here? Where's my father?"

The man's bewildered expression hardly changed as he looked up and met the challenge in her blue eyes.

"My dear girl," he said pettishly in an educated voice, "don't ask such ridiculous questions. For all I know I may be your father. I've not the remotest idea who I am or where I am."

CHAPTER II

THE NEWSPAPER CUTTINGS

Pollards,
Castle School,
Shrewsbury.

D EAR DAVID (wrote Peter),
Considering what you said about cricket in the summer
term taking up so much of your time so that you probably won't
have much time for letters, I think you're jolly lucky to get one
from me so quickly. And I may as well tell you right away that
it's going to be a long one—so long that it will be written over
several days whenever I can find the time. I can't think why
you imagine that it's only boys who have no time for writing
letters at school. It just shows how little you know about it, 'cos
if I've not told you before, I tell you now that everything at a
girls' school like this is so *organized* that sometimes I wonder
if they do it on purpose. Miss Cockshott—our loathsome maths
mistress—told us once that if you want a thing badly enough
you can always get it. The girls here who like maths think she's
very clever, but I don't think I've ever heard anything more
unintelligent, and I'm only mentioning it now because I want
you to see that although I haven't really got any spare minutes,
I'm jolly well going to find the time to write because what I've
got to tell you is important.

I hope you've settled down all right to your cricket. I may
have told you that we play cricket here, too, but I don't think
much of it. All rather pointless, I think. Things aren't too bad
here and you soon get used to it. I know I'm silly—is this a bit
like Jenny?—but sometimes at night before I get off to sleep

and it's very still, I can hear the trains. Just after ten there's a train going south to Hereford—I looked it up in the timetable. I can hear it start. I know exactly what it looks like and I expect I should know the guard, and I can almost feel it banging over the points. Then I think of all the stations—Condover, Dorrington, Leebotwood; then the hills close in on each side of the line and at Stretton there's steep old Caer Caradoc on the left and soon afterwards there's Onnybrook and the level crossing over the road up to Ingles and Witchend, and it's home. I don't suppose you can possibly imagine why I'm writing all this to you. I'm not quite sure myself except that I'm fairly sure you won't think I've gone completely soppy.

Now for the real business, and I expect you wondered whether I was ever coming to it. It's about what happened after I left you at Witchend last Tuesday, and rode Sally up to Hatchholt. I want to try and remember every little thing that happened because it seems that by having to come back to school we may have missed another adventure. Anyway, I didn't care much for what happened to me when I was alone.

By the time I was in sight of the cottage the sun had gone in, and I remember that it was dull and cool. I remember, too, that I had that odd feeling that something was wrong, like I did when we went up to the Chair the other night and we saw the burning plane. Anyway, I was hoping that Daddy would be at home and was looking forward to telling him everything that we'd been doing. I "cooeed," but Daddy didn't come out like he usually does. I hitched Sally to the gate and ran up the path. The door was open, and then, David, I realized what they mean when they say in books about your scalp tingling when you're frightened. The top of my head really did creep 'cos instead of Daddy there was a strange man sitting at the table. He stared at me—almost peered at me as if he couldn't see very well—

and looked sort of puzzled. His hair was long and untidy, and although he had a beard I'm sure he wasn't very old. His face was pale and scratched, with blood on it. He was wearing an overcoat, but had no hat and a thick leather case—a brief-case, I think it's called—was on the table. It seemed ages while we stared at each other without speaking, and then I said something about, "Where's Daddy?" or "Who are you?"

He kept on staring at me, and then, David, he said the most extraordinary thing. He said, "For all I know, young lady, I may be your father. I've no idea who I am or where I am," and as soon as he'd said it I was sure he meant it.

I s'pose you've already guessed what I guessed. This man must be one of the passengers from the plane who somehow or other had got lost and found his way to Hatchholt. I wish I could explain him to you, David. Except for his beard, he was very ordinary looking. His voice was ordinary, too—nothing special to remember about it, I mean, but quite educated. But his eyes were peculiar and I felt scared because I could see that he was frightened and puzzled, too. I can't remember exactly what we both said to each other, but because I was worried about Daddy I suppose I got annoyed, and I think I said, "Don't be silly. Of course you're not my father. I suppose you were a passenger on the plane that came down here last night?"

"I don't know what you're talking about," he snapped. "So far as I can remember—and that's not much—I've never seen this place before. Do you live here and where am I?"

This didn't seem to be a very good start, and I don't mind admitting to you that my knees began to feel wobbly. I had been riding for hours and was tired—which wasn't to be wondered at considering I had been up most of the night—and here I was alone with a man who didn't know who he was or where he was. I know I was silly, but I couldn't get it out of my head that he was just sitting there in our little room *waiting* for someone to come. I had a quick look round—and by now I was standing on the step—but nothing seemed to have been moved. He had just walked in and thought that this place looked as good as any other and sat down to wait for something or somebody to turn up, and I was the somebody. I s'pose I was staring at him because he said suddenly, "Don't look scared. I'm not going to hurt you. Just tell me who lives in this house and where it is."

I told him, and then asked him again if he was a passenger in the plane and whether he remembered it coming down and how long he'd been in the house ... You see, David, I couldn't make out how he had got in if Daddy wasn't in because he would never go out without locking up and leaving the key under our secret stone in the garden. Then I remembered that if Daddy had been telephoned for in a hurry to join a rescue party he *might* have forgotten to lock up. It wouldn't be like him, but he just might have done. I looked at the clock, and it was just half-past three, and that reminds me that it's now half-past nine and I can't write any more to-night.

Later.

I've just read through all I wrote last night, and if you've read as far you must be wondering when I'm going to get on with the story.

Well—there we were staring at each other and with me having the horrible idea that perhaps Daddy was in the house after all and maybe ill upstairs. Or perhaps a prisoner, which was so silly that I'm almost ashamed to write it down.

"Have you seen my father?" I asked him suddenly. "Was he here when you came?"

He said no he hadn't seen anybody and then, because I suppose I wasn't so afraid of him now, I asked him lots of questions and he put his hand to his head and said, "Look here, young lady. I seem to have lost my memory—or most of it, anyway—but I do remember something about a plane and somebody who might have been the Doctor shouting to me to 'hold tight,' and after that I remember running and falling down and running again. I got into a valley and fell into a bog and then it got light and I think I went to sleep for a long time because the sun was high when I woke and then I walked for miles before I found this place. The door opened when I pushed it. If you live here I wish you'd get me something to eat."

I didn't think a cup of tea would be a bad idea, and as he now seemed fairly harmless I came in and got out some food and put the kettle on, and it was when I was pouring the boiling water into the teapot that I suddenly realized what a fool I'd been.

"If you've forgotten who you are, surely you've got something in your pockets or in that case which will tell you. You must have your name written on something. And I ought to have told you before—we've got a telephone here so we can easily ring up the police and tell them you're here. If you were on the plane that came down on the top of the Mynd and caught fire then they ought to know about you."

And do you know, David, that the moment I said that I knew I'd said the wrong thing. He changed at once, and although he was stuffing bread and jam as fast as he could he peered at me suspiciously, and snapped, "Never you mind about my name. I've found it, but it doesn't mean a thing to me. I can't remember who I am or what I do or where I come from, and until I am sure you're not to ring up the police. Do you understand that? Where's the telephone?"

I told him upstairs in Daddy's bedroom, and he said, "Well, don't go upstairs then. I won't have it. Stop nagging and leave me alone for a bit. I'm beginning to remember a few things. I remember the Doctor, but he wasn't with me when I was on the hill. I'll remember more if you'll let me alone. I'm not doing any harm here, am I?"

I was beginning to feel frightened again now, so I grabbed my cup of tea and dodged round the table to the door again and sat on the step where I could watch him. I told him of course he wasn't doing any harm and I was sure Daddy would welcome him when he came home and would he tell me his name as I'd told him mine.

He just glared at me again and said I wasn't to go upstairs and that he meant this and did I understand that he meant it? I didn't have to pretend that I understood him, David, 'cos by now I was dead scared. He began to look very nasty indeed. He was very pale and there was a splodge of jam on the side of his face which he didn't even notice, and he banged his cup on his saucer and I was terrified he would break it because I knew Daddy would say that I ought to have given him a mug. Do you know who he reminded me of, David? A schoolmaster. An angry, untidy schoolmaster.

Well, he poured himself some more tea and gulped it down and wiped his beard rather disgustingly, I thought, and then he started asking me questions and he was getting more excited and nervous all the time. He asked me again who Daddy was and what he did and where was my mother. Then he asked if we'd got a dog and I said, "No, only a pony," and that reminded me that poor Sally was still hitched to the gate, but I didn't say anything because I got a wild idea that if the worst came to the worst I could dash out and ride back to you—all of you, I mean—at Witchend and that I jolly well would do this if Daddy didn't come soon.

Then he asked me about Hatchholt and the Mynd and exactly where it was and whether there were any houses or towns near.

There didn't seem much harm in answering questions like these, so I told him all he wanted to know and I got the idea, David, that all the time now his memory was coming back. There was an excited tone in his voice and a look in his piercing eyes that I didn't like at all. There wasn't a chance of getting to the telephone and I'm awfully sorry, David, if you've managed to read as far as this, but I've got to stop now. I ought to have been doing an essay, but I'll write some more as soon as I have time.

Later again.

It's three days since I wrote anything, but the summer term is so busy with cricket that we hardly have time for anything else! I'd a good mind to post you all that I had written, but it is rather like a serial story and it didn't seem quite fair to keep you waiting for the last instalment, although the term is now a week old and I haven't even had a picture postcard from you to say you've arrived safely, although I've had one from Mary, who is sometimes so nice that nobody would realize she's your sister.

I got to where my bearded stranger was bombarding me with questions about the district and wolfing our bread and jam.

"When you arrived," I asked him when he stopped for breath, "was there a note for me on the table or on the dresser? I'm worried about my father," and just at that very moment, while I waited for him to speak, I thought I heard voices. I shouted something to him, and before he could move I ran down the path to the gate. When I turned he was standing in the doorway, but he didn't follow me and I've never really understood why.

Coming round the edge of the reservoir was Daddy with another strange man. I think I shouted and I know I ran as hard as I could to meet him and was quite out of breath when he gave me a hug. The man with him was as different from *my* stranger as you could imagine. He was much older—short and thick-set, with lots of black hair streaked with grey. He looked important and rather fussy and silly, too, 'cos he was wearing a black overcoat and a black suit with striped trousers. It's funny how sometimes you remember things like that, but he looked so out of place walking with Daddy on the Mynd when he was dressed for London or Birmingham or some big town. One thing I noticed about him was his thick, bushy eyebrows, which jutted out and made his eyes look small. His shoes and the bottoms of his smart trousers were all dusty and because he hadn't shaved and his face was pale and dirty, he didn't look at all nice. I'm sure he was very tired and hot and angry.

You know how sweet Daddy is. He looked just the same of course and gave me his twinkly smile and then turned to the man and said,

"Petronella, my dear. This gentleman has had a nasty accident and a shock. He was a passenger in a small aeroplane which was forced to land on the Mynd early this morning. Fortunately, nobody was injured, but our friend here is most concerned about his companion, who apparently ran off as soon as the plane landed and cannot be found."

You know how slowly Daddy explains himself. He won't be hurried and, of course, I'd guessed right away that *my* bearded stranger was the one the man was looking for and I kept on trying to say so. I'm sure this man knew I had some news 'cos he suddenly interrupted Daddy rather rudely and said, "Yes, yes, Mr. Sterling. I'm sure your daughter understands, but I think she has something to tell us."

Then Daddy said, "Dear me. I am so sorry, my dear. Will you allow me, sir, to present my daughter Petronella ... Although I am delighted to have been of service to you, I do not think I have the pleasure of knowing your name?"

The stranger went very red in the face and then, through

his clenched teeth, said, "Never mind my name. Have you seen a young man with a beard wandering about these confounded hills, miss?"

His voice was quiet and sort of silky. I didn't like it much, but he seemed quite harmless and I could understand that he must be very tired and hot, walking about the Mynd for hours in his black, city shoes. I could understand him getting a bit exasperated with Daddy, too, because even I sometimes wonder when he's going to get to the point.

Anyway, I had my chance then and, as far as I remember, I said, "Yes. I'm sure I've found the man you're looking for. He's in our sitting-room now—or he was when I came out to meet you. I'm jolly glad you've come because I think there's something not quite right about him."

At this poor Daddy looked as if the world was coming to an end, but before he could say anything the man said, very quietly and urgently:

"What do you mean? What's wrong with him? Is he hurt?"

"I don't think so. He says he's lost his memory and can't remember who he is or what's happened and he won't let me telephone the police. Once or twice he said something about a doctor—"

"He did, did he?" said the man in his beastly quiet voice. "I am a doctor and I think he is my young friend."

Then he turned to Daddy and poked at him with a stubby finger.

"You have been very good to me, Mr. Sterling, and I am grateful. May I ask you a further kindness? My friend is, I fear, suffering from shock and I hope you will excuse me if I have a few minutes with him alone. If he has indeed lost his memory I think I shall be able to restore it. He is very highly-strung, but if I might have ten minutes I am confident that I can help him," and before either Daddy or I could say anything he trotted down the path and left us looking at each other in astonishment.

Of course Daddy wanted to know what had happened to me and what the man with the beard was like and whether he had annoyed me. I didn't tell him all that I really thought about him or how scared I had been, and, anyway, everything seemed to be different now that he was home again.

We sat down in the heather at the side of the path and then he told me that he had not heard the plane come down, but had been called at breakfast-time by the police and asked to keep an eye open for any strangers. They had told him that the pilot was safe and unhurt but that one man—it must have been my "beardy"—had jumped out before the plane had stopped and, so far as they knew, dashed wildly away into the darkness, so that story seemed to make sense. They also told him that a search party had gone up—I expect your father was in that, David— and that the Doctor had told the pilot not to worry about him, but he was going to find his friend. Daddy decided to go out by himself and see if he could help and found the Doctor over by the Gliding Station.

"I must admit that he is a very peculiar man, Petronella," he said. "I do not think I can claim to have met anyone like him and I can only wish that I found him more congenial. He was very angry when I hailed him and certainly very footsore. No doubt he would pass for an educated man, but his ridiculous comments about our mountain and his constant questions as to how lonely we must be and the distances from the nearest towns I found rather exhausting and boring … I am not inquisitive by nature"—he certainly is *not*, David. He's inhuman about that sort of thing and says very politely that he believes in minding his own business—"but I must admit that I could not understand his interest in this particular part of the country. He appeared to be astonished that Shropshire existed and amazed that here, in our own hills, we are so remote from what some people call civilization. I enlightened him as best I could, but he volunteered no information about himself and although he was obviously suffering great discomfort, he was very determined to find his friend who, from what you say, is even more eccentric … I don't think I should care to have him as my doctor, but no doubt I am prejudiced … Now we will go and see our guests, my dear."

Before we reached the gate the two men came down the path together and a very odd couple they looked, without their hats, and one smartly and the other shabbily dressed. The "Doctor"— we never found out his real name—looked grim but fairly satisfied, and my "beardy" seemed almost jaunty.

I introduced him to Daddy and he was quite polite—"beardy," I mean—and then he turned to me and said, "Thanks for the tea. I needed it. The Doctor tells me I must have got a bang on the head when I jumped out of the plane, but I've now got to the stage where I remember the plane coming down, and I do recall wandering about in the loneliest country I've ever seen in my life …"

All the time he was speaking, though, David, I got the idea that the Doctor was watching him suspiciously, as if he might say too much. He had one hand on his arm and at last he interrupted and turned to Daddy and said, "There is one final favour you can do for me, Mr. Sterling. Tell me the quickest way back to civilization and a car. We must go at once."

I told them to follow the pipeline down to Onnybrook and said I'd telephone for a car to meet them at the bottom of the track if they liked, and he agreed to this almost without a thank-you, and almost before we realized that we were alone again they were hurrying down the track. Neither of them looked back, but we could hear the Doctor's voice after they had disappeared round the first bend. Then I ran in to telephone the garage and when I came back Daddy was still standing at the gate looking thoughtfully down the valley.

"A very unusual couple, my dear," he said. "I do not wish to appear discourteous, but I am glad it is no longer necessary to offer them hospitality. My companion was very difficult to place, although he seemed relieved to find me for he was quite desperate about discovering his companion. It was almost, Petronella, as if he was afraid that anyone else should question him … At the same time he was not reticent about asking me questions. Most curious he was and I think I will now telephone to the police station and inform them that the two missing men have been discovered … I like everything to be right and proper and I am sure that the police should be informed."

It was while Daddy was upstairs doing his telephoning—and you know how he *loathes* that, so he must have thought that this really was his duty—that I found the newspaper cuttings that I'm sending with this letter. They were on the floor under the table and I'm sure that "beardy" dropped them out of his brief-case. I did just show them to Daddy, but he didn't seem very interested, but the more I examined them the more peculiar I think they are and I can't think why that man was carrying them round. Can you see any sense in them, David? You'll notice that most of them, with the exception of the one on the top which is a picture from the *Daily Picture*, tell how an attempted burglary was prevented by a dog giving the alarm, or has something to do with a dog preventing crime. One or two describe how police dogs are trained and how they help to track criminals and another one explains how some dogs are trained to guard aerodromes and army camps. The picture from the *Picture* is extraordinary because it shows an alsatian which has been trained by its master to know the difference between friendly and dangerous scents on handkerchiefs which may be doped by burglars. It says that the dog actually chose his master's handkerchief from several placed on the ground. The man in the picture used to be a policeman and he says he's forming "an emergency dog force" to help to beat crime.

I've been wondering whether the two men in the plane were detectives. They could hardly have been criminals, although they both behaved in a very peculiar way, because they wouldn't want to carry round cuttings describing what dogs were doing to prevent crime, would they? I mean, they'd know.

I can't help thinking, David, that perhaps we've missed another adventure just by going back to school, but I wish we were together just to find out whether we have.

Now I've tired myself out writing all this. It's taken me *days and days* and I don't think you really deserve it. You can keep the cuttings if you like because I'm sure we shan't hear anything of those two men again, but it was a peculiar adventure for me and I shall never forget seeing that man with a beard staring at me with his peering, brown eyes, and saying that for all he knew he might be my father. He was a very odd type, David, and I didn't like either of them. I don't think Daddy was very easy in his mind either, although of course we didn't have much time to talk about it before I had to come back.

Write if you can spare the time. I'd like to know what you think of the cuttings and of my news. Hope you're having some good cricket.

Love from

PETER

P.S.—I'm glad we went up the Dingle to the Chair that night and that, after all, nobody was killed when the plane came down. Perhaps I shan't be such a fool and never get really scared of the place again.

CHAPTER III

CLUB MEETING

THE summer holidays came at last and the Lone Piners, as they had so many times before, converged on Witchend with that wonderful feeling that these were the longest holidays of all and that it was almost impossible to see the end of them.

To David the term had gone quickly, with cricket the chief of his joys. There was no term to him like the summer term, with its bright mornings, long evenings and the smell of newly-cut turf on match days, and the feel of the seam of the new red ball between his fingers. This had been a good season, for he was now in the first eleven and he had not disgraced himself.

To Dickie, away on the Dorset coast, the term had not been so good. He detested cricket and, although nobody knew it, the summer term made him homesick. Not badly, because Dickie was really a tough little boy, but just enough to nag at him sometimes, particularly when he woke early and thought not only of his home in Hertfordshire, but of Witchend and the stream that came chattering so happily down the valley, and of Mary and Mackie and David and Peter and the others.

Mary enjoyed school—also on the south coast—very much more than she thought she would and the terms flew by for her. She was learning to enjoy life to the full and was finding, from a charming young mistress, the joys to be found in good reading. She kept her promise, too, and wrote to all the Lone Piners and had wonderful letters in return from Jenny and Peter.

Tom, not being at school, found his days very occupied at his uncle's farm, but without fully realizing it he was learning to love everything that happened at Ingles as the pageant of the seasons brought the harvest nearer. His uncle and aunt were always kind, and when they knew for certain that the Lone Piners were coming again to Witchend, Mrs. Ingles wrote to Mrs. Harman and suggested that Jenny should come over to the farm for a week or more, so that the children would be together, and she added that if Jenny would like to stay on and help Tom at harvest-time she would be welcome.

Naturally enough, this idea appealed to Jenny, who had not enjoyed the summer very much so far, although she had had plenty to keep her occupied. She had seen very little of the people at Seven Gates and had not once been up through the wood to the farm. Charles had stopped his van twice in Barton to speak to her and she had seen Trudie once in Bishop's Castle after school. She had kept her word and written long letters to Mary and to Peter and had welcome replies from them both, although the latter had not told her anything about her adventure on the last day of the Easter holidays.

David had written Peter a long letter in answer to hers, but had said that there wasn't much sense in discussing the two strangers and the newspaper cuttings until they all met again, but he had told her how glad he was to hear from her. And then, a week before the end of term, he had written again to tell her that they were all coming to Witchend in a fortnight's time, and would she call a meeting of the Club for noon the day after they arrived.

And now that day had come. Peter, from school, had posted the messages to all the Lone Piners, had enjoyed a lovely week at home at Hatchholt riding Sally and swimming in the reservoir, which was still so cold that the first plunge took her breath away, and just being alone with her father. The day on which the Mortons actually arrived she had to spend in Shrewsbury with Mr. Sterling. She would have liked to have been at Witchend to welcome them; Jenny and Tom had promised to be there and Peter felt disappointed that her father wanted her on that particular day. But she soon forgot that little pang of jealousy when she realized that Mr. Sterling had planned this outing a long time ago, because he hoped it would please her to be taken out to lunch and tea and told to buy herself a new frock.

When they were on their way home in the dear, familiar Midland Red bus, she had said,

"The Mortons will have arrived by now, Daddy. I think I told you that Jenny is at Ingles, so she and Tom will go along and see if they can help to get them straight."

"You can leave me at the turning, Petronella, and run along to Witchend and see them to-night, if you wish. I'm glad they've come again, for they're company for you. That David, now, is a very pleasant lad—always ready to listen to his elders without interrupting … And those comical twins, too. These valleys have never been quite the same since they arrived here with their dog. You must have them all up to tea, my dear, as soon as you like, but you must give me good warning and we will try and choose a day when you can all picnic out of doors, as our room is a little cramped for so many to eat simultaneously … Why don't you go along this evening?"

"No, I won't do that, Daddy. I'm riding Sally over in the morning and going to spend the day there. I'd rather spend the evening with you after such a lovely day," and the smile he gave her was reward enough for her unselfishness.

The next morning was blustery and not very warm. As she rode down the valley great grey clouds were sweeping over the Stiperstones from the west, and Peter wondered what everyone at Seven Gates was doing and how soon it would be before they went over to see them there. They had promised to visit Trudie one day, too; it was going to be fun planning the best ways in which to spend the wonderful holidays before them.

Sally knew the way to Witchend without being told and turned right at the fork. A million insects hummed in the green bracken, which was higher than her stirrups, and down here between the steep hillsides it was very quiet. She knew every inch of this narrow track. Here there was a boggy patch, which Sally always avoided by treading delicately over the rushes growing rankly across the path, and a little farther on, just before a sharp corner, a spike of golden broom from a bush on the hillside above her had to be pushed aside if she did not duck. Every time she came this way she wondered why she did not do something about it.

As she pushed it aside as usual, Sally's ears went back and she was not altogether surprised when they rounded the next bend to see the twins blocking the path. Peter blinked with surprise, for they seemed to grow more alike every term and if they had been of the same sex it would have been impossible to tell them apart. They were dressed alike, of course—grey shorts and gaily-checked "cowboy" shirts, which Mrs. Morton must have worked on in term-time, and sandals. Both were very brown and looked as if they had already been on holiday for weeks.

"Hullo, Peter," Mary smiled. "It's grand to be back. How are you?"

And, "Hullo, Peter," her twin said. "Somebody told me—I forget who—that you'd really sold that old horse of yours at last. I think it was David. He said he'd seen it in a milk cart in Shrewsbury."

"Of course it was David," Mary took up the challenge in a flash. "He said he thought it was cruelty to animals to keep poor old Sally alive just to cart you around in the holidays."

"You little liars," Peter said cheerfully. "Out of my way, or the milk-horse will ride you down ... Where's Mackie?"

PETER ROUNDED A BEND AND CAME UPON THE TWINS, WHO SEEMED
TO GROW MORE ALIKE EACH TIME SHE SAW THEM.

"He's temporary indisposed," Mary said with a winning smile. "He got excited last night when we came and ate a very dead rabbit."

"Daddy says he's lucky the rabbit only stayed with him temporary. He's convalescent now down by the stream. How are you, Peter? You never wrote to me."

Peter jumped down and helped Mary on to Sally's back and then groaned.

"Unless I get a lot stronger that's the last time I'll be able to do that. You're disgustingly fat, Mary. How are the others?"

"When you say 'others,' we know you mean David," Dickie said; "but all our family is very well, thank you."

"Are very well, twin. Do be careful of your grammar."

"A family is one thing, isn't it?" Dickie began fiercely, and then said, "What's the use of arguing about a stupid thing like that? We're on holiday and we've got a meeting at twelve o'clock, so let's buck up."

David jumped down from the top bar of the gate when Mary urged Sally into a reluctant trot, and went over to meet them. Meetings were sometimes more awkward than partings and neither David nor Peter seemed to know quite what to say, beyond "Hullo." Nobody would have described David as good-looking, but Peter was quite sure that no other boy could possibly look as friendly and nice, while David, not usually shy, suddenly realized that one day, and very soon now perhaps, other people would look at Peter and see that she was a very beautiful girl.

Mr. and Mrs. Morton came over from the house to greet her and Mackie, lying exhausted by the edge of the stream, feebly wagged his tail when Peter called to him, and then, two minutes later, they were all chattering at the same time.

"You'll come here whenever you like and whenever you

can, won't you, Peter?" Mrs. Morton said. "I'm only sorry we haven't room to sleep you, but I know you don't like leaving your father for too long. How is he?"

"Just the same, thank you, except that he's a bit more darling than usual. He took me to Shrewsbury yesterday and bought me a frock. That's why I wasn't here to welcome you ... No. I don't sleep away from home too often, but I expect we shall go to Seven Gates for a few nights. It's fun there and now there's the extra excitement of Trudie."

Ten minutes later David produced two heavy haversacks.

"It's a quarter to twelve, Peter. We'd better be going. Tom and Jenny will come the other way from Ingles. I think I've packed everything and I've told Mother we shan't be back to lunch ... Come on, twins. Are you bringing the greedy Macbeth? What he needs is a good dose of castor oil."

"You're disgustin'," Mary said, with her nose in the air. "Disgustin' and heartless. You know it was excitement made him sick. You're excited when you come back to Witchend, aren't you—"

"I should just think he is," Dickie broke in, and rolled his eyes in the direction of Peter.

"Well, anyway," his twin went on, "if you're excited, why shouldn't Mackie be? ... O' course he's coming. I'm going to carry him if he can't walk."

"Oh, no, you're not," Peter said. "You're going to carry a bucket and the kettle and fill them both at the stream. Mackie can walk. If you go on spoiling him like this he'll lose the use of his legs."

David led the way down to the stream and they both looked up at the lonely pine tree towering above the green sea of bracken about a hundred yards up the hill to their left. They walked along the bank of the stream until they came to the place where they had built a little dam so that they could fill their buckets, jumped over and began the steep climb through the fern. From previous experience they knew that the longer way round was the shortest way home, and David, who was now in front and struggling with the heavy bucket, bore away to the left towards the larch wood clinging, so delicately green, to the side of the hill.

When they reached the wood, which was dark and cool inside, they toiled up at its edge until they were level with the lonely pine. The gorse, blazing with golden blossom, still barred the obvious way to their secret camp, but they climbed a little higher, turned to the right into the thick bracken and then jumped down into the little grassy clearing, which was the original headquarters of the Lone Pine Club.

David and Peter slipped the heavy haversacks to the ground and then the former looked ruefully into the bucket.

"We're fools, you know. Why don't we buy another big iron kettle with a lid and use it instead of this? Even I spill more than half the water on the way up. Doesn't look as if anybody's discovered us yet, does it? You twins get back into the wood and fetch some larch cones and kindling and we'll get a fire going ... Surely Tom and Jenny ought to be here, Peter? It's after twelve."

Peter was lying flat on her back, looking up through the branches of the tree with half-closed eyes.

"You know, David, I'm sure that, however long we live or wherever we all go, we shall all of us always remember this place. I know I sound a bit soppy, and I suppose I'm being almost as dramatic as Jenny, but there's something about our Lone Pine which makes me feel rather peculiar."

David was leaning against the tree, looking down at her.

"I think I know what you mean and I'm sure you're right. We're all glad to get back ... I think I heard Tom's whistle."

Peter sat up and flicked back her plaits, put her fingers to her mouth and, in a most unladylike way, whistled the peewit's call, loud and clear. They listened, heard Mary's—or Dickie's—voice, and then the peewit's whistle from the edge of the wood.

Jenny, pink with exertion, freckled and beaming, slid down into the clearing first.

"Hullo, Peter," she began breathlessly. "Isn't this marvellous? I mean to be all together again. I've had the most horrible, dreary term, but I don't care what happens now. Do you know, I've been at Ingles for days already and I can stay as long as I like and I've been on a tractor with Tom … Where is he? He's always disappearing just when I want to tell him something interesting … How are you, Peter? Hullo, David … Yes, the twins are just coming. They tried to make me carry fir cones, but I told them that was their chore … What are we going to meet about? I reckon we ought each of us to make a suggestion about the best things to do these holidays and make them all last as long as we can …"

Then Tom jumped down, shook hands with Peter and winked at her.

"Everything O.K., Pete? Good … D'you know they could hear you chattering at Witchend, Jen? … And did you know, Pete, that we're teaching her to milk? What a life! I've got the afternoon off, anyway … Sorry we're late. I never can get away from Uncle Alf. Are we going to eat first?"

Mackie, apparently on the road to complete recovery, barked and led the twins, with their arms full of cones, down into the camp.

"I'll carry on with the cooking," Peter said as she undid the first knapsack and pulled out two loaves, a pot of jam, six apples, a jar of fish-paste, a tin of luncheon meat and a bag containing twelve brown eggs. "You get out the log-book, David, while

Tom gets the fire going. I'll hard-boil the eggs in the kettle and put the tea in after."

From his pocket Tom produced butter sent with Mrs. Ingles' love, and Jenny unloaded packets of chocolate from her blazer pockets.

"Fancy calling hard-boiled eggs cooking," Mary observed. "It's 'bout time somebody round here, besides Dickie and me, did some real hard work. Why can't we have sausages, I want to know."

"Because there aren't any left in the whole world," her twin explained. "We've had 'em all at school. It's always sausages and when they aren't in their beastly tough skins we have 'em naked in rissoles, if you know what I mean?"

"You're just about as clear as usual," David said, "and if you'll stand away we'll see if the Club's documents are still safe."

At the foot of the tree was a square patch of turf which did not look quite as fresh as the surrounding grass and as he lifted this with the blade of his scout knife he said, "We shall have to find a new place for the tin. A stranger would soon spot that the turf has been cut."

"Perhaps we ought to throw that bit away," Peter suggested as she raised a smutty face after blowing on the embers of the fire. "Maybe you could cut another piece exactly the same size from higher up the hill. I should hate to change our hiding-place."

David scraped up some soil and then lifted the original sardine-tin from its little grave, bent back the lid and pulled the rules of the Lone Pine Club out, all signed in the members' own blood.

"Still safe, anyway," he smiled. "All we've got to do now is to enter in our log the date of this meeting and who's here and sign it, and then we'll get down to the serious matter of eating … How are the eggs, Cook?"

"The water isn't boiling yet, but it won't be long. You're good with a tin-opener, Tom. Get to work on the meat-tin and ask Jenny to help you make some sandwiches."

While David was putting away the documents the twins climbed into the tree and watched their father and mother sitting in the porch at Witchend, down in the valley below. David sat with his back to the tree and tickled Mackie behind his ears as the little dog watched Tom's efforts with the tin of meat with an appreciative eye. He was evidently feeling better.

The wind was stronger now, and up here above the valley it was cool when the sun slipped behind the clouds which came sailing over the bulk of the Mynd from the west.

"All's well," Mary chanted from above, although nobody had asked her. "No spies in sight."

"It's about time we had some more spies," Dickie yelled. "We want something to liven us up a bit. I hope you've all got some plans for these hols, because we don't want to waste any time, and if you can't think of anything Mary and me will just go off and do something on our own. Something always starts up when we're about."

Nobody answered him, but Tom, still wrestling with the tin-opener, muttered to David, "That young brother of yours wants putting in his place. He's much too cocky. I don't think he's very funny, either."

"Oh, yes he is—sometimes," Jenny said. "They're both very comical and I only wish I was a twin."

"There could never be two like you, Jen," David laughed, and she wasn't sure whether this was a compliment or not, but decided to pretend that it was.

"I don't see how you can expect us little ones to have good manners," Mary shouted. "We don't get much of an example. We sit up and keep a look-out for you and every now and then

MACKIE WATCHED, WITH AN APPRECIATIVE EYE, TOM'S EFFORTS TO
OPEN THE TIN OF MEAT.

we say something sensible, like Dickie did just now, and nobody answers and nothing happens. You're all rude and puffed up with yourselves—"

"I wish I was puffed up, twin," Dickie replied. "I'm starving. They can't even boil eggs. I'm coming down to get things going ... Look out, David."

They enjoyed their lunch and took a long time over it, but when the last apple-core had been thrown on the embers of the fire Dickie said, "What we want now is ackshun. Quick ackshun. We want something to happen, or us to make something happen."

"What are we going to do first these holidays?" Mary echoed. "Watter we goin' to do to-morrow, f'rinstance?"

David shifted his back against the trunk of the lone pine.

"Peter had an adventure the very day we all broke up last hols," he said. "She's going to tell us about it presently, but it hasn't got anything to do with what we do, because it's all happened and over ... I propose that every member of the Club—and I wish Jon and Penny were here, too—take it in turn to suggest a scheme to start off these holidays. We've got to do something together fairly soon, before Mr. Ingles' harvest is ready, because we shall want to help him get that in."

"What we want to know," Mary said quickly, "is how David knows what happened to Peter after she left us all that morning after the aeroplane came down. It looks to me as if they've been keeping a private secret and we're FED UP with this sort o' thing."

"David knows because I wrote and told him," Peter said, quite sharply for her, "and *one* of the reasons I wrote and told him is that he's the captain of this Club and, if he doesn't mind, I suggest that the twins give us some of their wonderful ideas first and then I hope they'll keep quiet and give someone else a chance."

Mary looked at Peter under her lashes and went a little pink. She was very fond of Peter and realized that, for once, she was annoyed with them. Then she glared at Dickie, who seemed willing to argue, and he had the sense to keep quiet.

"All right, Mary," David said. "You start and try and be sensible."

"We haven't really talked about this much," Mary began, "but if Tom—and we know he hates us bitterly—has to go back to Ingles for the harvest soon, then we think it would be best to do something all together like a camp as quickly as we can. We can always come back here when we haven't got anything special to do and Dickie and me is—are—prepared to have Tom with us whatever we do, and we think that's jolly big of us, considerin' what he was mutterin' when we were up the tree—"

"Shut up, Mary," David said. "Don't start that nonsense. Where do you suggest we go camping?"

"Clun is too far," Dickie broke in. "Mary and me suggest Seven Gates if they'll have us. We can get there easily enough, and if it's wet it's just right 'cos we can stay inside HQ2 and shut the door and light the stove an' the lamp an'—"

"Suffocate to death, I should think," Jenny said unexpectedly. "It's all very well to say Seven Gates, but that's not much of a holiday for me. I've only just got here. I don't want to go back."

"All the most excitin' and mysterious things happen round there," Dickie persisted. "We all know they do. I'd like to do some real climbing with a rope tied round me. I'd like to explore right to the very end of the Stiperstones—not just the silly old Devil's Chair. I'd like to get inside the mine again and explore that with proper lanterns and nails in my boots—only I haven't got any boots except football boots, which aren't here. We'd like to go over to Greystone Dingle again and see where the river burst out of the lake underground* and explore inside there again … Do you remember what we did to Powerless Percy, twin? What a pity we shan't ever see him again."

"That's what we suggest, then," Mary said. "Seven Gates as our headquarters, which means we can see Charles again and Mr. and Mrs. Sterling, and then we try and do real exploring inside what Jenny called the neglected mountain … That's the best thing we could do. If it's too hot we shall be in the shade inside, and if it's cold and wet the weather doesn't matter if we're exploring caves … I've got a wonderful feeling about caves—creepy, but excitin'!"

"What do you think, Tom?" David said. "Any ideas?"

"I reckon it's a good scheme of Mary's to do something together as quickly as we can because in a week maybe we'll be hard at it on the farm, and it's decent of Uncle Alf to give me so much time off now. I'm not very keen on Seven Gates. We've been there plenty o' times, and although it's best if the weather is bad, I suggest we keep this as our H.Q. and go out for the day to different places. We could go on bikes or even by bus, but I'd like to go to Shrewsbury and Ludlow and Clun and maybe Hereford— each place a different day. I reckon we could have a jolly good time that way … Maybe if the weather is awful we might go to the pictures," he added wistfully, "and it's a jolly long time since I did that. I wouldn't mind seeing a real town again. What do you think, Jenny? You wouldn't mind that, would you?"

"No. No, I don't *think* I would, Tom," Jenny said a little doubtfully as she shook back her red curls. "It's just that I'm not sure that it would be frightfully thrilling and dramatic just to go to places like that. Of course, you never know what *might* happen to us, but I think I've got a better scheme."

Jenny did not often express ideas of her own, so they all looked at her expectantly.

* "Lone Pine Five."

"Mary said that the only times things happen to us is over my way—up Black Dingle and the like. I think we've had enough of all that, and what I'd like to do is go out exploring every day on our bikes until we find our gipsies—Reuben, Miranda and Fenella. You know how nice they are and Miranda can look at your hands and tell you wonderful things, and they let us ride on the caravan and have the most marvellous meals with them … I think they're wonderful people, and whenever we've met them we've nearly always had an adventure. I think they bring us luck."

"It's a good idea," Peter said. "I like them, too, Jenny, but we don't know where they are. We might have to cycle all over England looking for them."

"No, we shan't, Peter. They're not far away, I'm sure. I don't think I told you—and this makes my idea a better one—that there's a Fair coming to Bishop's Castle soon. It comes every year and stays two nights, and gipsies come with it and sell clothes' pegs and baskets like Miranda makes. Whatever happens, we must go to the Fair, and that might mean that we'd have to stay at Seven Gates just for a few nights. But let's find the gipsies. They're always romantic and thrilling and exciting."

Then Peter had her say.

"I like Jenny's idea—'specially the Fair. We *must* go there. And that reminds me that last hols, when she and Charles got engaged, Trudie asked us all to go over and see her. She wrote the other day and reminded me that I'd promised we'd all go and would I telephone her and make a date … Wouldn't it be a good scheme if we said we'd like to come the night of the Fair, and then if Charles comes over—which I'm sure he will—he could take us back to Seven Gates in the farm van and we'd spend the night there and p'raps walk back over the Stiperstones the following morning … Let's fix that as soon as we can. I'll go

103

down to the telephone-box at Onnybrook when we've finished here and ring her up. She'll tell us the date of the Fair and let us know right away whether we can go to her that day."

They all agreed that this was probably the best idea and that Bishop's Castle was a place which none of them, except Jenny, knew very well.

"It all depends on the day of the Fair really," Tom said, "but if it's not soon and the weather keeps good we'll be harvesting, and then I'll be spending 'bout twelve hours a day on a tractor, and that's not much of a holiday … Let's all walk down to Onnybrook with Peter now and then we'll know when we're going."

"Let's do that," David agreed. "We can have a chat with old Bob in the signal-box. I didn't see him yesterday when I came in by train … I s'pose we'd better wash-up. Mother said we needn't take the crocks back. We'll just hide them in the gorse tunnel … Come on, Jenny, you help me while the others tidy up."

The relief of not being told to wash-up was such a stimulation to Dickie that he had one of his bright ideas.

"I *got* an idea," he said as he hauled Mary to her feet. "I like this Fair idea very much and so does Mary, but when we fix the day don't let's all trail over in one huge gang … Let's split up in pairs and go different ways to Bishop's Castle and see who has the best adventures."

"I bet we do," Mary said. "Dickie and me—and Mackie—I mean. That's a good idea … I s'pose you two girls will go together and then the great big strong boys will be the last pair."

Peter and Jenny glanced uneasily at each other.

"Nothing of the sort," David said abruptly. "Peter will come with me. We've got Club things to discuss, haven't we, Peter? We never have time to write in the term—"

"Not *this* term, David," Peter interrupted sweetly. "Cricket takes up so much of our time, doesn't it? All the same, I'd like to come with you. The only trouble is Jenny. There's nobody left for our Jenny except Tom, and if he's busy with the harvest she'll be on her own."

"I won't," Jenny said, very pink and defiant. "I'll be helping with the harvest, too."

They pushed the clean cups and plates in the tunnel under the gorse bushes, threw away the dirty water, scooped the tea leaves out of the kettle and put them with the egg-shells and other rubbish in a paper bag for disposal on the Witchend compost heap. The twins took the empty bucket and kettle and the boys the two haversacks, and when the camp was really clean and tidy they crept out in single file and made their way down the hill by the side of the wood.

"I've got a better idea for our day out," David said suddenly. "I'll ask Father to work out three secret routes from Witchend to Bishop's Castle. We'll tell him which party is which and he'll decide when each one is to start and hand them sealed orders which they must swear to follow. It's up to him to make handicaps if he wants to, and we'll tell him it would be a grand gesture if he gave a prize to the party which gets in first."

"We'll give him some ideas for prizes," Mary said. "We shall win ... We shall just PRESS ON an'—"

"Press on with the uttermost determination," her twin finished triumphantly.

They paused at Witchend only long enough to dump the bucket, kettle and haversacks and wave to Mr. and Mrs. Morton, and went on down the lane to Ingles. Then they paused again at the farm—the pause here was a quarter of an hour—while Mr. Ingles roared at them from across the farmyard and Mrs. Ingles brought them out some hot scones.

It was after that, when they were walking down the long hill to the main road, that Tom said, "What were you going to tell us about, Peter? Something that happened to you when you got home at the end of last hols?"

"Of course I'll tell you. I've been wanting to ever since it happened, but it's such a long time ago now."

And, curiously enough, the events of that strange afternoon seemed to have faded in her memory, and she found it difficult to recapture the fear and surprise of seeing the young man with the beard sitting at her own table and saying that, for all he knew, he might be her father. She remembered the other man—the man they called "Doctor"—more clearly, but somehow she felt that the others did not think it such a very remarkable adventure and were wondering what all the fuss was about.

"I expect he just banged his head getting out of the plane," Jenny said brightly, "and then he forgot who he was. I've never fallen out of a plane, but I've banged my head sometimes and I go quite silly with the pain. I might even think I was somebody's mother. You never know."

"No, you don't," Peter snapped. "It's obvious you don't even know what I'm talking about. I'm sorry I'm boring you all. I wrote to David about it and sent him the newspaper cuttings my man left behind. Have you got them in your pocket, David? I'm sure they'd like to see them."

"Newspaper cuttings?" Tom said. "What on earth do you mean?"

"Cuttings *from* newspapers," Peter explained very slowly and carefully. "Cuttings all about dogs who had prevented crimes or were being trained to prevent crimes. A little bundle of them. All about dogs … Oh! Show them the cuttings, David."

David looked embarrassed.

"Sorry, Peter. I don't think I've got them now. I kept them

in my wallet with your letter for a bit. They might be at school somewhere—"

"Oh, *please* don't bother to explain. It's not of the slightest interest now, although it did all seem very peculiar and quite interesting at the time ... Anyway, we're not likely to see those two men again, and I don't suppose those newspaper reports about the dogs meant anything either."

But she was wrong.

CHAPTER IV

THE MAN WITH THE CAR

A FEW mornings later all the Lone Piners met again at Witchend at half-past ten. Tom and Jenny strolled up the lane from Ingles just in time to see David and Peter walking together down the track from Hatchholt.

Tom whistled the peewit's call and Peter waved in reply as the twins, with Mackie at their heels, came running from the house to meet them all.

"You two look jolly pleased with yourselves," Tom said as Peter and David came up. "What have you been doing? David looks as if he's had a bath."

"I have," David said. "I had an invitation to breakfast at nine o'clock, and I went at eight and to give myself an appetite I went swimming first ... I managed to beat Peter by about a yard, but if she goes on like this I shan't be able to catch her at the end of the hols."

Jenny looked at Peter ruefully.

"You did promise that I could come swimming with you before I go back to Barton," she said. "You haven't forgotten—"

"Of course I haven't. It was Dad's idea to ask David to breakfast. I can't think why, except that he says he's an intelligent lad and knows how to listen to his elders. I hated the idea of seeing him so early in the day, of course, but what could I say? ... We'll have a swimming party at the reservoir soon, but I think we ought to wait until Daddy goes to Shrewsbury or Birmingham for the day because he gets rather fussed when all the Lone Piners come to Hatchholt at the same time. It's just that he's afraid we shall spill things or spoil the polish on the table ... We'll fix it soon, though, Jenny. It'll be grand, although the water this morning was so cold we could hardly bear it. David was as blue as an ancient Briton covered with woad when he came out ... Is Mr. Morton ready for us, twins? Has he got the sealed orders?"

Mary nodded. "In his pocket. He's sitting in the porch looking mysterious and puffing at his pipe. We think this is a jolly good idea, but the waiting is awful. He won't tell us anything."

"I should think not," Jenny said indignantly. "You two get away with a lot, but Mr. Morton is always fair. Shall we go and ask him to put us out of this awful suspense? ... I read a book once about a man who was given a secret letter which he had to take to a distant kingdom ... And when he had travelled for a day and a night—I don't remember what distant kingdom it was—he opened the letter. I'm not quite sure *exactly* what was in the letter, but I know it led him in the end to a humble girl who was a servant in an old castle and—what do you think?"

"I bet she was a princess or a duchess or someone of noble lineage," said David promptly. "There you are! I knew I was right. It's just the way in which you tell the story, Jenny. That's what makes it easy for someone clever like me to guess."

"You can laugh at me, David," Jenny said as she laughed herself. "I don't care ... And it was a jolly good story 'cos I remember it very well even now. Let's go and ask Mr. Morton to start us off."

They opened the gate and walked across the grass to Mr. Morton, who was reading the newspaper which had just been delivered by their old friend the postman. They stood before him in a semi-circle with the twins in the centre and waited for him to speak. Inside the house Mrs. Morton was singing, but her husband looked almost stern as he glanced at them over the top of his paper.

"What a grand lot they are," he thought, "and mine are all the better for the friendship of the others."

Tom was at the far end of the line. Small, tough and very brown, with a cheerful grin on his face and a shrewd look in his eye as their glances crossed. Jenny next to him in a bright green blouse and grey kilted skirt. Her cheeky, freckled face was getting very pretty. Then the twins, and there wasn't much he didn't know about them, although he was amused to see that they were looking quite tense. Then David, of whom he was very proud, and next to David, Peter. How fond they all were of Peter and how nice she looked, upright, slim and yet so very feminine in bright blue summer frock with a new belt and a scarlet jersey over her arm. Her hair, bleached by the summer sun, was almost ash-blonde, and she gave him a lovely smile as she caught his eye.

"*Please* don't keep us waiting too long, Mr. Morton. We're all worked up with excitement."

"You're all on time," he said as he looked at his watch. "And I'm pleased to see that you're all taking this seriously. I've taken your suggestion seriously, too, in the preparation of your orders. Do you all promise solemnly to obey the orders which I am about to give you?"

Mary checked a giggle which was due to excitement rather than to anything funny.

"Of course we all swear, Daddy. Dickie and me have made a vow that we go out on this journey without scrip or purse and follow it to the bitter end."

"I don't think it will be as bad as that, Mary, and I don't see why the end should be bitter. Surely you're going to tea with Trudie Whittington, aren't you, and then on to the Fair? And what's a scrip?"

"Don't rag her, Dad," Dickie said. "Never mind about the scrip. As we're the smallest, may we go now?"

Mr. Morton shook his head as he took three envelopes from his pocket.

"No, Richard. You are not the first to leave. David and Peter first."

"But, Daddy," Mary wailed, "we're the smallest, and we shall have to take Mackie wherever we go, an' it's not fair to keep us back."

"Let me look at the envelope, David," Peter said. "It says 'Open at once.' ... Come on ... Let's take it where the others can't see."

"What do we do now, then?" Dickie protested as his father retired again behind his newspaper and David and Peter went over to the gate. "You've put those other envelopes away again."

"Tom and Jenny come back for their orders at ten to eleven and the twins at ten past eleven ... Sorry to keep you waiting, but you've promised to obey orders."

"I'm going in to see if I can help Mrs. Morton," Jenny said. "Call me when it's time, Tom. Of course you can come and help, too, if you like."

"Just a sec," Tom said. "I want to see which way David and Peter are going. There's nothing in the rules to say we shouldn't."

David was now pushing the crumpled orders into the back pocket of his corduroys and Peter was laughing at him. Then they looked up, waved towards the porch and set off along the side of the stream up the valley.

"They're going over the top of the Mynd," Tom said. "And that means they've got a long walk. That's why Mr. Morton sent them off first ... Come on, Jenny. Let's see if we can do anything to help indoors."

The twins went back to their favourite perch on the top rung of the gate, and exchanged views on the curious ways and habits of grown-ups and of parents in particular, and of the hard and bitterly unjust lives led by young twins.

They were still enjoying themselves in this way when Tom and Jenny received their orders and came and pushed them rudely off their gate.

"Cheerio, kids," Tom said. "See you at the Fair if you get there in time."

Then the twins went down to the stream, lay on their stomachs on the bank and put their noses as close to the running water as they could without wetting them. But after a few minutes this entertainment seemed to be as pointless as it was exhausting, so they rolled over, closed their eyes to the sun and tormented Mackie by urging him to show his affection by licking their faces.

Three times they went to their father, pointing out that, as they had not yet been given watches of their own, it was quite impossible for them to know how time was passing. But at last the summons came and Mr. Morton placed a bulky envelope, containing something fairly heavy which clinked, into Dickie's trembling hands.

"There you are," their father said. "Take care of yourselves. Obey the orders. Have a good day and enjoy the Fair. You can beat the others to Bishop's Castle even now if you hurry ... Good-bye."

They scuttled away to the gate with Mackie at their heels and opened the sealed orders. Two half-crowns fell out.

"Look at that," Mary gasped. "The letter, I mean. Daddy has printed it."

"Walk down to Onnybrook at once," the orders read, "and catch the 11.50 bus to Ludlow. At the top of Broad Street, on the left-hand side, just below the Butter Cross, is a café. At any

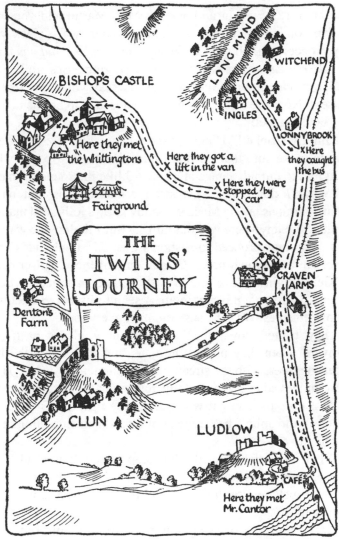

THE ARROWS ➤ ➤ SHOW THE ROUTE THE TWINS TOOK FROM
WITCHEND TO BISHOP'S CASTLE.

time after 12.45 go in and ask for Mrs. Martin and you will receive something to your advantage. After two o'clock you may proceed to Bishop's Castle any way you like, *but you must not take more than one bus*. Not even changing buses is allowed, but if you can find one that goes all the way you are at liberty to use it. No more money than that enclosed is to be spent. You may take Macbeth."

"Jiminy Cricket!" Dickie gasped. "Isn't this wizard? We'll have to make sure that we don't miss that bus. I wonder what we'll find to our advantage at a café—I like the sound of that."

"What *I* don't like," his sister remarked, "is that nasty remark about us taking Mackie. Daddy knows jolly well that we wouldn't go anywhere without him ... But I do like the way he says, 'You may proceed to Bishop's Castle.' I think that's very important and grown-up ... Gimme one of those half-crowns, Dickie. I ought to have one in case we get separated ... Let's pretend we're on a mission, twin. A secret mission. Something to do with spies. We'll be suspicious of everybody."

They trotted down the lane without a glance at Ingles farmyard when they passed the gate, and then down the hill under the trees, with the stream running under the hedge. They knew and loved every inch of this road and always remembered the first time they saw it when they rode up from Onnybrook station in old John's battered car and had their first glimpse of Witchend.

When they arrived at the bus stop in the main road three people, whom they knew by sight, were already waiting. They smiled a welcome to the twins and then looked astonished as Mary said,

"Good morning. We're going in the bus, too, but I'm sorry we can't talk too much to anybody 'cos we're on a secret mission."

"That's right," Dickie agreed. "You mustn't mind if we're rather aloof." The last word, which was one of his new possessions, he pronounced "aloaf" and was not in any way put out by the look of amusement on the faces of his listeners.

Macbeth liked buses and was no trouble on Mary's lap, so the journey, on the route they knew so well, was uneventful. They never tired of Ludlow, which their father had told them was one of the most unspoiled towns in England, and when they got out near the castle gates Dickie said, "It's only half-past twelve. The orders say the café after twelve forty-five, so shall we go up the castle or down by the river?"

Mary looked doubtful. "Mackie doesn't like those slippery stone steps inside the keep. He doesn't really like the castle much at all. He doesn't 'preciate old ruins, Dickie, and you ought to know that … Let's not go up to-day. Let's go and look in that nice bookshop in Broad Street and then go and see what's to our advantage."

Dickie made no objection. He wasn't very keen on ruins either, but he liked climbing to the iron cage on the top of the keep and looking out over the sweep of the river Teme below to the Welsh hills in one direction, to the forest of Clun, where they had had an adventure with sheep stealers one winter holiday, in another and northwards to the blue line of their own Stretton Hills.

They wandered back into the town, found the bookshop and were allowed to look round and pick up books and then, precisely three minutes late, they went back to the café. In the porch Dickie, although he knew them by heart, glanced again at the sealed orders just to make sure that the name was Mrs. Martin. Then he took a deep breath and opened the door.

The café was long and narrow, with lots of dark oak tables and pleasant pictures on the walls and coloured lamp-shades.

So far as they could see there were no empty tables. They were not particularly surprised to notice that the woman in a green overall by the cash desk was staring at them because people always *did* stare, and it was the sort of thing to which the twins became accustomed. But when the stare changed to what was surely a smile of welcome Dickie stepped forward and leaned across the cake counter.

"We gotter speak to Mrs. Martin," he whispered out of the side of his mouth, as he had seen those curious beings in slouch hats do in some American films. "Are you Mrs. Martin—?" he nearly added the word "Sister," but wisely thought better of it.

"No, I'm not," the woman replied, withdrawing herself a little from Dickie's out-thrust lower lip, "but, all the same, you're expected. Please wait there," and she beckoned one of the hurrying waitresses and whispered something which they could not hear.

Mackie sat down, sniffed the beautiful smells of cooking food and yawned audibly while his master and mistress looked at each other in astonishment. How could they be expected? They hadn't even given their names! It was all very mysterious.

Then a pleasant lady with grey hair came out of a door they hadn't noticed and stood before them smiling.

"You are punctual," she said. "I know you are Richard and Mary Morton—and the dog, of course, I recognize him—so will you please come this way?"

Mary went a little pale.

"It's magic," she whispered. "It must be. Do you think it's all right, Dickie?"

Her brother gulped, nodded and followed Mrs. Martin between the crowded tables to one in the corner on which was a card bearing the word "Reserved."

"Please sit down here," Mrs. Martin smiled. "This table has

been kept for you and you may have whatever you like to eat so long as it is on the menu … And you may have what you like to drink and ice-cream and raspberries afterwards … And if you think your dog would come with me, Mary, I'll give him a few tit-bits in the kitchen. How would you like that, Macbeth?"

Mary, still pale, rallied a little.

"He'd like that and we like it all, too, but it's only right to tell you that we've only got 'bout four shillings between us an'—"

"You don't have to worry about that, Mary. I have my instructions. Everything is paid for. All you have to do is to enjoy your meal. What would you like?"

It took a long time to decide and, in the end, they chose the most ordinary things—Dickie taking fried plaice and Mary bacon, egg and chips. They never knew what Mackie had, although it was obvious when he reappeared, thoughtfully licking his whiskers, that he had lunched well.

"I think this is marvellous of Daddy," Mary said ten minutes later as she bit into a very hot chip. "I think he's the most wonderful father. O' course, you realize he planned all this in advance. This is what we've found to our advantage, Dickie. I wish we could always find things like this to our advantage."

Mary had a very clear and penetrating voice. She was enjoying herself, had forgotten even about the race to Bishop's Castle and, for a moment or two, was not even aware that several people were listening to her and smiling at them. But Dickie, who had his back to the room, sensed that once again they were the centre of attraction and turned round to see the size and quality of their audience. He turned back quickly with a frown and said quietly to his twin, "Mary. There's a man. Quite an old man, two tables away on the left. He's by himself and he's lookin' at us hard … I think we know him, Mary. Who is he?"

Mary stopped talking and looked over her twin's shoulder.

Two tables away and watching them with a mixture of curiosity and benevolence was a short, stout little man with a rosy, innocent face, wearing spectacles with heavy horn sides. His hair was grey and several long strips were brushed across his pink scalp in a rather feeble attempt to hide his baldness. He was wearing a greenish tweed suit and from the hook in the wall above his chair hung a shapeless tweed hat of the same colour.

Mary's face went very pink.

"Dickie! Don't you know who it is? It's Mr. Cantor. The detective we met at Clun* and who took us for a walk and who helped us to catch the sheep thieves. I'm *sure* it's Mr. Cantor and I'm sure he's remembered us, too … HULLO, MR. CANTOR! How wonderful to see you. May we come and talk to you? Are you doing any DETECTING?"

These remarks were uttered in a shrill whisper which could probably have been overheard in the forecourt of the castle, and they seemed to embarrass the elderly gentleman, who put a finger to his lips as they got up and came over to his table.

"Richard and Mary Morton," he said, rather precisely. "How very curious to meet you here. How are you both—and all your other young friends?"

"We're very well, thank you. We're staying at Witchend for the holidays and now we're acting under sealed orders," Dickie explained. "I knew you the very second I saw you, Mr. Cantor. Will you whisper and tell us whether you're on the trail?"

"I'll not whisper anything, Richard, and I'll thank you both not to shout my business aloud. I should have thought that after our last adventure you would have learned a little more caution."

Although he said this so sternly that poor Dickie coloured with annoyance, there was a twinkle in his eye as he turned and smiled at Mary.

* "The Secret of Grey Walls."

"You must come outside and tell me all about yourselves. You must indeed. I shall be most interested to know how you are spending your time in these parts. I seem to remember that something was always happening when you and your young friends were about ... Have you finished your meal?"

Dickie looked embarrassed.

"Not exackly," he said. "We hope there's several more things to come. It's rather difficult to explain to you, but we're sort of guests here. Whatever we have our father is paying for ... Oh, no, Mr. Cantor. He's not here with us. He arranged all this and I 'spect it's all going on the bill."

"Dear me," Mr. Cantor smiled. "How very generous of Mr. Morton, whom I don't think I ever met. I hope he won't have too great a shock ... You know the bridge over the river at the foot of the hill? Come down and join me there as soon as you are ready. No need to hurry. Do not spoil your father's pleasure," and he reached for the floppy tweed hat which they remembered so well, and strolled over to the cash desk.

The twins went back to their table feeling, and looking, rather subdued.

"I s'pose we ought to go and speak to him," Dickie said. "Do you think we can spare the time? If we go, do you think we shall win the race to Bishop's Castle?"

"We're goin' anyway," Mary said. "I like him very much and I think that where Mr. Cantor is there might be an adventure ... Do you remember, twin, that after we found out who he really was he altered his voice and looked much younger? He had his old voice just now, so I'm sure he's in a sort of disguise ... Let's go down to the bridge and see what we can find out."

Ten minutes later, after raspberries and cream and double ices, they said "Good-bye" to Mrs. Martin and her friendly staff, woke Mackie from his sleep under the table and went out into the sunshine.

Mr. Cantor was waiting for them on the bridge. He was leaning over the parapet with his tweed hat tilted over his eyes and an old pipe between his teeth, and gave them a welcoming smile and a pat for Mackie when they came up.

"Are you *really* detecting now?" Dickie whispered. "If you are, can we help you? You'll never forget how jolly helpful we all were before, will you?"

"No, I won't forget that, Richard. I'll always ask your help if I need it—and yours, Mary. What are you going to do now?"

They knew at once that he did not intend to tell them any more than this and were a little puzzled to know why he had wanted to speak to them away from the café.

"Acksherly," Mary explained, after rather a long pause, "we have got special sealed and secret orders given us by Daddy, but we don't mind telling you that we're all meeting at Bishop's Castle to-night and we're goin' to the Fair. *And* we're going to a party first 'cos Peter's cousin, Charles Sterling, at Seven Gates, who is a very wonderful man, is going to marry Trudie Whittington, who we like very much—"

"So you're going to meet at Whittington's, are you? Well, well! I've known Mr. Whittington for many years and maybe I'll see you to-night because I may be over that way myself. I like fairs."

"You remember the gipsies, Reuben and Miranda, who helped us over at Clun, don't you, Mr. Cantor?" Dickie said. "Yes, I thought you would. Do you think they'll come to the Fair, too? We want to meet them again."

"I expect they'll be there, Richard. I'm sure they're not far away and all the Romanies for miles round will be at the Castle to-night and to-morrow … If I don't see you all later, pray convey my very best wishes and regards to all your young friends. I cannot recall their names, although I should recognize them, I am sure ... I wonder if you would permit me to provide something for your refreshment on your journey? Good-bye."

And almost before they could thank him, he gave them each half-a-crown, raised his tweed hat courteously and walked away from them up the hill.

"I love him," Mary said. "I always did and to-day he's more mysterious than ever."

"He's all right," Dickie agreed. "But, all the same, I'm sure he's sleuthing. Sometimes he used his real voice and then, just now, when he said, 'Pray convey my good wishes,' he was talking like the old Mr. Cantor we first knew ... I don't think we ought to go yet 'cos he might think we were trying to trail him. Wait till he's got to the top of the street. I reckon he's got a powerful police car hidden somewhere ... I hope we'll see him to-night 'cos otherwise I don't suppose the others will believe we met him ... Now we can go. We'd better look at the bus time-table, only I can never understand them properly ... It was jolly decent of him to give us half-a-crown. Shall we spend it or save it?"

"Save it for now," Mary said. "We'll want it at the Fair."

They soon found that there was no direct bus to Bishop's Castle and then decided to catch the first that came up the main road to Craven Arms and then walk or hitch-hike the remaining six miles.

"It sounds a long way," Mary said. "I think Daddy must have known very well that we'd have to walk a lot of the way ... He's been cunning about this, Dickie."

The bus journey did not take long, but the road to Bishop's Castle was not at all busy on this summer afternoon and they had walked for nearly half an hour with Mackie trotting happily between them when they heard a car behind them and turned to see whether there was any chance of a lift.

The car was small, noisy and old, and although neither of them made any signal, it pulled up with a screeching of brakes beside them. It was an open four-seater with the space behind the driving-seat covered by a waterproof sheet. The driver was a youngish man with a wild shock of hair and wearing horn-rimmed spectacles. His blue suit looked almost as grubby as his shirt. When he spoke his voice was quite pleasant.

"Good afternoon! Where are you going with that nice little dog? ... Here, boy! Come and say 'How do' to me," and he moved across to the empty seat, opened the door and clicked his fingers encouragingly to Mackie, who was looking at him with his head on one side.

They stared at him and, without any obvious reason, disliked him at once. His fingers were stained brown and there was a curious, wild look in the dark eyes behind the spectacles, but what surprised them most was that Mackie, who in the usual way would probably have snarled at a stranger, gave a funny little whine, wagged his tail and put his two front feet on the dashboard of the car.

"Mackie," Mary said sharply, "Come here."

The little dog stopped almost reluctantly and looked back at his mistress just as the stranger leaned forward and picked him up.

"Nice little chap," he began. "I like Scotties. Can I give you a lift anywhere? Where are you going?"

"Never you mind where we're going," Mary stormed as she went into action. "Put that dog down! He belongs to us. Give him to me," and, to Dickie's admiration, she put one foot on the running-board of the car and grabbed the struggling Macbeth from the astonished stranger.

MACKIE GAVE A FUNNY LITTLE WHINE AND WAGGED HIS TAIL.
"MACKIE, COME HERE!" SAID MARY SHARPLY.

"How *dare* you," she said with tears in her eyes. "How dare you trick him or speak to us? We don't want a lift anywhere, thank you. Please go away."

The man ran his fingers through his hair and gave them a wild sort of look.

"Walk if you prefer it," he said. "I thought you looked tired and I like dogs. Where do you come from, anyway? I've not seen you round here before, have I?"

"I shouldn't think so," Dickie said, and added, rather rudely, "I hope not."

They stood still, with Mackie still wriggling in Mary's arms, until the car had disappeared round the bend in the road. Then Mary put the dog down, looked at Dickie without a word and followed it.

Dickie spoke first.

"Why don't we like him, twin?"

"I don't know. Because he was peculiar, I s'pose. Why should he stop like that and say he likes Mackie?"

"And why did Mackie like him when we hate him? *That's* the most peculiar thing of all."

"There was something else, too, Dickie. His clothes had a strong smell. Not a nasty smell. A *different* smell. It's difficult to explain, but I noticed it most partickeler."

"I wish Mackie could speak," was all that Dickie said.

Ten minutes later a grocer's delivery van from Bishop's Castle came up behind them, and when Mary waved the man stopped.

"Thank you very much," she smiled. "We're going to the Fair and our little dog here is rather tired, so if you could squeeze us in the front there with you we should get there much more quickly."

The driver gave them an amused glance and opened the door.

"Plenty of room for three little 'uns. Hop in. We'll all be at the Fair to-night, I reckon." Then he looked at them again, blinked with astonishment and the van swerved. "Where do you come from? Don't seem to have seen you afore. Holiday-makers?"

"We come from Witchend by Onnybrook," Dickie explained. "We're not really strangers 'cos we come nearly every holidays … We're going now to Mr. Whittington's for a party."

"That's the way we go into the town," the man said. "I'll deliver you right to the door."

On their way they passed the field in which the Fair was going up. There were some gipsy caravans in the far corner, but there was so much noise and bustle round the nearly-completed stalls and side-shows, and as the driver did not seem inclined to wait they had no chance to see whether Reuben and Miranda had arrived.

The streets of the fascinating little town were steep and winding and the van stopped outside a pleasant, low, white-walled house with a porch supported by two pillars. On the left of the house was a cobbled yard and on the gatepost of this they saw a shining brass plate.

"Here you are," the driver said. "And you're welcome. I'll be bringing my youngsters along to-night and we'll look out for you. I reckon my Joan would like to meet you. She'll never believe me when I tells her how like you are."

Mary smiled at him sweetly and held out her hand, and as Dickie did the same at the same time, and as the driver had no idea they were going to shake hands with him, there was some momentary confusion.

As the van rattled off down the street Dickie grabbed his twin's hand and dashed into the yard.

"Quick!" he said. "We got to prove we got here first. That was Tom and Jenny at the end of the street."

125

As the door marked "Surgery" was closed the only thing to do was to ring the bell and hope that it would be answered before their rivals arrived.

Then they heard voices and footsteps behind the door, which was opened by the smiling Trudie. Before she could even say "Hullo" the twins jumped over the threshold.

"Sorry to be in a hurry," Mary gasped, "but we *are* the first, aren't we?"

"You'd swear anywhere that we're here the first, wouldn't you?" Dickie pleaded. "Tom and Jenny are only just down the street, and they might be jolly unscroopless—if you know what I mean, Trudie."

"Yes, you're first, twins, and it's grand to see you. You can come in this way through the surgery. Father is out now and I'm not sure when he'll be back. Come and wait in the other room while I finish speaking to this gentleman who has come in with his lovely dog."

And at that moment, just as with one ear they heard Tom and Jenny coming into the yard, a man's voice which seemed vaguely familiar came to them from the shadows at the end of the flagged passage.

"I'd bet any money in the world that's Richard and Mary Morton," it said. "Surely you don't know these two rascals, do you, Miss Whittington?"

"Oh, but I do. I've known them nearly six months. Surely they haven't got as far as Clun, have they, Mr. Denton?"

Alan Denton, of course! Alan, their friend the sheep farmer over in Clun Forest, whom they hadn't seen since their adventure with the sheep thieves round the house known as Grey Walls.

Mary rushed at him.

"Alan! How marvellous! Of course it's us, and if you can wait a little while you'll meet us all, except Jon and Penny, who can't come up here this hols … Here's Tom and Jenny, anyway, and Peter and David are on their way."

Dickie grinned at Tom.

"We beat you," he said. "Trudie will swear. You remember Alan Denton, don't you?"

And while they were all shaking hands with Denton, Mary noticed Mackie wag his tail and prance up the hall to meet Alan's lovely collie sheepdog, Lady. The bitch was sitting by the door of the surgery and did not take much notice of the little black Scottie, but Mary remembered her well and ran forward, crying her name.

"Be careful of her, Mary," Denton said sharply. "She's not been well."

But Mary was already on her knees with her arms round Lady's slim neck. The bitch turned and licked her face and then the little girl looked up and wrinkled her nose.

"That's funny. Lady's got a most peculiar smell. It reminds me of that man we hated, Dickie. I noticed how his clothes smelt when I snatched Mackie away from him."

CHAPTER V

QUIETEST UNDER THE SUN

THE sealed orders given to Tom and Jenny were brief and to the point.

"With the help of your bicycles find the quietest place under the sun. Look for a buffalo and find out what's good for you."

Tom pushed back Jenny's curls, which were tickling his cheek as she leaned over his shoulder.

"What's he mean, Jen? What's the quietest place under the sun?"

"Let me think. Whatever happens, we've got to win this prize, Tom. We've just got to get there first. We haven't got a second to waste, so let's dash down to the farm now and get our bikes and think while we run ... You know, Tom, this really is a wonderful and most exciting idea ... It's like a treasure hunt really ... *Come on*, Tom!"

She grabbed his hand as he crammed the folded paper in his pocket and pulled him down the lane towards Ingles.

"Steady on, Jenny," he protested. "There's no need to dash about like this. We'll get to the Fair and the party all right, and I don't see really that it matters very much what time we arrive so long as we all enjoy ourselves ... I can't think when I'm running, anyway."

Jenny saw the sense of this. Perhaps there wasn't, after all, any need to make a race of it. This day, with three pairs of Lone Piners each having an adventure and meeting in the evening, might be one of the very best days they'd ever had and could be a wonderful beginning to the holidays.

"All right, Tom. Let's do as you say. What do you think the

writing means? I'm sure I've heard something about quietest place under the sun before. I s'pose we ought not to ask Mr. and Mrs. Ingles, ought we?"

"I don't see why not. Nobody said we weren't to ask grown-ups; but I'd rather we thought of it ourselves ... Buffalo, Jen? That reminds me of something, too."

They had reached the farmyard gate of Ingles now and he stood on the bottom rung, leaned his elbows on the top bar and looked across at his uncle's golden fields. Suddenly he turned round and faced her.

"Got it, Jen! Don't you remember the Buffalo? It's a pub in Clun, up at the top of the street near the castle. It's such a rum name for an inn, and as we had that winter holiday there and all that business with the sheep and Alan Denton and the detective, Cantor, I reckon Mr. Morton was sure we'd remember it ... This is easy now, so I'll get the bikes, but I wish I knew what we're going to do when we find the Buffalo."

"I wish I knew what's going to be good for us," Jenny laughed. "But I think I've remembered about 'quietest under the sun'. There's a rhyme about it, but let's ask Mrs. Ingles—she'll know."

While Tom went round to one of the barns for the cycles Jenny ran into the kitchen.

As usual, Mrs. Ingles was cooking. Jenny had never known anyone who did so much cooking for so few people, but although she had not been at the farm many days her stay had been long enough for her to realize that Mr. Ingles ate more than anyone she had ever known and that for someone who was small and wiry Tom also did very well. Her own appetite was improving, too, and the fact that Mrs. Ingles baked her own bread may have had something to do with that.

"Hullo, Mrs. Ingles," Jenny said breathlessly. "We're just off on our adventure. It's supposed to be secret, but Tom and me are going to Clun first and then on to Bishop's Castle like we told you. We're going on our bikes now, so I've just come in to say good-bye."

Mrs. Ingles turned a glowing face from the oven.

"Good-bye, indeed! A body might think we were never going to see you again, Jenny love … You told me you'd be out for the day at breakfast time, so I've packed you up a bite in the old haversack, and I reckon you and Tom'll be all right till you get to the Whittingtons."

She crossed the room and drew Jenny by the arm over to the window.

"How many days have you been with us, Jenny? Only five? I was only saying to Alf this very morning that 'tis beginning to look as if Ingles suits you. You're looking bonny, love. Are you happy here?"

She looked down at the little tanned, freckled face and saw Jenny's grey eyes suddenly fill with tears.

"There, there," she said as she bent and kissed her. "We know you're happy and we're happy to have you here … There's too many men in this house, I was telling Alf and Tom only a week ago, and you being here evens things up a bit … 'Tis nice to have a girl about the place, I must say, and good for us all."

"You're very, very kind to me, Mrs. Ingles," Jenny gulped. "You mustn't think I'm not very happy with you, 'cos I am."

"No more Mrs. Ingles," the woman said as she looked out of the window over Jenny's auburn head. "I'm Aunt Betty to you, same as I am to young Tom … Now be off with you and have a good day with all your mysteries and adventures and the like … Take the haversack, and I'm not forgetting you'll be sleeping at Seven Gates to-night with the others … God bless you, love."

Jenny reached up and kissed her, grabbed the heavy

haversack and ran for the door. Out in the yard Tom was whistling cheerfully as he pumped up the back tyre of her cycle. He grinned when he saw the haversack.

"We'll never starve when Aunt Betty's about, Jen. Did you remind her we wouldn't be back to-night?"

"She'd remembered. She's marvellous. Nobody could have a more wonderful aunt than Aunt Betty. ... Don't you forget to go and say good-bye to her."

Tom looked surprised at this outburst, but had the sense to say nothing. Women were very odd. But he did go in and say good-bye to his aunt and thanked her for packing up the food and this seemed to please her very much.

Ten minutes later they were on the main road and heading south.

"We won't try and cut across country, Jenny," Tom said. "Let's go to Craven Arms first and then maybe we could have an ice or something, and then take our time going to Clun ... Are you in a special hurry now, anyway? I can hardly keep up with you."

Jenny laughed.

"Not really in a hurry. When I'm happy I pedal very fast—if it's not uphill. Sometimes I think bikes are the most loathsome sort of torture, but other times, when I'm in a good mood like now, I like them very much ... Sometimes when I'm biking to school and the wind and rain is against me, do you know what I do, Tom?"

Tom could never be sure what Jenny did.

"I just *cry*, Tom. I sob with fury, Tom. Sometimes I shout out awful curses at the wind, but it never makes any difference, except that it beats me and I have to get off and walk as a punishment."

"Do you really curse, Jen?" Tom seemed amused. "What do

you say? I've heard Uncle Alf say a thing or two, but I didn't know you could curse."

Jenny went a little pink.

"I couldn't tell you, Tom. I've got a secret curse I made up about the Devil's Chair. You mustn't ask me, Tom. Honest you mustn't!"

"O.K.," Tom laughed, and he didn't ask her, which was rather annoying.

"Let's wait here for a bit," Tom suggested when they reached the oddly-named Craven Arms. "I could do with an ice. We'll find a place and I'll treat you."

They found a café where two lorry drivers were having a friendly argument with the girl behind the counter, but who soon turned their attention to Tom and Jenny. But Tom didn't care. He bought Jenny a double ice and then ordered himself a ginger beer with an ice-cream in it, and sucked up this peculiar mixture through a straw, and when the men began to tease him he was so good-humoured with his answers that one of them insisted upon buying them both ginger beers.

"I feel blown up like a balloon now," Tom said as they jumped on their bikes again. "Maybe the exercise will do me good. Let's get there as quickly as we can. This is the road we came the very first day we came to Clun. D'you remember, Jen? You went in the bus with the twins and Mackie, and I cycled with Penny and David and Jon. It was jolly cold, too … Here's our turning. See the signpost?"

Jenny squealed with excitement and wobbled dangerously.

"I forgot to ask Aunt Betty about the rhyme, Tom, but I've just remembered it. Now I know what quietest under the sun means. The names of the places on the signpost reminded me, but I think it was a difficult clue of Mr. Morton's. We'd never have guessed it if you hadn't been so clever about the hippopotamus."

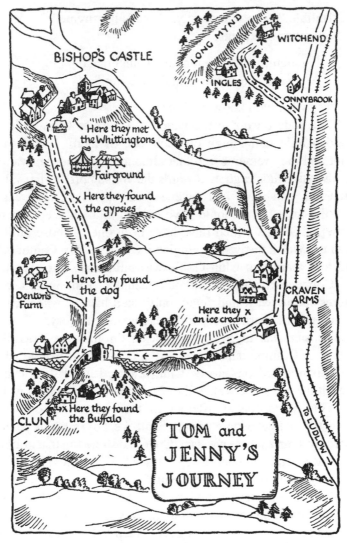

BISHOP'S CASTLE

Here they met
the Whittingtons

Fairground

x Here they found
the gypsies

Denton's
Farm

x Here they found
the dog

Here they x
an ice cream

LONG MYND

WITCHEND

INGLES

ONNYBROOK

CRAVEN
ARMS

x Here they found
the Buffalo

CLUN

TOM and
JENNY'S
JOURNEY

TO LUDLOW →

FOLLOW THE ARROWS → → FOR THE ROUTE TAKEN BY TOM AND
JENNY FROM WITCHEND TO BISHOP'S CASTLE.

"Buffalo," Tom said quietly. "What's the rhyme?"

"Something like this:

'Clungunford and Clunbury, Clunton and Clun,
Are the quietest places under the sun.'

It's easy when you know, isn't it?"

They rode on down the valley of the river Clun with the wooded hills rising high on each side of them. It was very quiet and they remembered that although the road did wander westwards rather vaguely towards the Welsh border after it had left Clun, that there had never seemed any very real reason why the little town should have existed at all. Except for the castle, of course, which must have been one of those built to keep the Welsh away from England. Or was it Mr. Cantor who had told them that Clun Castle was built soon after William the Conqueror? They couldn't remember. Tom wasn't very interested, anyway, and Jenny only liked history when it was about people—particularly if it was romantic history.

The sun was high as they cycled through the straggling village of Clunton, and it was just after half-past twelve when they dismounted on narrow Clun bridge, leaned their cycles against the old stone wall and looked down into the cool water.

"This place looks different in the summer," Tom said. "Actually a few people about! Shall we go and look at that boarding-house where we stayed? We had some fun that holiday, didn't we, Jen? I wonder if we shall see those gipsies? Have you got any money to spend at the Fair?"

"Dad gave me ten shillings and I've got seven left. I'm going to buy something for you, Tom. I want you to have a souvenir of the Fair ... No, don't let's go to 'Keep View'—that was the name of the boarding-house. Let's go to the Buffalo right away and see what's good for us. I'll never dare go in."

"I don't know that I will," Tom admitted. "You're not supposed to go into pubs until you're eighteen, but maybe there's a door at the side. I believe it's a sort of hotel ... Come on. Let's get it over."

Tom was right. There was a glass-panelled door under a porch with a bell-push set in the wall, and it was obvious that this was not the door used by those who wanted the bar. Tom took a deep breath and pressed the bell. Nothing happened. He tried again and this time the door was opened by a girl in an apron and a print frock, who looked at them curiously and then smiled a welcome. She could not have been many years older than Tom.

"I reckon the Guvnor's expecting you two. Come in," she said.

Completely mystified, they stepped into the cool, dark hall, and followed the girl down the passage into a room furnished with a sofa and chairs to match, with hard, black, shiny seats, a sideboard and table of gleaming mahogany and an aspidistra in a pot which stood on a small bamboo table in the window.

"I'll tell the guvnor," the girl said and went out.

They stared at each other as her footsteps receded down the flagged corridor. Then they heard a burst of loud talk and laughter as a door opened and closed.

"This is a rum go, Jenny," Tom whispered. "What's it all about?"

"I'm sure it's going to be all right, Tom. Mr. Morton would never do anything to make us really frightened, but he knows we like adventures, and he's giving us one ... Listen. I think someone's coming."

She was right. The door to the bar opened again and they heard the sound of men's voices and then the footsteps coming nearer.

Jenny moved away from the table and stood close to Tom, who had his back to the window. The man who came in was small, brown-faced and wrinkled. He was in his shirt sleeves and wearing a pair of green corduroy trousers, and there was very little hair left on the top of his head. At once Jenny was reminded of a gnome. He stood just inside the door and smiled at them—a pleasant, crinkly smile.

"So you've come to see what's good for you," he said in his slow, country voice. "You must be Tom and Jenny, I reckon, come to find the old Buffalo … I've been expecting you this half-hour gone, and told young Jessie to be looking out for you."

"That's wonderful," Jenny laughed. "But how do you know our names, and will you tell us what's good for us?"

"And have you got any other message for us?" Tom said quickly, remembering that they didn't know what they were supposed to do next.

"Aye, that I have, Tom. First of all you're to have what you like to eat and drink here—that's what's good for you—and not a penny to pay. You've only to say what you want and young Jessie will come in here and lay the cloth. I don't keep ice-creams here and I can't offer you a steak, but there's some cold ham and red-currant tart."

Jenny looked ruefully at the heavy haversack which Mrs. Ingles had packed for them and then at Tom.

"It's very, very good of you, Mr—"

"Jenkins is the name, Jenny. Jim Jenkins of the Buffalo."

"Mr. Jenkins. But I don't see how we can possibly waste all the food Mrs. Ingles packed up for us. I'm so sorry I can't manage two dinners. Could you, Tom?"

Tom looked doubtful. "Not if one of 'em is cold ham and the other has been made by Aunt Betty. I tell you what I think we ought to do, Mr. Jenkins. We'll take our picnic up on the hill by the castle and eat it there, but if you could let us take up some bottles of ginger beer that would be grand ... What was the other message?"

Mr. Jenkins twinkled at them.

"I was to tell you that you're not to leave Clun for Bishop's Castle until five o'clock and you can come back here to tea if you like, for everything is paid for ... You can take any bottles you like and I'll lend you an opener if you'll let me have it back with the empties."

"This adventure is like a fairy story," Jenny said. "I know it's all been arranged by Mr. Morton, but it's wonderful for us to be expected like this. You're very kind, Mr. Jenkins ... You're rather like a good fairy yourself," she added unexpectedly.

The little man roared with laughter, and after telling them to make themselves at home said that he would put the bottles and the opener in the hall and would see them at tea time.

The ruined castle of Clun stands bravely on a high green mound, round which the river, like a moat, slides on the three sides farthest from the town. Tom and Jenny remembered it well, for it was here that they had got to know Jon and Penny Warrender and under the same grey walls that these two cousins had been made members of the Lone Pine Club and signed their names in their own blood in the register. The Lone Piners called Clun Castle "HQ3" because it was the third place which they had used as their headquarters. But until now they had only seen Clun in winter, when the days were short, and a cruel, cold wind came sweeping over the heights of the old forest.

To-day, as Tom and Jenny climbed up the steep slopes of the hill, it was very different. To-day the sun shone and the sky was blue and a gentle breeze played with the heads of the mauve scabious and the golden buttercups in the grass, while below them the river lay like a silver ribbon. Away to the south the Welsh mountains piled up against the sky, while to the east, on their left, were the more open hillsides where it was possible to pick up prehistoric arrowheads of flint, and where the great artificial ditch known as Offa's Dyke ran straight as a ruler through the border lands of England and Wales.

They sat with their faces to the sun and with their backs to the warmth of the stone wall of the castle and munched in silence. There was a lot to munch, for Aunt Betty had no half-hearted ideas about meals. The drinks were good, too. It was warm, they had been up early, and although they had not really come very far they were pleasantly tired.

Jenny put down an empty bottle, moved a little so that she would be fully in the sun, stretched herself out on her back, put her hands behind her head and closed her eyes. Far, far away she heard Tom tidying up—picking up bits of greaseproof paper, rustling paper bags and whistling quietly to himself. Tom had a lovely whistle. Tom was a very nice boy. Tom was always wonderful to Jenny. So many things were either wonderful or terrible to Jenny. There wasn't much in between. Tom was the best friend she would ever have. Peter was wonderful, too, but she was a girl and that was different ... The sun shone warm and pink through her closed eyelids. She heard the hum of summer insects ... The sun was wonderful ... She slept.

When she awoke the sun was behind a fat, woolly cloud, and the air was cool. Tom, who did not at first realize that she was awake, was sitting with his hands clasped round his knees staring straight ahead of him over to the west.

"Hullo, Tom," she said as she sat up. "I've been asleep. What are you thinking about?"

He didn't say "I was thinking about you, Jenny," as she hoped he would. What he did say was rather surprising.

"I know you've been asleep. You snored. It's funny, but somehow I never thought of girls snoring ... I don't know why, Jenny, but I was thinking about that rum business of Peter's at the end of last hols—that business of the two men who were passengers in the plane that came down on the Mynd. She said something about newspaper cuttings that one of the men left behind at Hatchholt ... Something about dogs."

Jenny got up and brushed down her frock. She wished her legs would get nicely brown instead of pink. It was the same with her arms. All that seemed to happen when she lay in the sun was that she got more freckles. It was very disheartening for a girl who wanted, so very badly, to look smart and beautiful. And Tom didn't even look at her when she sat down beside him.

"Peter said the cuttings were all about dogs who had helped to prevent crimes or been responsible for catching criminals. But why are you thinking about that now, Tom? Let's do something exciting until tea time."

"All right, Jen. I was thinking we'd take the bottles and the haversack back to Mr. Jenkins and then get our bikes and see whether we can find Alan Denton's farm. What was it called?"

"Bury Fields, I think ... Yes, Tom, let's do that."

On the way down the hill she asked him again why he had remembered Peter's story.

"I dunno, really. It struck me as being rather rum. Peter was mad with David because he'd thrown those cuttings away and mad with us because we didn't seem to reckon it was much of a story. But it was rather odd, you know, Jen. How would you like to go back to your house and find a stranger sitting there who said that for all he knew he might be your father?"

"I should hate it. It's the sort of unlucky thing that might happen round our village, or Seven Gates, or the Dingles, but not at Hatchholt … Tom, why is it I'm still scared of the country round the Chair? I am, you know. I wouldn't tell anybody in the world but you, but I am."

Tom shook his head. He would have liked to have understood Jenny, but what she was saying didn't make sense. If and when she was frightened he would do all he could to help her, but although he thought the Stiperstones and all that country very gloomy, he wasn't afraid of it. Tom liked company and so was not very keen on lonely places, but he wasn't afraid of them and couldn't quite see how Jenny could be. What he did know, as all the other Lone Piners did, too, was that Jenny was not particularly happy at home with her stepmother. She adored her father, who had been away during the war, but had never really got used to the new Mrs. Harman, who seemed to have no time or sympathy for children.

"Don't worry about the Stiperstones now, Jen," was all he said as they reached the Buffalo again. "We're having this day on our own and going to the Fair to-night … It's only just after two, so we'll take our bikes even if we have to push 'em up the hill over the bridge, see if we can find Bury Fields and get back here just after four. It won't take us long to ride to Bishop's Castle from here, although it's very hilly."

Mr. Jenkins came out to see them off and Tom asked him the way to Bury Fields.

"We met Mr. Denton once and now we're over here we'd like to see him again … We'll be back by four for tea."

"I don't reckon you will be if Alan's mother is at home, and she generally is. She'll make you stay for tea. Remember my message. You're not to leave here for the Castle till five. Bury Fields be fairly easy to find, though 'tis wild country."

His directions were clear, and as they rode over the bridge and then pushed their cycles up the long hill they remembered some of the more familiar landmarks. At the top they turned and glanced back at Clun and its castle.

"It looks like one of those toy villages you can make yourself," Jenny said. "I like looking down on things."

"He told us to take the second gate on the left," Tom said, "but that the track was good enough for our bikes. I think we'll remember it when we come to it."

They did remember it, but had not realized that the track was so bad.

"This is the only way to the farm, I s'pose," Tom said, "and as Alan would have to bring his car this way to the main road it's no wonder it's so rough ... I wonder if he'll remember us?"

"Of course he will ... Sorry, Tom. I can't ride on this. It's too bumpy. I'm going to walk for a bit."

It was soon after this that Tom saw the dog standing in the track about two hundred yards ahead by another gate.

"Didn't he have a collie sheep-dog like that, Jen? I'm sure he did. What was her name?"

"Lady, I think. It looks like her. Whistle her, Tom."

Tom whistled and the dog moved a little, but did not come to meet them. It just stood there with its head up in their direction and its tail down.

"Lady! Lady," Jenny called as they got nearer. "Please don't forget us, Lady ... Tom! Surely there's something wrong with her?"

As they came up the bitch moved her head from side to side almost pathetically, but when they spoke to her again she bared her teeth in a snarl.

"Don't touch her, Jen! There is something wrong, I'm sure. I wonder if she'd follow us. I'll open the gate and see if she'll come down to the farm."

Jenny moved forward and the front wheel of her cycle

touched the dog gently. She backed away with a growl and banged into the back wheel of Tom's bike as he swung open the gate.

"Tom!" she gasped. "*I think Lady is blind* ... She didn't see my bike and she banged into yours ... How *awful*, Tom. Whatever has happened to her? Hold my bike a sec."

She went on her knees in the dirt in front of the dog and held out her hand.

"Lady! Lady darling. We won't hurt you. Come here!"

The dog moved forward cautiously, but brushed by Jenny's outstretched hand without seeing it. "There you are, Tom. *She can't see* ... I'll stay here with her if you'll ride down to the farm and fetch Alan or Mrs. Denton. You *must* find Alan 'cos I'm sure Lady won't come with us, though I suppose if you've got a hanky or a belt we could fix it to her collar and lead her down."

"We won't try that," Tom said. "She might turn on us. If she runs off, though, Jen, you mustn't follow her far, else you'll get lost, and we shall have the bother of searching for you ... Don't fuss or touch her, but keep talking to her so that she doesn't wander away ... Promise you won't go off by yourself."

Jenny nodded her red head. It was nice to have somebody a little worried about you and she was glad it was Tom.

When he had disappeared down the hill she sat back on her heels and spoke to the dog, who was now looking very dejected. There was no doubt that she was blind. She moved her lovely head to and fro and held up her muzzle as if trying to sniff what she could not see. After a little she crept forward and when Jenny's hand caressed her silky head she did not start away and made no protest when the girl put her arm round her and drew her close as she sat in the heather at the edge of the track. She stroked her gently until her trembling ceased and it was soon

"TOM," GASPED JENNY, "I THINK LADY IS BLIND." SHE WENT ON HER
KNEES IN FRONT OF THE DOG AND HELD OUT HER HAND.

after that they heard voices. Lady struggled, barked and ran into the closed gate as she heard her master's voice, and so it was that Jenny's face was wet with tears as Alan Denton shook hands with her and then stooped to the dog, who whimpered and licked his face.

"Of course I remember you, Jenny. I knew young Tom as soon as I saw him trying to break his neck down this track. 'Tis grand to see you, and he's been telling me you'll all be over at the Castle to-night for the Fair ... You can leave your bike here if you like and save yourself pushing it up the hill when you go. Nobody will take it ... Mother's in Bishop's Castle all day and I've promised to pick her up in the car to-night. You must come over again and see her."

While talking he was running his hands over Lady's coat, feeling her legs and examining her eyes. His face was very grim when he said, "I'll have to take her to the vet. right away. Man called Whittington in Bishop's Castle, so I can give you a lift now if you like. Your bikes can be strapped on the back of the car."

"But what's happened to Lady?" Jenny said. "It's awful to see her like that. Was she lost? Is she hurt in any other way?"

"She doesn't seem to be, Jenny. She was all right last night. Never better. She sleeps in the summer in the open barn across the farmyard. I don't tie her up at night, but she couldn't get out unless I left the yard gate open by mistake ... I must have done that last night because I noticed this morning it was open ... Unless—"

"Unless what?" Tom prompted.

Denton laughed grimly and picked up Lady as he started down the hill.

"Unless someone else opened it," he finished.

"But wouldn't Lady have barked at a stranger?"

"I reckon so, but she's not really a watchdog. She's a sheep-dog, as you know ... It's odd, but now I come to think of it I believe I heard a car in the night."

"But *why*?" Jenny began. "I mean have you been looking for Lady all day? How could she suddenly go blind?"

"I missed her at breakfast time and kept hoping she'd turn up. I took Mother into the Castle this morning, and after lunch I began to search for Lady ... Here we are. Give her a drink, Jenny, and see if she wants any food—I left her dish by the back door—and I'll get the car out. She'll stay with you."

All the fun seemed to have gone out of the afternoon now. Jenny stood with her hand on Lady's collar as she lapped her water and Tom stood moodily by with his hands in his pockets.

"It's no more than three o'clock, Jenny," he said at last. "We've promised not to leave Clun until five, and I told Alan that so I reckon we stay on our own. We'll ask him to leave a message for us at Mr. Whittington's. We'll want to know about Lady."

Jenny nodded and bent and kissed the top of the dog's silky head. When Alan had backed the car out of the barn, they went over and told him that they would go back on their bikes.

"It's difficult to explain," Jenny said, "but we're sure you'll understand that we promised. We'll come over and see you again—all of us, maybe—as soon as we can. If you're not at Mr. Whittington's when we get there, will you leave a message so that we know about Lady?"

"Of course I will, Jenny ... Here, Lady."

At the sound of his voice the bitch, still nosing in her dish, looked up and moved towards them with the tip of her tail moving.

"She's better," Tom shouted. "I believe she can see something."

Lady moved towards Tom on her way to her master and banged into him, but when she reached Alan she put one paw up and tried to reach his leg.

"I'm going to get to the bottom of this," the farmer said grimly. "If Whittington isn't in I shall wait for him, so I may see you two there ... I reckon you're right, Tom. She can see more than she could half an hour ago. If anybody has been tampering with her I'll catch him and wring his neck if it's the last thing I do ... Sure you two will be all right? So long, then. Hope to see you later," and he lifted Lady into the back of the car, closed the rear windows and drove off up the track.

Tom and Jenny took their time on the way back and did not really do full justice to the magnificent tea prepared for them in the parlour of the Buffalo. They were served by Jessie, who made many excuses to come into the room and join in their conversation.

Mr. Jenkins, she told them, had gone to Bishop's Castle and when he came back she was going in for the Fair.

"Everybody goes," she said, "and maybe I'll see you, although I shall be with my Bert."

This hint of romance roused Jenny's interest. "How lovely, Jessie. I do hope we meet you."

"You two haven't had a row, have you?" Jessie went on maternally. "You're not the same as when you come. If you don't cheer up you'll give me the miseries ... Oh, well, if you don't want to talk, I s'pose I can't make you. I like folks to be a bit friendly, and I can't see that you two kids have got anything to be stuck up about ... Just because somebody sends money in a letter to the guvnor and makes all this fuss about you—"

Jenny got up from the table and, with memories of some of those curious, old-fashioned romances which she loved so well, she said, coldly, "Thank you, Jessie. That will do. You may clear now," and the girl was so astonished that she had no answer as Tom, with a laugh, followed Jenny into the hall.

As the last stroke of five sounded from the church tower they jumped on their cycles and pedalled furiously along the road towards Bishop's Castle until they had to dismount for the first steep hill which climbed and twisted between the trees until, once again, they were able to look back and see Clun far away below them. Soon afterwards they overtook the first caravan.

"I'd forgotten all about the gipsies," Jenny yelled over her shoulder as they swooped past. "P'raps we'll see Reuben and Miranda after all."

They were within a mile of the town, pushing their cycles up the last hill, when they turned a corner and saw, but fifty yards ahead, the smartest of all caravans. Red and yellow were the sides and yellow and red the wheels. The roof was bright green and, although they could not see them, they knew that the shafts were green, too, and that on the driving-seat a handsome, brown-faced gipsy in an old hat and with a short, black pipe between his gleaming white teeth would be singing as the well-kept horse plodded up the hill. Then the caravan stopped and Reuben himself, with his wife Miranda, jumped down to lessen the load.

Jenny shouted at the top of her voice and Tom jumped on his cycle again and, standing on the pedals, forced his way up the hill. Jenny could see the welcoming smiles on their faces as she toiled towards them.

There was Miranda. Just the same, with a scarf round her head and her big gold earrings shining. And, sure enough, there was little ten-year-old Fenella on the driving-seat with a nondescript black puppy wriggling with excitement in her arms.

"Well, pretty one," Miranda smiled. "Shall I read your hand for you again? Did I not tell you last time we met that you would learn not to be afraid?"

147

"Yes, you did, Miranda. And you were quite right. I'm hardly scared of anything now. Are you going to the Fair? All the others will be there … Peter? Of course she will, and of course we'll all come and see you in your caravan if we may … Hullo, Fenella. Do you remember us?"

The little girl nodded and beamed.

"Is she still as shy as she used to be?" Tom asked. "I don't reckon she's ever had a word to say to me … May I come up and see your puppy, Fenella? Hold my bike a sec., Jenny."

Tom had a way with little girls, and Fenella made room for him on the driving-seat and pressed the squirming little dog into his arms.

"I reckon you've got a fine dog here," Tom said as the puppy nipped his exploring fingers with sharp teeth. "What do you call him, Fenella?"

"Elizabeth," the gipsy girl whispered, "because of the new queen."

Tom nodded sympathetically.

"I bet he—she—is worth a lot of money."

Fenella became really talkative.

"Yes. Elizabeth is. Two days back a man in a car stopped by our van when we were eating at the side of the road. What do you think he did?"

Tom had no idea. Elizabeth, with wildly thrashing tail, growled and worried at his coat sleeve.

"He wanted to buy Elizabeth for ten shillings and when we say 'No,' he say 'one pound,' so we say 'No'."

Reuben looked up and laughed.

"'Tis right, Tom. A stupid man to offer so much for such a pup that cost us nothing. Maybe we are stupid too not to take such easy money, but Fenella like to keep him, so we say, 'No,' and the strange man is angry."

Tom smiled at Fenella and jumped to the road.

"We'd better get on now, Jenny. We'll tell the others you're at the Fair, Reuben, and come and see you to-night ... Good-bye."

"You're looking very worried and cross, Tom," Jenny complained as they rode into the town. "What are you thinking about?"

"A pound for a pup like that!" was all that Tom would say.

CHAPTER VI

THE HIDDEN HOUSE

D AVID and Peter opened their sealed orders down by the gate, where none of the others could watch their reactions. Peter felt ridiculously excited as David slit the envelope. She knew it was silly. Really they were getting too old for this sort of thing, but all the same this was going to be a grand day, whatever they were told to do. First of all, a day with David and then the party at Trudie's, which would mean meeting Charles as well, and then the Fair with them all, and, finally, a night at Seven Gates and the fun of cooking their own breakfast over the old stove at HQ2 and seeing Aunt Carol and Uncle Micah, and then—

"What's the matter with you?" David was saying. "You're looking quite soft. What are you dreaming about? Look at this. They don't seem to be very difficult orders."

Peter flushed and snatched the paper.

"Make a day of it and enjoy yourselves," she read. "Up and over the Long Mynd, whichever way you like, cross-country to the Hope Anchor, where you will find a meal ready for you, and then up to the Devil's Chair. From there you can make your way to Bishop's Castle as you will."

"I don't suppose your father knows how I loathe the Chair, David," she said. "You've never told him, have you? I'll never forgive you if you have."

"Of course I haven't, and you don't really loathe it now, anyway. Let's kill that bogey once and for all to-day, Peter. Come on. We've no time to waste, for it's a long walk."

"All right. It can't be worse than our crazy trip up the

Stiperstones in the middle of the night, although I bet it thunders when we're up there. It did the first time I met you at the Chair, if you remember. You can laugh at me, David, but every time we go there something unexpected or beastly happens, so let's hope to-day is different."

They turned to see the others watching them curiously, waved and set off in single file along the track by the side of the stream.

The little valley narrowed as the hills closed in. Overhead, against the blue of the sky, a hawk hovered and then dropped like a stone. Rabbits frisked their little cotton-wool tails as they bolted for the cover of the bracken, and the brook sang at their feet.

"Bet we don't meet anybody until we get to the Hope Anchor," David remarked after ten minutes' silent walking. "It's too early for holiday-makers up on the top. Sometimes I think this is the loneliest country in England."

"You've forgotten that the R.A.F. have taken the old house on the top. I told you so last hols."

"So you did. What do they do there?"

"No idea. I don't think there are many of them, but they've got a wire fence round the place. Something very secret. I hate secret things like that. It seems all wrong to have something to do with war up here."

"Maybe what they're doing up here will help to prevent war," David said seriously. "I know how you feel, but that's what Dad told me once. I'll be going into the R.A.F. in two years, Peter. P'raps I'll be sent here? That would surprise you, wouldn't it? But perhaps you won't live at Hatcholt then? It's odd to think we're getting old so quickly. I don't think I like it."

"I don't either. On a morning like this I want to stay this age. Sorry I said that about the R.A.F. It was stupid."

Their feet were squelching through boggy ground now, for they were nearly at the head of the valley and the source of the Witchend stream. Then they were up, with the great tableland of the Mynd rolling gently as far as they could see to their right and left. For twelve miles, thrust up from the earth's cooling crust millions of years ago, this strange mountain straddled the coloured Shropshire fields which lay between its bulk and that of the gaunt ridge of the Stiperstones over to the west.

"It's always the same and yet it's always different," Peter said quietly. "I never get tired of it, David, and the way I feel now I could never leave it. I've seen it covered in snow when I didn't dare go farther than the top of Hatchholt, and I've been up here on midsummer night on Sally and ridden the whole length. It's not far from here that I first met you and the twins and we had our first adventure. I've seen it in the spring when it looks green and quiet, and now when the bilberries are turning purple. I told you in that long letter I wrote you at the beginning of the term how I hear the trains coming this way, didn't I? You never answered that letter properly, so I don't suppose you understood, and I suppose you think I'm crazy now. But I'm not—or only crazy to tell you, I s'pose."

"You say things like that more easily than I can, Peter. I was glad you wrote me that letter and I'm glad you can talk about it now. Straight across towards those trees now, I s'pose? Is that where the R.A.F. place is?"

"Just below the trees to the right," Peter explained. "We've got to keep more to the left and go down by the Gliding Station."

They went on for another ten minutes of friendly silence, striding through the bilberries, and then were startled to hear a distant shout, followed by a shrill whistle.

"There he is," David said, pointing ahead. "A chap running,

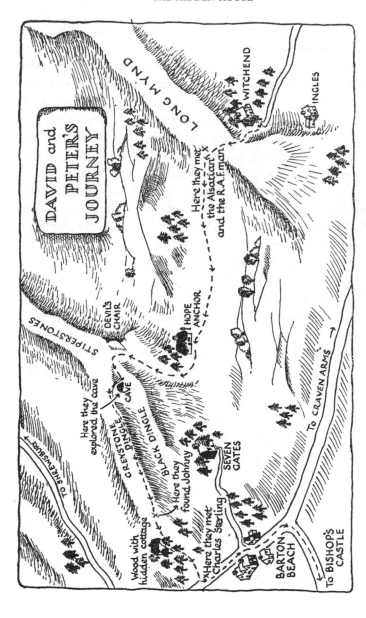

DAVID and PETER'S JOURNEY

LONG MYND

WITCHEND

INGLES

Here they met the Alsatian and the R.A.F.man

STIPERSTONES

DEVIL'S CHAIR

HOPE ANCHOR

GREYSTONE DINGLE CAVE

BLACK DINGLE

Here they explored the cave

Here they found Johnny

SEVEN GATES

To CRAVEN ARMS

Wood with hidden cottage

Here they met Charles Sterling

BARTON BEACH

To SHREWSBURY

To BISHOP'S CASTLE

THE ARROWS → → SHOW THE WAY DAVID AND PETER TRAVELLED FROM WITCHEND TO BISHOP'S CASTLE.

and I've lost my bet almost as soon as we've started. What does he want, I wonder?"

Before Peter could answer an enormous alsatian dog came bounding towards them from a hollow about twenty yards to their right. A thick leather lead was trailing from his collar, his mouth was open and his teeth bared. At the sound of the whistle he stopped, turned his head for a second and then jumped towards them again.

There wasn't much time for David to show how scared he was. He liked dogs just as much as most people, but he had never liked alsatians, and in the split second when he instinctively pushed himself in front of Peter, he remembered another occasion over at Clun when a large dog had been set on them, and how then Peter had stepped forward and calmed it while they had all been ready to run for their lives.

She did exactly the same now as she stepped forward and said, "All right, David. I'm not afraid of him."

The dog stopped short, growled and then, as Peter spoke to him and put a hand on his head before picking up the lead, he looked up at her and slowly wagged his tail.

"I think he was excited, that's all," she said. "Let's take him to his master ... It's one of the R.A.F. men.

David wiped his forehead.

"Excited, was he? Poor little chap. P'raps you'd like to tell him that I was excited too ... They're dangerous, Peter, and it's only because you've got this knack with animals that he's not attacking us now.

"They're fierce if you train them that way," Peter laughed, "and they're wonderful watchdogs, but I think they know if you're afraid of them. I'm not, though I'm scared of the Stiperstones. Funny, isn't it?"

A very red-faced but nice-looking young man in uniform came up and looked at Peter admiringly.

"That was cool work," he said. "It looked to me as if you just stepped up to Rolf and picked up his lead, and that might have been dangerous. This chap has got a very nasty temper."

"You couldn't know that she's an animal trainer," David laughed. "Take him away now, will you? I've had enough of him."

Peter patted the dog again and passed over the lead.

"You training them up here for something?" she asked. "You don't have to worry about telling us any secrets. We both live near here in the holidays. Did he slip his lead?"

"Yes, he did. My fault, though. I was lighting a cigarette and not paying much attention. He's a grand chap really, but it's no secret to tell you that he's being trained to attack inquisitive strangers. I don't think he would have gone for you, although he was excited at escaping. He's very high spirited."

"So we noticed," David said dryly. "I don't think he's fully trained yet, because he didn't give any sign of realizing that we're not really strangers to these parts and neither are we inquisitive!"

Then Peter told him who they were and where they lived and that they were on a day's tramp over the Stiperstones to Bishop's Castle.

"I s'pose we're not really allowed to ask," she finished, "but we could guess that you're training dogs to guard your place over there. I know we mustn't ask what you do there, and if you like we'll swear not to tell anybody about the dogs—but I'd like to know all the same."

The man laughed. "I'm being tempted by a beautiful blonde spy … Take her away, young man, and think yourself lucky that she has a way with dogs. We shall have to look out for her up here … So long!"

"That's all very well," David remarked. "I didn't expect him to tell us what they are doing, but I think he was a bit cool about it all."

"One of those newspaper cuttings which you lost was about alsatians being specially trained to guard camps and factories," Peter said as they went on their way along the steep track leading down the western slope of the Mynd. "Perhaps this place is where the R.A.F. train their dogs to guard their aerodromes ... If you look carefully now you can see the Devil's Chair on top of the Stiperstones there. It's clear enough to-day. Perhaps that means rain. We've still got a long way to go, David."

"Hope Anchor is on our way really, and we shall be glad of a drink and a meal. I remember that place, Peter. The first day we came to Seven Gates and met you up by the Chair in a thunderstorm I stopped there with the twins and Sally. Do you remember how we had loaded her up with all the baggage and called her a pack-horse? She took a very poor view of it so far as I remember."

Down into the lovely country between the two mountains they strode. The sun was hot now and the black rocks on the summit of the Stiperstones seemed to get no nearer as they left the Long Mynd behind. They were very tired and thirsty when, at half-past one, they flopped down on the bench against the whitewashed walls of the little inn.

"You're a fine couple to be sure," said a pleasant country voice from the porch. "I've been expecting you this last hour. You'll be David and Peter, I suppose, though why a girl as pretty as you, my dear, should have a man's name is none o' my business. Would you like a drink before the bite of dinner I've got ready for you in the parlour? Just wait there and cool off while I fetch you two tankards of ginger beer. Very special tankards they be, but you're welcome."

She was plump and short and rosy-faced, and wearing a print apron, and for some reason, which she couldn't possibly explain, reminded Peter of Grimm's Fairy Tales.

"It's wonderful of your father to have fixed all this up, David. He must have written to her … I s'pose you know that it's getting heavy and sultry—just because we're in sight of the Chair. Perhaps it's that makes us so tired … Good. Here are the drinks."

David glanced at the lettering over the doorway of the inn as he took the two tankards.

"Thank you very much, Mrs. Sandall. This is wonderful," he said. "What have you got for our lunch?"

"You're welcome, young man, but I'd like to be told how you know my name?"

"He read it over the doorway," Peter laughed as she put her nose in the tankard and drank deep. "But all the same he's got very nice manners sometimes … Do tell us what you've got for us to eat?"

"Sorry I am that I haven't had more time to get you something nice," Mrs. Sandall beamed. "But there's plenty of ham and eggs and some new bread that I baked but yesterday. And I've done some new potatoes for you—and very sweet they are this year from my own bit o' garden here. Come inside when you're ready."

The meal was as good as its description, and they did not hurry. It was fun to be out alone like this, and long before they had finished they were roaring with laughter over the curious habits and appearance of some of the masters and mistresses at their respective schools.

But when at last it was time to go and they had said good-bye to the friendly Mrs. Sandall, they noticed that clouds were gathering over the Devil's Chair.

"What did I tell you?" Peter said. "It's always the same, but to-day I don't care. It's nothing to do with you being with me, David, so don't flatter yourself."

"When you can't see the Chair the Devil is on his throne is what they say round here, isn't it? I'm sure Jenny believes it … Anyway, if the clouds come low over these rocks now we'll walk right under the Chair just to show his Satanic Majesty that we mock him … It's no good rushing at it, Peter. Never hurry uphill and you'll go twice as far is my motto."

"Sometimes, David," she said, "you're so maddeningly right that I hate you … I'll run up here if I choose."

David put his hands in his pockets and whistled cheerfully. The path steepened and it was hard going because of the loose stones. This mountain was very different from the Long Mynd which, although lonely and wild, was not cruel and hard like this one. As he puffed up the steep path behind Peter he was reminded again of Jenny's apt description—the neglected mountain. The sky darkened and it was very hot. A solitary black crow flapped sullen wings overhead and there was no other living thing in sight.

At each side of the path jagged rocks pushed their sharp edges through the heather, and David was just thinking that an aeroplane which tried to make a forced landing here would have a very poor chance of survival when Peter stopped suddenly and gave an unexpected squeal. When she turned round her face was white under her tan.

"That's one of the things I hate about this place. That was an adder. Just about two feet away. I might have stepped on it."

"Adder? Are you sure?"

"Idiot! Do you think I've lived all my life in these hills and don't know an adder when I see one? Of course I'm sure."

"Sorry. Let me go in front for a bit."

"No, thanks. You wouldn't recognize a poisonous snake when you saw one, and it's a bit late to offer now, isn't it?"

David looked as astonished as he felt, and suddenly she

flushed and said, "I'm sorry, David. I'm behaving like an idiot. It must be this place that makes me squabble ... Of course you can go in front, but there may be some more snakes. They like the warmth and they could easily bite you above your rolled-down socks. Better pull your socks up, David!"

He laughed and went ahead, and soon after they reached the top of the steep path which now wound ahead between the piled and broken rocks along the top ridge of the mountain. A quarter of a mile ahead the black rocks of the Chair reached up fantastically towards the darkening sky.

"It's not going to thunder after all, Peter," he said. "We'll go and sit in the Chair if you like, just to show him."

"I believe it was you—or it may have been Tom—who said once, 'Fun's fun, but you can't be laughing all the time'. I don't think your remark about sitting in the Chair is at all funny."

Strangely enough, the sun came out soon after and Peter had forgotten all her fears when they walked through the shadows under the rocks supporting the Chair. A little farther on they found a patch of ripe bilberries and stopped long enough to stain their mouths and fingers.

"Shall we go down through Black Dingle and through Barton or walk farther along the top here and go down Greystone?" Peter said as she sucked her fingers.

"Let's go Greystone and have a look at the cave where we found the hidden lake. I've often wanted to go back there. This would be just our chance."

Peter looked at him doubtfully.

"Greystone if you like, but I shouldn't think there's much sense in going into the cave without torches. I wonder whether that lake has filled up again? Let's have a look at the cave entrance, anyway."

They passed the track running down into Black Dingle, up

which they had toiled on the last night of the Easter holidays, and kept on along the topmost ridge. Behind them to their right was the long, smooth, whale-backed bulk of the Long Mynd across which they had been walking only a few hours ago.

At the top of Greystone they lay on the top of a flat rock and basked in the sun. They were still on the neglected mountain and had not seen a soul since they left the Hope Anchor, and Peter at last seemed not to have a care in the world.

"Don't let's hurry," she said. "This is a grand place, so let's stay until the sun goes in. It doesn't matter what time we get to Bishop's Castle so long as we're there by six ... That business with the dog this morning reminded me of those newspaper cuttings and the two men off the aeroplane. It was all very peculiar, David. It really was. Who do you think they were?"

"They might have been who they said they were. A doctor and a friend who was very highly strung and lost his memory after the accident."

"Yes ... They might have been, but somehow I'm not quite sure. Why those cuttings about the dogs, and why was the Doctor so keen to speak to Beardy before Daddy or I could get back to the house?"

"Don't let's worry, Peter. It was all over months ago ... Let's go and look at the cave."

Peter sat up and stared at her slim brown legs.

"All right ... All the same, it *was* very peculiar. You didn't see them both, else you wouldn't be so offhand."

The upper part of Greystone Dingle was very like Black Dingle except that on their left the mountainside came down abruptly, and in places was almost precipitous. The valley was steep and narrow at the top, but lower down it broadened out and there was a wood at the bottom. The cave which they were anxious to explore again was the scene of another of their adventures. Inside it they had found an underground lake which, after many weeks of rainfall, had overflowed, burst out into the Dingle and swept down the wood, exposing on its way some Roman treasure and part of a Roman pavement. Inside the neglected mountain were still the galleries of old lead mines, and it was possible once to find a way right through it to Black Dingle on the other side. Exploration, however, was very risky owing to the constant falls of rock.

The entrance to the cave was from a grassy plateau about thirty feet above the stream running down Greystone. They remembered this stream because in places it ran underground and made unexpected appearances in unexpected places.

"We called this HQ4 once, didn't we?" David said as he climbed up to the plateau. "We must all come here for the day, Peter, and have a look round. Let's just see that the cave hasn't fallen in."

He led the way into the cool darkness.

"I just want to see that the passage at the back isn't blocked," he went on. "Come in with me."

She took his hand as he crept forward. She heard him mutter something under his breath as he banged his head on the roof and then stooped as he drew her forward.

"We're at the beginning of the passage now," he said, and his voice went echoing weirdly round the walls. "There's plenty of draught, and that means that the way down to the lake is open. We must explore that again, Pete. I can't think why I didn't suggest it the other day …? I s'pose it's no good going on now?"

"No, it isn't. What's the sense of breaking our legs in the dark when we can come back another time with torches? Let's get on to Barton now, David. I want my tea."

When they were out on the little plateau again David saw an

empty cigarette carton. He picked it up and noticed that it was fairly clean and dry.

"That's a pity," he said. "Someone has found our cave, Peter, but I don't quite know what we can do about it."

They went on cheerfully down the dingle, recalling their first adventure here in the rain. Grass was growing now where the portions of the Roman pavement had been carefully lifted and taken to the museum in Shrewsbury, and soon they came to the wood through which ran the road to the village of Barton Beach. It was a thick pinewood which they did not remember exploring before, and as soon as they stepped into its shadows they seemed to be in a different world. It had been quiet enough in the dingle with only the occasional murmur of running water to break the silence, but once they were between the trees with their feet sinking into the soft carpet of pine needles they were almost scared to speak to each other.

Suddenly a wood pigeon cluttered up through the branches and then Peter laughed and said, "When I'm in a wood like this, David, I'm always reminded of Hansel and Gretel. It's these pine trees, I suppose."

David opened his mouth to reply, and then suddenly put a hand on her arm.

"Listen," he whispered. "Surely I can hear Hansel or Gretel?"

From far away down in the depths of the wood they heard the cry of a child. Not a cry for help, but almost a cry of despair. They stood in silence, listening and staring into the shadows between the trees.

The cry came again. Nearer this time, and followed by the pathetic calling of a name which sounded like "Sandy! Sandy!"

Peter lifted her head and called, "Hullo, there! Where are you?"

The crying stopped. Silence surged back into the wood.

"You heard it, too, didn't you, David?"

"Yes ... Call again."

"Hullo, there! Are you lost? Shout or whistle and we'll come to you."

Silence again. Not even an echo.

"Whoever it is didn't sound very happy," David whispered. "Let's just see whether anything's wrong, Peter."

She nodded and they turned in the direction of the last cry. There was nothing else to guide them and soon, to their surprise, they found themselves on a fairly wide track rutted by the tyres of a car.

"I s'pose this must lead eventually into the Barton road," Peter said. "I don't remember it. It wasn't the way we came into the wood before, because, you'll remember, we couldn't find a proper path at all."

While she was speaking David was staring ahead.

"Don't move for a sec," he whispered under his breath. "There's somebody hiding behind that tree on the bend. I'm sure of it. Silly if we've got to play a game of hide and seek ... There! It's a boy ... Hi, George, or whatever your name is, come out of there and help us. We've lost our way."

A fair-headed boy of about eight stepped out into the track and looked at them suspiciously. He was sturdy, grubby and dressed in patched corduroy shorts and a blue shirt. He stood with his hands rammed into his pockets and waited sullenly for them to come up. When they were close enough they saw that his eyes were very blue and that his face was streaked with dirt and tears.

"Hullo—George," Peter smiled at him. "Can you help us get out of this wood, please?"

They could see the battle going on behind those blue eyes.

Were they to be trusted? They were strangers. Or were they? The girl in the blue frock and the plaits. She didn't live in the village, but surely he'd seen her there some time?

"What's your name—George?" she smiled again.

He sniffed and gave in.

"'Tisn't George. 'Tis Johnny."

"You're just the chap for us, Johnny," David said. "Can you show us the way out of this wood? We've never been here before and we want to get to Barton ... You live at Barton?"

The boy nodded and gave a suspicious gulp.

"I lost my dog. My Sandy. He's locked up in liddle stone house yonder. I can hear him crying ... He must a' took him yesterday ... 'Tis all locked up."

Peter pretended not to see his tears and took his hand.

"You just show us the way to liddle stone house, Johnny. If your dog is shut up there we'll soon get him out. I don't like people who shut up little dogs and then go out and leave them ... Tell us all about Sandy and what happened."

There didn't seem anything which David could usefully do, so he just walked behind and listened to a rather curious conversation.

Johnny could not seem to explain what sort of a dog Sandy was, but David guessed that perhaps anybody would find that difficult. What was painfully clear was that, apart from Dad and Mum, Sandy was the most important thing in Johnny's life, and that yesterday afternoon Sandy was took and that he, Johnny, had been searching for him ever since, and now he'd found him.

"I bin calling him in the wood," Johnny admitted, "but he's in the liddle house. I heard him."

The track turned unexpectedly to the right and there the little boy stopped and pointed.

"There it be," he said tersely.

Below them, in a gloomy hollow overshadowed by the pine trees, stood an old stone cottage with a slate roof. It was surrounded by a crumbling wall inside which a tangle of undergrowth rioted over the lower part of the walls. The door was closed, the windows blank and no smoke issued from the chimney. The walls were patched with damp and the paint peeling from the door. To one side of the cottage a small clearing had been made, and it looked as if a car often stood there.

"Well, well," David said, rather unintelligently. "If this is a fairy-tale wood, we've found the witches' cottage. Who lives here, Johnny?"

"Young chap. My dad says he's barmy. Liddle ole car he got," and he ran down the weed-choked path, pulling Peter with him, and banged on the door. David would not have been altogether surprised if the latter had opened suddenly to disclose a wizard in a pointed hat—or the devil with horns and tail—but nothing did happen except that they could certainly hear the muffled whining of a dog.

"I tole you ... I tole you!" Johnny yelled. "That's my Sandy. We'll smash this liddle old house down and get him out."

They had trouble with Johnny then, for he was inconsolable. They could not shake his conviction that Sandy was inside and that, as they couldn't get in by the door, they should smash the windows. David had to hold his arms as he struggled to pick up a stone and although Peter, as usual, was prepared to go to the rescue of anybody or any animal being ill-treated, she realized that they could hardly smash the windows of an occupied house. It was obvious that Johnny had no proof that his dog was inside, for one dog's whimper is very much like that of another.

"You stay here with Johnny," she said to David. "I'll have a look round the back."

She was back in three minutes to find David amusing the little boy with his pocket compass.

"I'll tell you what we'll do, Johnny," he was saying. "We'll come back to Barton with you now, and if we meet the man in the 'liddle ole car' you told us about, we'll stop him and tell him you've lost Sandy and that there's a dog in his cottage because we heard him ... Nobody would want to take Sandy and lock him up, Johnny. I expect he lost himself, and maybe he'll be at home when you get back."

Johnny managed a watery sort of smile that almost brought the tears to Peter's eyes.

"Maybe he'll be back home now waiting for me?"

"He might be," she said. "I can't see him through any of the windows, but if he isn't at home, Johnny, I promise we'll do something to find out about the man who lives in this house. I'll ask my cousin Charles Sterling who lives at Seven Gates to help. We're seeing him this evening at the Fair. He'll help us, Johnny, if Sandy doesn't turn up."

Johnny walked away between them with his chin high and without a backward glance, while David gave Peter a smile of admiration over his head. She certainly had a way with her and Johnny now had hold of her hand as if he would never let it go.

Charles Sterling, in the farm van, drew up beside them on the outskirts of Barton.

"What are you two doing here at this time?" he said. "I thought you were all at Trudie's. I've had special instructions to be there on time to meet you all ... Who's your young friend?"

"We'll tell you all about it, Charles, and we are on our way to Trudie's now, and you can give us a lift. This is Johnny. He lives somewhere in the village and he's lost his dog."

Johnny glowered at Charles, and then, with a quick grin at Peter, dashed off down the street.

"Jump in, then," Charles said as he opened the door. "Tell me about your adventures on the way. How are the others? And don't look so worried, Peter."

"I am worried, Charles. We found young Johnny wandering about in the wood at the bottom of Greystone Dingle crying for his dog, which he said was lost yesterday. He took us to a nasty little damp cottage where he said the dog was shut up. There's nobody in the house now, and we could hear a dog whimpering. The boy said something about other dogs round here disappearing, and if that is so and animals are locked in empty houses we ought to do something about it. Do you know who lives in that place, Charles?"

"I know where you mean. That cottage has a bad reputation, but somebody did tell me that some misguided chap had taken it a month or so ago. Somebody who wants peace and quiet, I s'pose. Some writing chap, or somebody like that."

"I don't think it's an author," Peter said quietly. "Not unless he's writing something jolly technical—school books, I mean. I went all round the house and looked in the downstairs windows. The place is fearfully untidy and there are some books about, but what I noticed particularly was a bench down one side of the room under the window covered with chemistry things. You know what I mean. Flasks and test tubes and glass jars. And I saw a pair of rubber gloves on the bench, and I think it's all jolly mysterious, and I wish I knew about that dog, too ... There's another thing, too, Charles. I promised young Johnny I'd tell you all about this and that you'd help him to find his puppy. What do you think?"

"I think it's all very curious," Charles said as he changed gear for the hill up to Bishop's Castle. "I think I'd like to know more about this mysterious gentleman. Maybe some of us will go and pay him a duty call to-morrow. Care to come, Peter?"

CHAPTER VII

THE FAIR

D AVID and Peter were not really surprised that they were the last to arrive at the Whittingtons' when Charles drove them into the yard, but they had certainly not expected to see Alan Denton surrounded by Lone Piners.

Trudie was standing in the doorway to the surgery with her hands over her ears, and Peter noticed again how pretty she was when she looked up and recognized them.

"Hullo, darling," Charles said as she came over. "So the circus has arrived? I've brought the rest of it ... Surely that's Alan Denton from Bury Fields?"

"Yes, it is. All the others know him, too, so I've asked him to stay until father comes back and have a meal with us. He's worried about the dog. He says that she's been blind, but is now beginning to see."

Alan pushed his way through the crowd and shook hands with the new-comers.

"Jenny and Tom found Lady when they were on the way to Bury Fields. She disappeared in the night and was certainly blind when they fetched me to her. Curious thing is she seems O.K. now. Nothing much the matter with her, as you see, but I want Mr. Whittington to look her over, and as I'm not meeting my mother for an hour or so I'm very glad to stay ... Nice to see you all again. I must say you're getting a big girl now, Peter," and he gave her such an approving look that she blushed and went over to where Mackie and Lady were exchanging courtesies.

"We're used to nobody taking any notice of us," Mary said

loudly. "It's just because we're quiet and retirin', but I'd like to say good evening to you, Mr. Sterling."

"*And* to inform our brother," Dickie went on, "that we jolly well got here first, which Trudie will perform."

They all looked puzzled until a happy smile of understanding spread over Mary's face.

"How silly you all are. We mean *confirm*, o' course. Just a slip of the tongue, and you all look blank. We got here first, though Tom and Jenny ought to have the sort of prize that you get when you try very hard and just don't."

"Don't what, twin?"

"Don't get it ... We're jolly surprised that David and Peter have got here by now, considerin' they left first. We s'pose they've been *lazin'* at Seven Gates all day. Have they, Charles?"

Charles laughed and followed Trudie into the house as she called over her shoulder:

"All come in. Get yourselves clean and then come into the dining-room when you're ready."

The Whittingtons' house was shabby and rather untidy, but the dining-room, the windows of which looked out over the garden, was very gracious.

Dickie's eyes widened with appreciation when he saw the table.

"Is it anybody's birthday?" he asked reverently. "I wish it was ours, twin."

"Have you really done all this yourself, Trudie?" Peter asked as she sat down next to her. "If I hadn't been so jolly selfish I'd have come over early and helped you. Not that I'm much of a cook, but I can cut sandwiches."

But it was Jenny who put into words what they all wanted to say.

"We'd like to say thank you very much for such a wonderful

welcome and for taking all this trouble, Trudie. I expect we've all had a lovely day, and now this is just the right beginning to a thrilling evening."

At this Dickie clapped and Jenny went on:

"And there's another thing. We all think Charles is jolly lucky to marry you, Trudie, and if you don't ask us all to the wedding we shall come just the same."

"Well said, Jenny," Charles laughed. "I agree with every word, and we wouldn't dream of getting married without you. We wouldn't dare. Now, please, may we start? I didn't have any lunch because I wanted to do justice to this party."

There were plates of sandwiches of all sorts, two boiled eggs each, a dish of cold meat and an enormous bowl of salad; jellies, blancmanges and raspberries and cream, and six different sorts of cakes. There was tea for those who wanted it and cold drinks on the sideboard for those who didn't.

When the babel had died down a little, Charles suggested that, in turn, each pair of Lone Piners should tell their story.

The twins, interrupting each other skilfully, spoke first, and their story of meeting Mr. Cantor and then of the mysterious young man in the car was very well told.

"You swear you're not making up that bit?" David said when Mary said that Lady's coat smelled the same as the man who offered them a lift. "All right! All right! Sorry I mentioned it. It's just that it was rather a coincidence."

Then Jenny told their story and Alan Denton confirmed their meeting with him, and they were all delighted to hear that they would see the gipsies later.

"I'm still puzzled about a man who would offer young Fenella a pound for a puppy somebody would be glad to give away," Tom added. "I'm going to ask Reuben more about that when I see him."

But it was while Peter was telling them about Johnny and his lost Sandy and the mysterious house in the wood that everyone listened so quietly.

"And I wish now, Charles, that we hadn't been in such a hurry to come on with you. I feel we've let Johnny down. You will promise to help us do something about that missing dog of his to-morrow, won't you? We shall be at Seven Gates, anyway, so perhaps you'd come to the village with us and see what we can find out. I promised Johnny that you would help him."

Charles passed Trudie his cigarette-case.

"Of course I will. I told you coming along that somebody ought to pay that chap a visit ... I suppose you all realize what's common to all three stories?"

"I do," David said quietly. "And I don't like it."

"What do you mean, David?" Jenny asked. "Don't be so mysterious."

"I think Charles means that we've all been different ways and done different things as Dad planned for us, and that in one way or another there was a dog somewhere in each adventure. That's what you meant, isn't it, Charles?"

"That's it. What do you think, Denton?"

Alan had been looking more and more puzzled while they told their stories, but before he could answer there was the sound of a cheerful whistle in the hall and Mr. Whittington came in. Trudie went over and kissed him.

"I did warn you about this, Father. I told you at breakfast. They're all very nice really, and we're going to the Fair presently. Mr. Denton from Bury Fields is waiting to see you, so I asked him, too ... Come and sit down here and relax with a cup of tea, and then, when you've got over the shock, I'll introduce you to them all."

Mr. Whittington was small, almost bald, with a little clipped moustache. He was wearing a shabby tweed jacket, breeches and polished leggings, and round his neck was a black ribbon and an eyeglass.

He smiled round the table, sat down next to his daughter, put his eyeglass in his eye and looked at them each in turn. Then he looked for a second time at the twins.

"Ha!" he said suddenly. "Delighted to see you all. How are you, Charles, m'boy? And Denton? Sorry to keep you waiting, but if you can spare five more minutes I shall enjoy my tea. Surely that's your bitch in the hall playing with a rascally young Scottie?"

"It's Lady I've come to see you about, Mr. Whittington, and please don't hurry your tea. The Scottie is nothing to do with me. Belongs to your youngest guests."

The eyeglass went in again, and when he saw the expression on the faces of the twins he smiled at them so disarmingly that their resistance to him melted away.

"Nice little dog," he said. "You know how to look after him."

While he was drinking his tea Charles re-told the Lone Piners' stories and Denton added his evidence.

Mr. Whittington was interested.

"Glad to hear all this," he said. "Not altogether surprising. Never had so many calls to dogs in my life as I've had the last few weeks. I'm worried. Can't put my finger on the trouble. Feel a fool at my time of life to admit that I don't know."

"What's happening to dogs?" Denton asked. "Mine's been blind for most of the day. Now she can see, I think, but we've done nothing for her, and I want you to examine her."

Mr. Whittington looked round at the eager faces.

"I'll examine her, but I'll find nothing. I believe she's been blind for twelve hours and is now none the worse for it. I've had three similar cases during the last fortnight, and four of deafness. All the dogs have recovered, and they all have one thing in common—they disappeared from home and were found wandering like yours."

Lady walked into the room with Macbeth just behind her. Mary leaned down and scooped up the latter into her lap as Mr. Whittington lit his pipe and went on:

"I shouldn't like to think that somebody round here is experimenting with dogs, but all the cases I've seen are within ten miles of the Castle ... It's possible that they're picking up a virus, but I must admit I'm baffled. I've written to London about it, but I've had no reply yet ... Bring her into the surgery now, Denton, and we'll have a look at her, but I'm as certain as I can be that she'll be none the worse for this experience. None of the others were. I don't like it."

The two men went out of the room and Lady followed at Denton's whistle.

Mary's face was stricken as she looked up.

"Did you hear what he said? Somebody might be *experimenting* with dogs. I've never heard anything more awful. Mackie will have to sleep with me every night, whatever Mummy says ... Did you hear what Mr. Whittington said, Peter? You look frightened."

Peter tried to smile.

"Yes, I heard, Mary. Don't you worry about Mackie. We shall all look after him ... When are we going to the Fair, Trudie? Can we go as soon as we've washed up?"

"Of course. I've been looking forward to it all day. I'm going to take Charles on everything—even the horses on the old-fashioned roundabouts."

By the time they had all helped to clear away the three men came out of the surgery. Denton said, "Lady is all right now.

Perfectly normal. Mr. Whittington can't understand it, and neither can I ... I can't tell you how much I enjoyed your party, Miss Whittington. I think the last one I was at was when all these youngsters and two more of their friends from the south came to Bury Fields in the winter ... You must all come over again as soon as you can. I'll speak to my mother, who will be sorry to have missed you, and she'll write to you at Witchend ... Cheerio."

Peter and David went out with him to his car and as Alan turned to shake hands with them he said, "What's on your mind, Peter? You look worried. You two haven't squabbled, have you?"

Peter flushed. "Don't be silly, Alan. It sounds rather priggish, but the Lone Piners don't squabble—not much, anyway. It's just that I hate anything happening to animals. I'm puzzled about that boy's story this afternoon and the house we found in Greystone ... I'm glad Lady is all right now, anyway," and she bent and kissed her head.

"Don't be old before you've got to be, Peter. It's selfish to say don't worry about other people's worries, I know, but you kids ought to be enjoying yourselves. Why don't you go off to the Fair now?"

Lady jumped into the car beside him, and they waved as Denton drove away.

"Just a sec, Peter," David said. "Don't go in yet. You've got something special on your mind, haven't you? Care to tell me now?"

She shook her head.

"I can't tell you yet. We ought to go back and help the others. I will tell you later, David. Honestly, I will," and he had to be content with that.

Half an hour later they were all on their way to the Fair in the big meadow just outside the town. Peter seemed to have forgotten her worries and the only one of them who was not up to form was Mary. She had been persuaded to leave Macbeth behind with Mr. Whittington, who said that he wouldn't be able to concentrate on a Fair this evening and that Mackie would hate the noise and the people, and that it would be cruel to take him. Privately Mary had the fear that Mr. Whittington might be called out and would have to leave Macbeth in the house alone, a thing the Scottie would hate worse than the Fair, but in the end she gave way.

"I've been looking forward to this Fair all my life," she confided to Jenny as they set off down the hill, "and now the evening is spoiled because my darling has to be sacrificed … An' that reminds me, Dickie, that you didn't stick up for me much jus' now. I'm beginning to wonder whether we're twins or not. It's no use being a twin if the twin doesn't stick up for the twin."

"Mackie would hate the Fair, Mary. You know he would, an' that's nothing to do with twins."

They turned the corner of the street and saw the Fair already alive and gay with lights below them. And on the wind came the sound of music. Not the music of a band or the radio, but the cheerful clang of the roundabout's brazen song, the shouts of the showmen and the jolly noise of hundreds of people enjoying themselves. "If we miss each other," Charles said over his shoulder, "we all meet at Trudie's at ten o'clock. Look after the twins, David, and see they don't get trodden on. Enjoy yourselves," and he took Trudie's arm and hurried ahead.

The light was fading as the shadowy shapes of the swing-boats blotted out the first stars in a sky of deep velvety blue. There was a smell of crushed grass and fried fish as they hurried into the meadow, and the air was thick with shouting and the shrill laughter of girls.

"Let's try and stick together, Tom," David said. "We must keep an eye on the twins, but we dare not let them think we're looking after them."

Tom nodded.

"O.K. I'm going to buy Jenny one of those hats first. Which one would you like, Jen? What about the one with 'Kiss Me Quick' on it?"

"Thank you, Tom," she said demurely. "I'd like that one very much," and he tried not to look surprised as he went over to buy it from a jolly gipsy woman. David and Peter roared with laughter when he brought it back and Jenny said, "It's for Mary, Tom. She's just the right age to wear it," and Mary agreed and wore it proudly throughout the evening.

Then they tried everything in turn, beginning with the swing boats, from which Dickie alighted after only two minutes looking very pale and thoughtful. The roundabout was a success, and so were the Dodgems, although as the twins refused to be separated and tried to control a car between them they precipitated four crises in the same number of minutes. David and Tom had a shooting match, which the latter won. His prize was a hideous green china dog, which he hastily presented to Jenny.

They were no good at the coconuts and not much better at darts, but they did enjoy rolling pennies at which Peter and Mary were very successful. Mary, indeed, was so entranced by this apparently simple scheme of getting her money back that the others had difficulty in dragging her away.

All the lights were blazing now and Jenny had to scream to make herself heard above the blaring of the roundabout and the shouts of the showmen.

"I want to find Reuben and Miranda now," she yelled. "We promised that we'd look for them. Who'll come with me?"

"We'll all come," Peter said. "I want to see them again. I

THEY ALL LAUGHED AS JENNY PUT THE FUNNY HAT ON MARY'S HEAD,
SAYING "MARY'S JUST THE RIGHT AGE TO WEAR IT."

wondered if Miranda would be helping somewhere but I haven't seen her."

"I've seen some gipsies strolling about," Tom admitted. "I reckon they don't mix much with all these show people, and I don't really know why they come to fairs. I think the caravans are up in the corner of the meadow against the hedge … Let's get out of here and see," and he led them out of the brilliance of the lights into the shadows, where the engines of the lorries were throbbing and electric cables, like long black snakes, twisted over the grass.

"We'll have to search all round the field," Peter said. "It's difficult to see now we're away from the lights."

Just then a little girl, with her arms full of greasy newspaper, dashed between two lorries and almost knocked Dickie over.

"Hi! Look out!" he yelled, and then, "It's young Fenella. You are Fenella, aren't you? I mean, you would be if I could see you properly."

It was Fenella, and she dropped the fish and chips she was carrying as they all crowded round her. They helped her to pick up the remnants, licking their fingers appreciatively, and then followed her over to her caravan. There was not room for them all inside, where Miranda was busy with a large black teapot, so after the first greetings, and after Fenella, with Mary to help her, had been sent back for more fish and chips, they grouped themselves on the steps. Only Peter stayed inside, and that was because she had once saved Fenella's life by stopping the runaway horse in the caravan. Reuben and Miranda had promised never to forget what she had done, and to help her whenever they had the opportunity. They did not often meet, but Peter soon learned that she really had found fine friends in these wandering Romanies, who were so different from the rascally van-dwellers which many people miscalled gipsies. All the

Lone Piners liked them, too, but perhaps it was because Peter had such a love and understanding for the country and all wild things, and because she was so straightforward in her dealings with everybody, that she really liked Reuben and Miranda and the shy little girl whose life she had saved. Miranda had always been particularly quick to understand her—sometimes her sympathy was almost embarrassing—but she was always kind and generous.

So while the others chattered outside on the steps of the caravan and ate their supper out of newspaper, Peter and Miranda gossiped inside the caravan.

"Do you often come this way now, Miranda? Do you know a little stone house in the wood at the bottom of Greystone Dingle? We had a funny sort of experience there to-day, and I wondered if you knew who lives there?"

Miranda laughed as she heaped tea into the big black pot.

"You are always having what you call 'funny' things happening to you, my pretty ... No, I do not remember the house in the wood. I do not think we have been in that wood since we met you all that day in the rain ... Now let us see if those greedy ones have eaten our supper. The tea is ready."

They had hardly joined the others, crowded round Reuben, who was showing them how to make a whistle from a piece of wood from an elder tree, when a quiet but familiar voice said:

"Good evening, Reuben. Good evening, Miranda, and a very good evening to all my young friends," and there was Mr. Cantor looking as cherubic and benevolent as usual. He beamed upon them all, but looked slightly taken aback when Mary jumped off the steps, took his hand and said, "What do you think of this hat, Mr. Cantor? Jenny made me wear it, but I only agreed 'cos I was sure we should meet you."

Mr. Cantor bent and kissed her, looked round as if waiting

for the applause to die down and said, "Any other lady?"

The gipsies and Mr. Cantor respected each other. The detective knew how honest and trustworthy they were, and Reuben knew that if he was ever in trouble Mr. Cantor would be glad to help him. Gipsies are often accused of many things unjustly, but in their wanderings they pick up a lot of information; and when Miranda handed the detective a cup of tea she knew at once that there were questions he wanted to ask them. Peter had just asked her an odd question, too. She looked at her husband and wondered whether he had noticed anything and was sure that he had.

"Listen to me a minute, *please*, Mr. Cantor," Mary was saying. "You haven't asked where Mackie is. We'll tell you. He's staying with Mr. Whittington 'cos I didn't dare bring him to the Fair in all this noise and fuss. Mr. Whittington is guarding him for us."

"He needs a special guard now," Dickie went on. "We'd like a special detective to help look after him. There's awful things happening to dogs round here. Dogs going blind like Alan Denton's Lady, an'—"

Mr. Cantor stepped forward and put his hand on Dickie's shoulder. When he spoke his voice was different—not quite so vague and kindly as usual.

"I know about the dogs, old chap, and there's no need for you to shout. That's why I want a word with Reuben and Miranda—privately, if you please. Don't look so upset. It's only that Reuben may be able to help me, and I don't want to discuss it with anybody else."

"Let's see if we can find Charles and Trudie," David said. "They've been missing long enough. You come, too, Fenella, and show us round … We'll come back presently, Reuben."

They found Charles and Trudie at the shooting booth.

"Peter darling," the latter said as soon as she recognized them, "do make him stop. He's spending all the money he ought to be saving for our new home just to win these three mugs, which I don't think are really very dainty ... Of course, it's wonderful to have your man shoot things for you, but I'm getting bored."

"Very well," Charles said. "I'm going to win something for the girls. A green dog, perhaps."

"I've got one, thanks," Jenny said quickly, "but Peter hasn't. David didn't even try for her."

Then Trudie noticed Mary's hat and Mary knew that she'd noticed it. Would she behave like a real grown-up and tell her to take it off, or would she just be as wonderful as she'd always thought her to be? Trudie did the right thing. She just smiled and said, "While Charles is wasting his money why don't you twins come over and bring me some luck at the rolling pennies?"

It was dark now but for an orange glow below a ridge of cloud over to the west, and the fairground was packed. Dickie yawned when he was sure that no one was looking, and Mary tried to keep the tears back when a man trod on her foot. Neither of them would be likely to mention it, but if someone else suggested going home now they wouldn't mind. It had been a long day.

Trudie rolled three pennies without success, and then, after a glance at the shooting booth, said, "Do you know what I should like more than anything else, twins? I should like a cup of tea at home and a word with Macbeth. Let's tell the others, shall we? Or would you rather stay a little longer?"

"I think Mackie is lonely by now," Mary replied. "Of course, he's enjoyed Mr. Whittington, but he misses us very much. Let's go back and see him."

The others were still shooting—Tom and David had joined in again—but they agreed that Trudie and the twins should go home first, and that they would join them after they had said good-bye to the gipsies.

An hour later they were all—including Mackie—back at Seven Gates. There had been room for Trudie in the estate van, so she had come over to finish off the evening and Charles had promised to take her home later. As soon as they had both gone indoors the Lone Piners opened up HQ2 and were thrilled to see that Mrs. Sterling had been in and unrolled their bedding and lit the oil-lamp. There was a note on the top of the stove, too.

"Welcome back again, Lone Piners. Help yourself to milk and cocoa from the scullery if you'd like some. The back door is unlocked."

"That's the sort of aunt to have," Peter said. "Isn't she wonderful? Anybody want anything to eat?"

Nobody did—not even Macbeth—and when Peter suggested that Mary might like to go up to bed first she yawned, said good night and went up the ladder to the girls' dormitory without further comment. Dickie gave in, too.

Peter wandered out into the farmyard and the others followed her and stood with their backs to the big white gate and looked over the roof of the house to the Stiperstones.

"What did Reuben say to you, David?" Tom asked. "I saw him whispering to you. Was it anything to do with old Cantor?"

"Yes, it was. I asked him straight out what Cantor wanted to talk to him about."

"Did he tell you what he said?" Peter broke in. "I've got some ideas about this, too."

"He told me Cantor has asked them to keep a look-out for anything or anybody who might have any connection with these queer happenings to dogs. I think he told Reuben that quite a lot of dogs are disappearing, so what that kid Johnny told us this afternoon may be right."

"But *why*, David?" Jenny said. "I can't see why all this is happening."

"Neither can I, Jenny. Apparently Cantor suggested that all cases of injured dogs might lead to something more serious. Burglars, perhaps? ... What do you think, Peter?"

"I'll tell you. What Mr. Cantor says only makes me feel more certain that I'm right. I've been thinking about those newspaper cuttings which you lost, David. I told you they were left at Hatcholt by the man with the beard after the plane came down, and were all about dogs who had saved their masters' property ... I believe there is some connection between those two men and what is happening round here now to these dogs. I s'pose Mackie went up with Mary, by the way? Did you actually see him, Jenny? Good ... I think we all ought to go to-morrow—we'll ask Charles to come, too—to that stone house in Greystone wood, and have a good look round. And there's another thing you could do, Jenny, and it's jolly important. Would you go and ask your father directly after breakfast if he knows anything about the man in that house? If he ever gets any post Mr. Harman would know about it, wouldn't he? I mean it would go through the post office; and if you could *persuade* your father to tell you his name and whether he gets lots of post and whether he calls for it ... Things like that would be useful to know. Will you do that, Jenny?"

"Of course I will. Dad will tell me even if I have to lure him a bit. I'll find out."

"Let's go over to say good night to the others, then," David suggested. "But we'll wait till morning before we remind Charles that he's promised to come to the house in the wood with us. We must tell him as soon as possible, though, because I think I heard him say something to Trudie about urgent business in Shrewsbury ... I don't know what we should do in this Club without Jenny."

Jenny looked at him gratefully, but her smile changed to an enormous yawn.

"I'll do anything for the Club, David, but Tom will have to come with me in the morning."

CHAPTER VIII

LITTLE STONE HOUSE

TOM was the first of the Lone Piners to wake the next morning. He turned on his back and drowsily watched the sun coming through a crack in the wooden walls of the barn and lighting up the cobwebs hanging from the beams. David was breathing gently in his cubicle next door, while Dickie, on the other side, was much more obvious.

He looked at the watch which Uncle Alf had given him at Christmas. Ten past eight. What was it they were going to do to-day? He tried to collect his wandering thoughts and then remembered the Fair and the adventures they had all had yesterday, and that Peter had asked Jenny to go down to Barton this morning and ask her father about the man who lived in the house in Greystone Dingle. And Jen had said that she would go if he'd come too, and although he didn't think much of Mrs. Harman he would be glad to go with Jenny, of course.

But if it was past eight it was time they were all moving, because Tom was quite sure he wasn't going to do any detective work on an empty stomach.

He reached out for his shoe and tossed it over the division between the cubicles, and with a grin of satisfaction heard it land on something soft and then David's muttered, "Shut up. Go away."

"Wake up!" Tom shouted. "It's past breakfast time. Wake up, David! Rouse Dickie while I shout up for the girls."

He wriggled out of his sleeping-bag, groped for his shorts and then pushed back the big doors so that the sun streamed into the barn. Next he went to the bottom of the loft ladder and yelled, "Wake up, you girls! We've had our breakfast, but you can't stay up there any longer. If you're not moving in five minutes we'll come and fetch you."

The only effect of this awful threat was to bring Mackie to the trap-door at the top of the ladder. He barked a welcome, and as he was plainly asking to be brought down Tom climbed up until the little dog was able to lick his face and then tucked him under one arm and jumped to the floor.

"Mackie, my darling," wailed Mary's voice from above, "those brutes have kidnapped you."

"Get the other two up, Mary," Tom shouted. "Just remind Jenny that she's got to go down and see her father and that if she's not quick she'll have to go without me."

Dickie was stirring now and David was rather petulant.

"Can't you make a little less row, Tom? You're disgustingly hearty this morning just because you woke up first."

"Light up the stove, David; I want my breakfast, and do get Dickie moving. When you're conscious you'll remember we've got a lot to do to-day," and he went out whistling into the farmyard.

Charles had often told the Lone Piners that they weren't really campers at all because the girls used the bathroom upstairs and the boys, if they felt they couldn't get really clean in a bucket filled from the horse-trough, were allowed to use the scullery sink. Tom preferred the bucket this morning, and while he was still drying his back the girls, with macks over their pyjamas, strolled across the yard to the back door.

"Good mornin', Thomas," Mary said cheekily. "I think we've made up our minds—us girls, I mean—that we're all going to be late for breakfast."

"Make the tea on Mrs. Sterling's kitchen stove for once, Peter," Tom called over his shoulder. "Don't you remember you asked Jenny to go down and see her father about this chap in the mystery house? We want to get on the trail, don't we?"

Jenny squealed with excitement.

"I'd *forgotten*, Tom. I'd forgotten what Peter said. I won't be a sec."

It wasn't what Dickie called a super-breakfast—just cornflakes, cream, brown bread and butter and marmalade—but it was a quick one and did not leave much to wash-up.

"We'll clear up here while you've gone," Peter said as Jenny drained her second mug of tea. "Come back as soon as you can, 'cos we don't want to do anything more until we know what Mr. Harman—or anyone else in the village—knows about the man in the little stone house. While you're away I'll ask Charles if he can come with us. But do be as quick as you can, 'cos we'll be waiting for you."

"All right," Jenny said. "If anybody in Barton knows anything about that man, I bet it's Dad. We won't be long. Come on, Tom."

They turned and waved at the gate and set off together down the hill through what Jenny still called the "whispering wood."

"This might be the beginning of another adventure for us, Tom. It might be, mightn't it? I mean it would be wonderful if we really did find out something from Dad and then went back and told the others and then we started on the trail of something exciting and they said—"

"Who said?" Tom asked. "You're making me out of breath. Who said what?"

"The others. Peter and David and the twins and— Oh! don't be so grown-up and ridiculous, Tom. I want the others to be able to say, 'If it wasn't for Tom and Jenny we would never have found a clue about this. Not a single solitary clue. We can always trust Tom and Jenny to get on the trail …' Do you see what I mean, Tom?"

"I s'pose I do, though I can't see that it matters. I s'pose your father will be home now, won't he?"

"I'm sure he will. You just leave this to me, Tom."

Soon they had fastened the last of the farm's seven white gates behind them and were in the lane leading down to the village of Barton Beach. Barton was not a pretty village and seemed somehow to have suffered from being under the shadow of the Stiperstones. The street was long and straggling and there were very few shops, for now most of the inhabitants went into Bishop's Castle for their marketing. But Jenny knew everybody, and everybody liked her and had been sorry for her when her father had gone off to the war, leaving her alone with her elderly and not very sympathetic stepmother. There was a baker's shop and a small butcher's and one other grocer's besides Mr. Harman's general store and post office. Tom always wondered secretly why anybody at all came into the shop because it was so dark and gloomy.

"You know that boy, Johnny, Peter told us about?" Jenny said as they passed the baker's.

"No, I don't, Jen. Never seen him."

"I mean, you remember her telling us about him? I can't think why you don't understand what I say the first time, Tom. I do hope you're not getting dull … Anyway, I'm sure the boy Johnny who lost his dog is Johnny Ellis at the baker's. I didn't know he had a puppy, but we'll go and see him after we've spoken to Dad."

"We'll have to go back and tell the others our news first," Tom reminded her. "We promised to do that."

"We might have more news after I've had a chat with Johnny. Anyway, let's see what Dad says about the stranger."

As usual, the swinging bell on a spring clanged as they opened the shop door, and, as usual, Tom tripped over the step.

The small post office counter was shrouded in gloom at the rear of the shop and the "general stores" counter was on the left. There were articles for sale in this small shop which fascinated Tom—such things, for instance, as peculiar patent medicines, green brilliantine, combs on a card, a tray of hideous birthday cards, rabbit snares, anti-flea powder for dogs and shampoo powders. He was sure that nobody ever bought a bottle of the green brilliantine because there had been just three bottles in their box on the counter ever since his first visit. One day he would have to buy one just to help Mr. Harman and for the relief of seeing two bottles instead of three.

"It's all right, Dad. It's only us," Jenny was calling through the curtained doorway. "I want to see you very specially, Dad."

Mr. Harman, in a grey alpaca jacket, emerged from the living-room behind the shop.

"Hullo, lass," he smiled as he gave her a kiss. "Can't keep up with you and your friends. You're all too quick for me ... How are you, Tom? Nice to see you ... What made me think you were over at Ingles, Jen?"

"I can't explain now, Dad, but we are still there really and I'm having a wonderful time, but we were at Seven Gates last night ... Where's Mum?"

"Gone to the Castle on the first bus. She'll be sorry to have missed you."

"Yes, Dad, I'm sorry, too ... There's something very special we want you to help us about, Dad. It's nothing much really, but it's important to us because we're nearly mixed up in another adventure."

Mr. Harman twinkled at his daughter and Tom saw where she got her smile.

"Better ask me quick afore a customer arrives," he suggested. "I'll do my best ... I shouldn't have thought you ever used brilliantine, Tom, but if you'd like one of those bottles you're very welcome—with the compliments of the management! Can't think why I bought 'em. Nobody round here seems interested … Here you are, boy. Put it in your pocket, but I should be careful how you use it. Shouldn't be surprised if it didn't smell rather strong … Now, Jenny, tell me the worst."

Tom hadn't the heart to refuse the dusty bottle and felt rather ashamed because Mr. Harman had caught him staring at it. But before he could say "Thank you," Jenny was firing a number of confused and breathless questions at her father.

"Steady. Steady," he said with his hand to his head. "The man in the old house at the bottom of Greystone? Of course I know who he is! Name of Robens. I reckon he's been there about six weeks. Crazy to take the place, o' course, but he's no worry to anybody so far as I know."

"Does he get a lot of post, Dad?"

"Yes, he gets a bit and calls here for it two or three times a week. Says he doesn't want it delivered because he's busy and doesn't like being disturbed in the mornings."

"Is he a mystery, Dad?"

"Folks here say there must be something wrong with him, but I reckon he's harmless … Quite a young chap. Excitable, but civil."

He moved behind the post office counter.

"Funny you should ask about him, because about five minutes before you came in they telephoned through a telegram for him, and I was wondering how to get it out there. Young Jimmy Barlow generally delivers for me—when we get a telegram, which isn't often—but he's away. Sounds an important message, so maybe you two would like to take it over to Greystone as you're so interested in him."

Tom opened his mouth to reply, but Jenny was before him.

"*Of course* we will, Dad. We'd like to help you and Tom can borrow your bike, and I'll borrow Mum's because we've left ours at Seven Gates. We'll be back in half an hour. Is it a very important and urgent message, Dad? I'm afraid of telegrams."

Mr. Harman pushed the pad across the counter.

"It's against the rules, of course, but it looks as if he ought to have it as soon as possible. I'll be glad if you two will deliver it."

Shamelessly they read the pencilled message.

"Robens, Greystone End, Barton Beach. Doctor free noon Wednesday call without fail."

There was no signature and the wire had been handed in at Shrewsbury half an hour ago.

"But to-day is Wednesday," Tom said. "Of course this ought to be delivered. It sounds as if he's been trying to see a doctor, and this is fixing up the arrangement. We'll take it, Mr. Harman."

"I'll be obliged," the postmaster said. "And I'll be obliged, too, if one of you would tell me what all the excitement is about, and why you want to see this chap. You're not up to anything, are you?"

Jenny barely hesitated.

"We are a bit, Dad, but I promise you we shall be all right. Really we will. It's just that Peter and David met young Johnny Ellis in Greystone Wood yesterday and he told them that the man living in that house had stolen his puppy and kept it locked up while he was away. They went along with Johnny and heard a dog whining, but couldn't make anybody hear ... It's just that we all hate cruel things, and I told the others that you would be sure to know something about that man. Oh! And Johnny also told them that several people round here have lost dogs lately. Have you heard anything about that, Dad, and do you know what Mr. Robens is *doing* there by himself?"

"No, o' course I don't. I don't ask him and he doesn't tell me. I'm not the nosy sort, as you know, Jenny. I reckon he's a writer or is just studying. Something like that … As for this business about dogs, seems all nonsense to me, although, come to think of it, there was some talk about a dog disappearing, but I can't for the life o' me remember whose it was … And I wouldn't take too much notice of young Johnny if I were you. He's a bright spark and always got his fingers into something … Here's the telegram, and better ask if there's an answer."

Tom put the orange envelope in his pocket.

"What does he look like, Mr. Harman?"

"Youngish. Thin. Untidy. Long hair. Heavy spectacles. Decent voice … Cheerio to you both. Take care o' my bike, Tom, and I'll give Mum your love, Jenny … Look in on your way back."

As soon as they were outside Tom said, "That was a bit of luck, Jenny. One of us ought to go back to the others now and tell them what we're going to do. Shall I go to Greystone while you go back to Seven Gates and tell them what's happened? They'll be worried waiting for us."

"Let them be worried for a little while longer," Jenny said surprisingly. "Of course we want them to know what we're doing, but *I'm* not going to Greystone by myself, Tom, and I don't want you to go either. As soon as we've delivered the telegram we really will have some news for the others. We shan't be long on our bikes."

"I'm not so sure," Tom said gloomily. "I've ridden on your Dad's bike before. It's too big for me and it's torture. I think I'd rather run all the way."

"Don't be silly, Tom. Will you please pump up my tyres while I run down to the baker's and see if Johnny is there? I'd like to know whether his puppy has come back."

Tom wandered round to the shed and was not surprised to find that both tyres of Mrs. Harman's bicycle were flat. He was still working on them when Jenny came back.

"Do *please* hurry up, Tom. I've seen Mrs. Ellis and she doesn't know where Johnny is, and the puppy hasn't come back, so we must hurry."

They caught up with Johnny at the edge of the wood. His face was white and his eyes swollen, but there was a stubborn look about his mouth that Tom liked.

"Don't you worry, old chap," he said. "We're going to the cottage with a telegram, and you can come too and have a look for your dog. We'll help you to find him."

"There were a girl and a big chap yesterday—" he began sulkily, and then Jenny interrupted him and told him that it was because of Peter and David that they were here now, and that Mr. Sterling had been told as well.

Tom flung Mr. Harman's detested bicycle in the undergrowth and advised Jenny to do the same with her mother's.

"I'm quicker on my feet, anyway," he said, "and if I ride it any more I shall be a cripple for life ... If we have to make a dash for it we know where we left them ... Come on."

When they were within sight of the cottage, which looked to be deserted, Tom told Johnny to run on ahead, and if he could not see anybody, to hide at the side of the porch until they came up with the telegram.

"If the man is there," he went on, "we'll try and keep him talking and you can either nip round to the back and whistle your dog, or call him through the front door. If you're sure he is there, then we'll do something about it. If you see the man watching you from the window, just wait for us at the gate, and we'll go up to the front door together."

Johnny nodded, dashed into the wood like a rabbit, and a

minute later they saw him peeping over the garden wall.

"All right, Jen? Not scared are you?"

"I'm shaking all over, Tom. I feel a bit sick. I'm terrified, but I wouldn't be anywhere else for anything."

Tom laughed. "I'm scared, too. Come on. Let's get it over."

The cottage looked as gloomy as usual. Outside the wood the sun was shining, but beside the garden path the weeds grew rank, and pale fungi thrust up their curious shapes under the dank walls.

Johnny was standing against the wall between the door and the window when Tom, whistling loudly and with Jenny beside him, banged on the door so hard that several flakes of faded paint fell to the dirty stone step. Jenny was almost choked by her heartbeats when they heard the sound of a step and the door was flung back.

Tom played his part well.

"Name of Robens, sir?" he asked. "We've brought you a telegram. Mr. Harman of the post office asked us to bring it quick as it might be urgent."

The man's appearance was not very frightening. He looked dirty, wild-eyed and unkempt and almost bewildered as he stared at them.

"Are you Mr. Robens, sir?" Tom repeated. "I've got a telegram for you."

The man nodded and held out his hand, which was covered with brown stains. "That is my name, but I am not expecting a telegram."

He slit the envelope and read the message which they already knew, and it was obvious that he had forgotten that they were still waiting.

"Nonsense," he muttered. "Absolutely ridiculous. I can't get there by noon. Experiment won't be over for an hour or more."

"Is there an answer, sir?" Tom asked. "I was to be sure and ask you that."

"Certainly not. I'll come when I can—" but before he could finish this curious sentence there came a yell of triumph from somewhere behind him.

"I got him! I got my Sandy. He's tied up."

Robens' face flushed with fury, and he swore as he turned and tried to slam the front door. But he was not quick enough for Tom, who put his foot in the crack and dashed into the house after him. Jenny, terrified but wildly excited, followed.

The room on the right of the narrow passage ran from front to back of the house and had a window at each end. Johnny had obviously found the back door open and slipped across from the scullery behind Robens' back while the latter was talking to Tom and Jenny. They saw him now on his knees with his arms round a little black and tan mongrel tied to the leg of a table which was loaded with piles of papers, books and a collection of dirty tea-cups.

"Leave that dog alone and get out!" Robens snapped. "Who are you, anyway? ... And you two get out, too. There's no answer to that telegram."

Jenny noticed that although he was angry he was not very confident; while Tom, standing in front of her, was almost enjoying himself.

"Look here, Mr. Robens," he said, "that dog isn't yours. It belongs to this boy from Barton. He's been searching for it for two days. Do you mind telling us where you found it? ... Here, Johnny, cut the string with this," and he threw over his pocket-knife.

Johnny was not ashamed of his tears now, and, indeed, did not even know that he was crying. The little dog, frantic with excitement, was crying and whining, too, but did not seem any the worse for his captivity. Tom looked carefully to see whether it was blind or deaf, but it seemed to be normal and not particularly cowed.

Johnny stood up with the puppy in his arms.

"You dirty bully! You dirty thief! I'll tell my dad. You stole my Sandy. Yes, you did. What you done to him?"

"Yes, that's it," Jenny said suddenly. "What have you done to him? Why was he tied up to the table? Was he tied up alone in there when you went out yesterday? Johnny thought he heard him then."

Robens moved over and stood in front of the open door. His face was twitching, but he made an attempt to smile.

"Now look here, all of you. We don't want any fuss and bother about this, and I'd like you to forget all about it. I'd no idea the puppy belonged to this youngster. He just turned up here, so I kept him until I had time to take him in to the police station."

"When did you find him?" Tom asked.

"Never mind when I found him. If he belongs to this kid here I'll be glad to buy him. I rather like the little chap. How about ten shillings, son?"

Tom knew what Johnny's answer would be. He looked round the room carefully. He wanted to remember everything in it. Under the window facing the back garden was a wide bench covered with chemical apparatus—glass jars, test-tubes, flasks, rows of brown bottles, little brass scales and methylated spirit burners. The only easy chair, which was very shabby, was piled with papers, and on the walls were pinned charts with red and green lines straggling up and down them and rows of figures underneath. And there was something else even more noticeable—a strange, unrecognizable but not unpleasant smell. Suddenly Tom was sure that there was nothing more which they could do here, and that it would be unwise to stay.

"YOU BULLY! YOU THIEF! YOU STOLE MY DOG!" SAID JOHNNY. "WHAT HAVE YOU DONE TO HIM?"

He was no longer nervous of an unknown adventure, but very much afraid of something he couldn't quite explain. Robens himself was not explainable. He obviously had a quick temper and was working on something secret. Just as obviously he was nervous and excited. Tom remembered what he had muttered when he had read the telegram—something about the experiment not being over for an hour or more. Was the experiment on Sandy? And had he started it yet? Was Sandy going blind in an hour? Had Robens got any more dogs tied up for his horrible experiments, and what did it all mean? Whatever the answer, Tom knew that Charles Sterling must be told about this at once.

"I wouldn't sell him for any money," Johnny said. "Not a billion pounds. Not anything."

"But you don't understand," Robens pleaded. "How could you? I want that little dog. I must watch him for the next few hours. I'll give you—" and here he put his hand in his pocket.

"Quick, Johnny!" Tom said. "Run for it! We'll catch you up."

Even as Robens turned the boy, with the puppy in his arms, slipped past him and out into the hall.

"We'll go, too, Jenny," Tom said with a shaky smile. "I'll tell Mr. Harman there's no answer to the telegram, Mr. Robens."

Robens coloured with anger again as he made an effort to control his words.

"Just listen to me for a minute," he said slowly. "I'm not doing any harm to that dog, but I must have him for a few hours. I've told you I'll pay for him—"

"You're too late," Tom said grimly. "You'll never catch him now."

He took Jenny's hand and pulled her quickly out of the front door.

"And I wouldn't advise you to try and steal him again, Mr. Robens. We'll have the whole village of Barton on the look-out for you ... Come on, Jenny."

Johnny was already out of sight by the time they reached the bicycles.

"He must have gone another way," Tom gasped. "He'll be all right, won't he, Jen?"

Then he noticed that she was crying.

"I'm frightened of that man, Tom. What shall we do? We ought to be doing something quickly 'cos I saw his old car by the side of the house and he might come racing after us ..."

Tom was scared, too.

"Come on, then," he said. "If he comes after us we'll leave the bikes and make a dash for it each side of the road ... Do you think Johnny is all right?"

Jenny was already pedalling ahead as hard as she could.

"Of course he is," she said over her shoulder. "He'll never be caught by that man. He'll be nearly home by now ... We must tell the others and Charles, Tom. That's what we've got to do right away. Let's go straight to Seven Gates."

Poor Tom was positive that he would never be able to go straight anywhere on Mr. Harman's bicycle.

"It's Mr. Cantor we ought to find," he gasped. "There's something very wrong about that chap and all that chemistry stuff in the room ... He wanted to do something to Sandy, didn't he, Jen? P'raps he's done it already and soon the puppy will be blind like Lady."

Jenny sniffed. She was crying again, so Tom concentrated on the bicycle.

Just as they were entering the village they heard a car honking behind them. Tom dared not look back, and as Jenny was now nearly twenty yards ahead he stood on his pedals and made desperate efforts to catch her. Surely Robens would not dare to threaten them in the street?

It was not Robens. It was the Seven Gates estate van with Charles driving and the others shouting at them as they passed and then drew up at the curb.

"You must be crazy," David laughed. "It's too hot for bike races, and, anyway, Jenny was well ahead. We got sick of waiting for you, so as Charles had to go to Shrewsbury he gave us a lift down to see if we could find you. What have you been playing at, and what have you found out?"

But Peter had just seen Jenny's face.

"Shut up, David," she said. "Something's happened," and she jumped out of the van.

"Peter and me will take the bikes home," Jenny gulped. "You start telling them all about it, Tom. We'll be back in a minute."

Tom thankfully handed over the hated bicycle, got into the van and wiped his face, and by the time Jenny and Peter had returned he told the others their story.

The twins for once were silent. Charles looked puzzled, but obviously had something else on his mind, so it was left to David to make the most practical suggestion.

"Tom says the telegram to Robens was handed in at Shrewsbury this morning. Charles has got to go in there, so I suggest we go with him. There's just a chance that we might see Robens, but I'm sure we ought to tell Cantor all we know now, and the only way we can get hold of him is through a police station."

"P'raps Cantor isn't his real name—just a detective's name," Dickie said. "You know—a disguise name. If it is we wouldn't know who to ask for at the police station ... Mary and me don't mind *asking*, mind you. We like police stations."

"Whether it's his real name or not," Peter put in, "any

policeman would know him if we described him. I'm sure he's not disguised as much as that ... The only thing about going to Shrewsbury is that I feel we're running away from here. Perhaps we ought to see if your Johnny has come home safely. I did promise yesterday to look after him."

"You needn't bother about that," Jenny smiled for the first time for an hour. "Here he is, and there's nothing the matter with Sandy."

Johnny was almost swaggering down the street with his hands in his pockets, but as Sandy was trying to undo his shoe-laces his progress was not really very dignified. They waved as he went by on the other side of the road, but he did not even see them.

"What do you think, Charles?" David asked.

"Robens seems to be an unpleasant chap, I agree, but nobody can prove that he stole Sandy. I dare say he did, but that's not enough to tell the police about. And it's not a crime to keep chemicals in your house if you like it that way ... And it's no use you looking like that, Peter. I know you're furious with me and Robens and lots more besides, but I can't have you kids spying round a house that belongs to somebody else and suspecting all sorts of things that can't and haven't happened. We could certainly tell your detective if we can find him, but I've got business in Shrewsbury and I must go now. Are you all coming?"

David answered for them all, and although Peter still looked mutinous she did not think of any real reason for not going until they were ten minutes on their way.

"We might have gone over to Bishop's Castle again and had a word with Reuben and Miranda, and perhaps we would have seen Mr. Cantor there."

Five miles from Shrewsbury, Charles pulled in to a petrol

station, and while his tank was being filled Mary gave a loud shout of triumph.

"Look, Dickie!" she yelled. "That's the car that offered us a lift yesterday. There couldn't be another one like it!"

They crowded to the side of the van as a dilapidated open four-seater car with the back seats covered with a waterproof sheet roared past.

"That's the man," Dickie shouted. "That's the man who wanted Mackie ... Buck up, Charles. Follow him."

"Did you recognize him?" Tom said to Jenny. "That's Robens on his way to Shrewsbury to keep his appointment."

"That settles it, then," Peter said as Charles let in the clutch. "We've got to find Mr. Cantor now. You will help us, won't you, Charles?"

"If you want me to catch the crazy fool in that car, I'm afraid I won't. He must have been doing fifty. I shouldn't worry, though. We'll be able to pick up the bits of his car soon. It can't hold together much longer."

"You'll help us with the police, I mean? You'll make them do something?"

"Not now I won't," her cousin said. "I've got my business to do first, but perhaps we may catch Robens up at the traffic lights, and then I don't see why we shouldn't follow him carefully and see where he's going, and then perhaps some of you could amuse yourselves by keeping an eye on him ... I promise you I'll think it over, and if you do discover anything else suspicious we'll telephone the police and try and find your detective."

"He told Reuben that he wanted any information about anybody who seemed specially interested in dogs," David said. "We've got that information now, and we know that Robens is the man who tried to get Mackie. I bet he's the man who poisoned Lady if we could only prove it."

"And the man who offered a pound for young Fenella's puppy," Tom added.

"You see how it all fits in, Charles? You've got to help us."

"But it doesn't really fit in yet, and there's next to nothing we can prove ... There he is now, stopped by the traffic lights. If he doesn't take me miles out of my way I'll follow him, and although I hate to suggest it, I think you all ought to lie on the floor. It wouldn't help you much if he suddenly turned round and recognized the twins and Tom and Jenny ... And don't look so rebellious, Peter. I'm sure it's no good rushing at this."

This remark was received in silence and the van moved forward as the lights changed. Robens was forced to drive more carefully now. There was no difficulty in following him because he soon turned into the residential part of the town and within five minutes he stopped half-way down the right-hand side of a pleasant avenue opposite a stuccoed, double-fronted house called The Limes, with a monkey puzzle tree in the front garden.

"Can't stop now," Charles muttered. "I must pass him. Don't let yourselves be seen, but have a look at the house as we go by."

Robens hurried up the path and did not even turn as the van drove slowly past and stopped round the corner of the next road.

"What do you think of that?" Tom said. "Lone Piners on the trail again, and all because Jen made me ride her father's bike down to Greystone."

"There was a plate on the gatepost," David said. "Did you tell us that chap looked ill, Tom? Maybe The Limes is his doctor's house, although why they call it The Limes when it's got a ridiculous monkey puzzle in front of it I don't know."

"I didn't say he was ill," Tom replied. "I should think he's crackers, and it's not an ordinary doctor he needs. What shall we do?"

"Let the air out of his tyres first," Dickie hissed. "If you like I'll crawl along the gutter and do it. I'll stab 'em all with knives."

Charles Sterling looked round at their excited faces and lit his pipe.

"Now listen for just three minutes," he began. "I've got to go now, but you must promise me that you won't do anything stupid. All that we're sure of is that this man Robens kept that boy's dog after either stealing it, or finding it. We believe that he was going to experiment on the puppy, if he has not already done so, and it is possible that Robens is responsible for the blindness of Denton's bitch and of other dogs, too ... Almost all these points are suspicions and not facts, and if you could find Mr. Cantor there's no reason why you shouldn't tell him what we know, but I think you'd do more good to the cause if you just keep an eye on The Limes and see what Robens does when he comes out."

"I can tell you what he'll do without waiting for him," Peter said angrily. "He'll get into the car and drive off, leaving us, without a car, standing over there behind the pillar-box ... I can't understand you, Charles. You're not being like you at all. Why are you so horribly cautious? You know as well as we all do that everything about that man Robens is wrong and suspicious, and that something very peculiar is going on. You promised to help us get to the bottom of this, and you're just about the only grown-up we like to help us, and now you've got nothing to say at all except that we're to be careful."

Her voice was very choky when she finished this long speech, and she got out of the van so that the others shouldn't see her face. Charles, with his pipe in his hand and his mouth half open with surprise, heard her in silence, but he did look shaken when first David and then Mary jumped out and stood beside Peter.

"I'm sorry," he said, and they knew he meant it. "I'm not really deserting you. Come back here so that I don't have to shout ..." He put out his hand to help Peter in, and she gave him a watery smile. "The truth is," he went on, "that I don't like this any more than you do, but I have got to meet a man in ten minutes on business—important business about the farm, which means a lot to us all—and when I've got it settled one way or the other I'll be able to decide what's the best thing to do about Robens. I'm sure this isn't the sort of thing in which you should be interfering. You've found out a lot, and if you can get in touch with Cantor by all means do so. But don't do anything stupid or dangerous, *please*, until we meet outside the main post office in three hours ...

"I've got to trust you all, but specially David and Peter because they're the eldest. In spite of Peter's temper, I do see what she means about being marooned on the pavement without a car when Robens drives off, but I still think it would be a good idea to stick around until he does go ... If the police really want to know about this man, we have at least found out where he goes in such a hurry."

"It must be his doctor," Jenny interrupted. "The telegram said that. 'Doctor free noon come without fail,' it said, or something like that."

"Good enough, then," Charles agreed. "Maybe he is ill and maybe that's his doctor's house, but you have got to promise me not to do anything silly or dangerous. From what Tom and Jenny told us, he's not a very pleasant chap. Promise?"

"We can't promise not to do anything, Charles," David said, "but we will promise to look after the twins. You'll have to trust us because we've made up our minds to do all we can to solve this mystery of the dogs. We don't like people who hurt animals."

"It's one of our rules, Charles," Peter said quietly. "We can't break our solemn vows and you wouldn't expect us to … I'm not angry with you any more, but you can trust us. We'll be at the post office in three hours."

"Why don't you go down to the river?" Charles said. "Or would you like me to give you all a lift into the town? As Peter says, you'll never know where he goes when he drives off, so why not enjoy yourselves?"

Peter glanced quickly at David and winked.

"Yes. Do that then, please, Charles. Just drop us at the nearest shop where they sell ices."

The others followed her lead, and five minutes later they were all sitting round an oil-cloth covered table in a small café with their heads almost touching. Six ices came and vanished, and then, when the woman who had served them had gone back to her parlour behind the shop, Peter said, "This is it. This is what I've got to tell you all because when Charles was talking just now about the doctor who must live in that house I had my terrific idea. I don't know whether I ever told you that the man with a beard, who lost his memory that day at the end of the Easter hols when the plane came down, called the other man who was so anxious to find him, 'Doctor'."

"That's right," David interrupted. "You told me that in your long letter," and pretended not to see Dickie and Mary wink at each other. "Go on, Peter."

"I remember that man well, and that I hated him, and although I've never seen either of those two men again so far as I know, I'd like to find out for myself whether this crazy Robens has now shaved off his beard and is the man I found at Hatchholt that day. I'm going back to where I can keep an eye on The Limes and the people in it. Robens knows Tom and Jenny from this morning, so they've got to keep out of the way. He'll remember the twins, I should think, because he offered them a lift, but he may be a bit puzzled if he sees only one of them. We can't all go, but I've made up my mind that I'm going to try and get into that house and I think I'd like Mary to help me. Little Mary can have a terrible pain and want the doctor quickly. Will you help, Mary?"

Mary looked at her twin doubtfully and at David quickly, and then nodded.

"Course I will. I s'pect Dickie and me could do it better on our own, but p'raps he'd better keep guard somewhere near with David … *And* it's no use looking like that, David. Nobody can hurt us if we're together and you stay on guard … There's another thing. I'm quite glad we left Mackie safe and sound with Aunt Carol. They'll look after each other."

CHAPTER IX

INSIDE THE LIMES

IN a large room at the back of the house with the monkey puzzle tree in the garden two men sat facing each other across a wide desk. It was a room which was not quite what it pretended to be. The furniture was solid and old-fashioned—glass-fronted bookcase, two easy chairs with shiny, black leather seats each side of a tiled fireplace and a small mahogany table—but most of it was dusty. The desk would have looked magnificent if it had been polished and kept tidy, but the beautiful wood was stained and grubby and the top was covered with loose papers, a bottle of beer and a dirty glass, two ashtrays full of cigarette stubs, a cheap bottle of ink and a stained plate.

The room should have looked like a doctor's consulting room, but it did not. The man behind the desk should have looked like a doctor, but he did not. Like the room, he was a sham, and Robens, to whom he was speaking, knew it, as he lit a cigarette and flicked the spent match towards one of the ashtrays.

His companion glared at him through heavy horn-rimmed spectacles. He was a gross man, thick-set, with greying hair brushed back from a wide forehead, and a florid, clean-shaven face. His clothes were like the room—uncared for.

"Thought we ought to have a chat, Robbie," he said. "I'm not too happy about things, and it's time we got some results. I want to know how you're getting on."

"Is that why you sent that absurd telegram?" the other snapped. "I thought you'd got more sense. I'm doing important work and I don't like being interrupted, and I told you that months ago when I agreed to come to that God-forsaken cottage. You seem to think that you've only got to send an idiotic message and I can solve a scientific problem which may take me months longer ... And another thing. Don't call me Robbie. I don't like it. It's not my name."

The "Doctor"—for Peter's guess that he was the man met by her father on the Long Mynd was correct—gave his companion an ugly look and then, after a long pause, leaned back in his chair and laughed.

"You know perfectly well that I shall call you what I like as often as I please. You seem very sure of yourself to-day, Robbie, but I don't want to have words with you now. Better pour yourself some beer and calm down. You'll find a glass and some bottles at the bottom of the book-case ... What's wrong with you, anyway? Have you got the formula yet, and if not how long will you be?"

"I don't know. No scientist could answer such a ridiculous question. You don't know what you're talking about. I thought, by your telegram, that somebody was suspicious of you. I noticed that your plate outside gives the name of Barnett. I suppose you know that you wouldn't deceive a baby for five minutes with the idea that you're a doctor? ... Now I must go. I had some bad luck about one of the dogs this morning, and I've got to find some more."

"No, Robbie. You are not going—just yet. You know very well that you can't give this up now. We're in it together, and I must remind you that I have been paying you for six months and the time has come for me to know how you are spending the money. I want to know how long you are going to be, Robbie."

"I tell you I don't know. The more you worry me the longer I shall be. I can't work that way. Nobody is suspicious, are they? I think you're a fool to set yourself up here as a doctor."

"I do not intend to be a doctor. The plate on the door was put there by the man from whom I bought this desirable residence. If strangers choose to think that I am a retired doctor, I do not trouble to deny it. Don't worry about me, Robbie. Just look after yourself and get on with your work. How soon will you have this ready? I've got several important customers waiting, and I'm getting a little anxious and suspicious of your ability to perfect the formula. I have reason to believe that you have been making some ridiculous mistakes."

The relationship between these men was curious. It was obvious that they disliked and distrusted each other. The "Doctor" was the stronger personality, but Robens the better educated, and although he was pretending that he was as good as his master, he was nervous and highly strung, and not a very good bluffer. He gave the impression that he would like to make a fight of it, but would never quite be able to find the courage. Perhaps the "Doctor" knew too much about him. Whatever the reason of the older man's domination, it was clear that he was a criminal; it was probable that Robens was only an unwilling one.

While the "Doctor" was talking in his threatening, silky voice, the younger man went over to the book-case and got a bottle of beer.

"That's better," the "Doctor" went on. "Make yourself at home, calm down and let's see where we stand. I know you wouldn't try to deceive me, Robbie ... Let's go over everything from the beginning and then you'll see why you've got to bring me results—quickly."

"Very well," Robens replied in a tired voice. "Try not to bore me, but do hurry."

"It won't do any harm to remind ourselves of our contract, Robens. I have it constantly in mind, and I want you to remember it, too ... I do not think we need dwell on the rather painful circumstances of our first meeting, but you must not forget that this idea is mine. *Mine*—and not yours. It was I who realized that a drug which could put a dog out of action for a few hours without any after effects would be worth a great deal of money to those immoral people who make a living by stealing. Almost every day now we read in the papers of how a dog has saved his master's property. Now I don't believe in house-breaking, Robbie—not doing it myself, I mean—but many misguided people try to make a living that way and they'll make it more quickly if the watchdogs are given a sniff of your formula, which will put them out for two hours without any ill effects. It's so simple, isn't it? You say you can make the stuff, I pay you while you're working it out and find you a nice cosy little cottage where you can work undisturbed, and I pay you very much more when you actually produce the goods and I can sell them ... How do you give it to the dog, by the way? In a pill?"

Robens put down his glass and stared over his confederate's shoulder into the back garden.

"You're a fool," he said at last, "but of course I must make excuses for you because you just don't know. I think you're greedy, too, but I gave you my word to produce this for you and I shall stick to it so long as I'm sure that you're playing the game with me."

"Get on," the "Doctor" snapped. "How do you give it to the dog? Why doesn't it give the alarm before it takes the drug?"

"I'll tell you, and then perhaps you won't bore me by asking again. My formula, which is nearly complete and which I call R.6., is most powerful when sprayed in the air a few feet from the dog. It has a very strong and distinctive scent—possibly you can smell it from my clothes now because apparently you never open a window. This scent delights the dog—no doubt you know how strong their sense of smell is—and although there is a risk that he might bark *before* he was fascinated by the smell and before the operator can use the pocket sprayer such as the one with which I am now experimenting, I consider the risk slight. No doubt you will also be able to go into business with the sprayers eventually?"

"I most certainly shall," the "Doctor" roared delightedly. "I'd thought of it as soon as you mentioned it, Robbie … Now tell me seriously what's going wrong? You'd better not make a fool of yourself and of me, too. That would be most regrettable. I've heard that dogs are disappearing every day and that some of them have gone blind for a few hours—"

"How do you know that?"

"—I make it my business to know a lot of things. What I have heard is true, isn't it?"

Robens twisted his stained fingers together.

"I tell you I can't help it, Doctor. I'm doing my best and every experiment brings me nearer success. My trouble is that I haven't got enough dogs. I try it on them and let them go and they find their way home so far as I know. Just now it's true that they're going blind, but it's only for a few hours. They're all right afterwards. *But I've got to have more dogs.* I've got to and you'll have to help me find them if we're going to get this through together."

The other stood up and stretched.

"I've got to help you? You've got to help me, Robbie. You've got to solve your problems in forty-eight hours, else I'm going to do something—something you won't like."

Robens stood up, too, and faced him across the desk. His lips were twitching and his face flushed.

"You don't understand. Can't you see that all that matters to me is the solving of this problem and I'm very near to doing it?

The trouble is that the cottage is unsuitable and too far from the village—"

"That's what you asked for. Exactly what you wanted. Perhaps, you don't remember anything about our plane coming down that night in March, when we were on our way to Ireland to find a place, and Providence put us down in one of the loneliest parts of the country. If you're careful there's no reason why anybody round about there should think you anything but a harmless lunatic. I bought you a car, and the only things I can't manage for you are a telephone and a modern laboratory—and, I remember, you told me when we made our bargain that you could do perfectly well without either ... Now we've had enough of this nonsense, Robbie. *How much longer are you going to be?*"

"I might have got the answer to-day if you hadn't sent that telegram. Now I've lost the dog I was working on. I was really getting somewhere."

"What do you mean?"

"Didn't it occur to you that if you send me a telegram it's got to be delivered to me by hand as I'm not on the telephone? Three children turned up at the cottage this morning—one of them saying that he was the owner of the dog. Very unfortunately they got inside, rescued the dog and escaped. It's very upsetting because now I've got to get more dogs and start all over again. You don't realize how difficult it is to get hold of these dogs. It's true that people seem to be complaining. There's a vet. over at Bishop's Castle making a lot of fuss, but what can I do? *I've got to have dogs.*"

For a moment the "Doctor" stared at him unbelievingly but when he spoke his voice was dangerously quiet.

"You mean to tell me that you're such a bungler that you allowed three kids inside the cottage and that they got off with the dog? Who are they?"

"How should I know? Two of them came from the post office in the village, I suppose. They brought the telegram."

"You've got to be very much more careful, Robbie," and although the words he spoke were not very menacing the other man got up from his chair and moved back into the room. "I think I must come over and see that nice little place I found for you very soon," the "Doctor" went on. "I must see for myself how you are getting on. I may consider it necessary for you to move house. Obviously it is really wiser for us not to be seen together; but as you're not to be trusted to work properly on your own it could hardly be more dangerous if you came to live here for a while, although I do not think my respectable neighbours in this very respectable road would understand your curious appearances and behaviour. This matter of the supply of dogs also presents a problem. I think perhaps it would be advisable for you to move. If you've bungled this, Robbie, you're going to be sorry ... Now you'd better get back as quickly as you can, and just remember that everything now depends on you getting this formula right. I'll come over to-day or to-morrow; but if you try any funny business I can promise you that you'll be sorry." As he stepped from behind the desk Robens retreated towards the door, but before he had reached it the silence was broken by the ringing of a bell.

The two men stopped and glared at each other.

"Is that housekeeper woman of yours here?" Robens whispered.

"She's not. I sent her out for the day when I decided to see you ... Stay here, Robbie. It's only somebody at the front door."

The elder man's face changed as he forced himself into the part of retired professional gentleman. He flicked cigarette ash from his black jacket, adjusted his tie, stroked his hair and then walked out into the hall, leaving the sitting-room door open behind him. He glanced at the glass panels on the front door, but could not see the shadow of anyone waiting on the step and wondered whether the ring was a tradesman at the back door, although his housekeeper had received instructions that only milk was to be delivered regularly. The "Doctor" did not encourage visitors.

The bell rang again and he stepped forward and flung back the door. On the step, smiling at him shyly, stood boy and girl twins of about ten years old. They were dressed alike in blue shorts and checked shirts and looked grubby, but attractive. The girl, whose big eyes were brimming with unshed tears, spoke first.

"Good morning, sir. We're sure you must be the doctor, and we're very pleased to see you, 'cos we're just visitors in this town and we were walking along while Daddy and Mummy left the car and have gone off to do some grown-up things "

"You know how it is," the boy interrupted in exactly the same tone of voice as his sister's. "You know, sir, how grown-ups go off and do things, and say to little children like us, 'Jus' you go off and amuse yourselves for two hours. Here's two shillings for ices and you can do what you like so long as you don't get run over or fall in the river.' Well! That's what's happened to us this morning, an' we were just strolling along these nice quiet roads an'—"

"Suddenly," Mary took up the tale, "absolutely *suddenly*, my little brother here, whose name is Richard, did something terrible to his knee and fell down in the gutter. He says he thinks he's twisted his knee off and the pain is absolute agony—"

Here Dickie let out a wailing cry, staggered across the top step, clapped both hands to his left knee and slipped into a fairly comfortable sitting position.

"I've been attacked by somethin' terrible," he wailed. "It's a disease. I jus' got to see a doctor an'—"

"*Please*, please, my dear children," the "Doctor" said with rather an anxious smile. "Do please be quiet for a moment and let me explain. I am not, you see, an ordinary—"

"Oh! Oh! "Mary cried out as she clapped her hand to her side. "You know what it is with twins, doctor. Generally when one of them is ill the other is, too. I gotta pain now. In my side—"

"Will you be quiet, *please*?" the man said. "I am not an—"

"We can't be quiet," Dickie yelled, and was pleased to see that the man's face was getting red and that perspiration was glistening on his forehead. "We got pains and we spoke to a man up the road there an' he said that there was a very *kind* doctor lived at The Limes."

"This *is* The Limes," Mary explained with tears in her eyes. "It says so on the gate, and you are the kind doctor, 'cos it says that on the gatepost, an' *please* will you help us?"

The "Doctor" gulped and ran his finger round the inside of his collar.

"My dear children," he began, and fortunately did not realize that Dickie's agonized hiccup was really a smothered laugh, "I am not an ordinary doctor, but a rather special sort of doctor. I have nearly finished my life's work now and have retired here. I only see a few special patients now by appointment and am very much afraid that—"

"But we don't mind a *bit* making a 'pointment," Mary groaned, thinking that this was all too absurdly easy and wondering whether Peter, hiding behind Robens' car, had seen enough of the man on the step. "We'll make the 'pointment now, and, of course, you'll have to send your bill to our parents—"

"Daddy will pay," Dickie added. "We've often heard him say that he's always paying. I'm sure you won't be any change—I mean jus' your bill won't make any real difference … Please may we come in so that you can look at my elbow—my knee, I mean?"

He staggered to his feet and felt Mary's hand in his back, pressing him forward. So they were after all to get into the house?

"Go away!" the "Doctor" shouted. "I can't do anything for you. I'm not that sort of doctor. Go away at once. I'm busy. I can't be bothered. I can't help you. *Get out!*"

But he was retreating into the hall now. The twins were both shouting at the same time. He lost control of himself and shouted back. Whichever way he turned there was a twin. Then another voice joined in the clamour as Robens dashed out of the back room and yelled:

"Get them out! Get rid of them!"

The twins retreated. The two men followed into the porch and abused them. Mary dragged Dickie to one side so that Peter should have an uninterrupted view of their victims.

"Will you GET —OUT?" the "Doctor" spluttered.

"Certainly we will," Dickie said. "We're not welcome, twin. He doesn't want us. He's rude. He's angry. I don't think he's a real doctor at all."

"He said he wasn't," Mary replied sweetly. "He says he's a special sort. I think he looks it … And I'll tell you something else, twin. I'm feeling better. The pain seems to have gone."

Before Dickie could answer the front door slammed and they were alone. They grinned, turned about and, hand in hand, marched down the path, past the monkey puzzle. As they closed the gate Peter dodged from behind Robens' car.

"That was marvellous," she said. "Quick as we can now. David is waiting round the corner."

"Could you hear us?" Mary asked. "I'm glad we arranged

for Dickie to come after all, 'cos I don't think it does matter if Robens reckernized us and p'raps he didn't. I couldn't have done so well without my twin."

Peter pulled them round the corner by the pillar-box where the three of them leaned breathless against the hedge of another respectable garden.

"They were wonderful, David," Peter gasped. "It was one of their very best acts, and although I couldn't hear everything I saw them both writhing with pain. They certainly needed a doctor badly."

David hardly looked at the twins, who were, naturally enough, feeling rather pleased with themselves.

"What about the man living there? Could you see him well enough to be sure?"

"Yes. I'm sure he's the same man Daddy brought back to Hatchholt that day after the plane smash. I'm positive. I can't be so certain about Robens because I only got a glimpse of him just now and of course his not having a beard makes it difficult to tell; but I'm positive about the other man. What shall we do?"

"We'd better find Tom and Jenny now, and then ask the police station for Mr. Cantor before we meet Charles … What's wrong, Dickie?"

His brother, who had hidden himself behind the pillar-box on the corner, dashed back to them.

"Lucky you got a good spy in this party. Robens is getting into his car, and I think he'll come this way. Let's hide in this garden till he's gone by. I don't think he ought to see us again."

They opened the nearest gate and without a glance at the house hid behind the tall privet hedge until Robens' car had gone by.

"I couldn't see his face," Peter said, "but I'm sure he's livid. I hope so. Let's get back to the town and find Tom and Jenny.

Did we say outside the post office? ... What on earth are you doing, Mary?"

"Just waving a nice friendly wave to the old lady watching us from the front window. I s'pose this is her house. She looks a bit worried."

"She must think we're mad," David muttered as he opened the gate. "I suppose I ought to go back and apologize, but I don't really know what to say."

"Say nothing," Peter said. "Come on."

Ten minutes later they found Jenny, white with excitement, outside the post office.

"We've seen him in his car," she hissed. "He went down that side street and stopped in front of a shop. Tom's gone down there to see what he's doing ... We were just standing here waiting for you, only about five minutes ago, and we saw the car. He was looking most peculiar and worried. I want to know how you all got on ... Wasn't it clever of Tom and me to see him like that, David? Here comes Tom."

"Hullo," Tom grinned. "Has Jen told you we saw Robens in his car? He stopped down there at a horse-meat shop, and it looks as if he's buying a lot."

"If he wants dogs' food he must have some more dogs somewhere," David said. "We'll have to tell Mr. Cantor about all this, but it's going to be the Lone Piners' job to find the dogs ... Come on!"

CHAPTER X

ROBENS LEAVES HOME

A S soon as the "Doctor" had slammed the door on the twins he turned on Robens and snapped, "D'you know those two? Are those the kids who got into your place this morning?"

"They were not, although I believe I've seen them before … Were they asking for a doctor? They must have been surprised when they saw you!"

"Just a minute, Robbie, if you please. You say you've seen them before?"

"Think so. You don't see many about like that. Wish I'd heard all your conversation now, but what I did hear I thought amusing. I hope you persuaded them that you really are a doctor, else they'll get talking and you may find some of the citizens of Shrewsbury becoming rather curious. Why did they want a doctor?"

"Said they were ill. Kept on contradicting each other, but of course it was an act … Why did they come here? They must have followed you."

"They couldn't do that. I came in the car. Quickly, too … Now I'm going, and please don't send any more ridiculous telegrams. If you've got any news write care of post office. I go into the village every other day."

"If *I've* got any news," spluttered the other. "It's you who will come to me, Robens. You're forgetting yourself."

"No, I'm not. I'm remembering a lot. I'm going on with the job, and I'll let you know when I've got anything to tell you. I've got to find more dogs before I can finish my work, and meantime I'll look forward to entertaining you at Greystone

End. That will be very pleasant if you bring your own food and drink, and it doesn't rain. I don't recommend the cottage at any time, but it's very depressing when it's wet because so much water comes through the roof," and before the "Doctor" could stop him he opened the door and stalked down the path.

He got into the car and drove off almost without realizing his actions. He was shaking with rage and trying to decide what he was going to do.

John Robens was not altogether bad. It was true that not very long ago, soon after he had left his university, he had made a bad mistake and by chance had been helped by the man he knew only as the "Doctor." He was a very able young scientist, and this particular problem of the dogs had interested him very much. Because he had been in trouble and short of money the "Doctor" had persuaded him to come into partnership and had paid him well. But the longer he had known him the more Robens had detested him he hated his sarcastic, silky voice, his pretence of friendliness, his cunning and the way in which he fooled everybody and apparently made a very good living by his wits. He was ignorant, too. He pretended to be clever and to have some culture, but when he lost his temper as he had just now, his background was obvious.

But Robens had brains and knew it. He realized, too, that he was capable of good work and was on the edge of a big discovery, and as he swung the car round the corner towards the town he knew that whatever else he did not do he was going to finish this experiment and that the answer, when he got it, was more important than the use to which it was put.

There was not much time if the "Doctor" was really coming over to Greystone, but there were two things he had to do—find at least three more dogs, and possibly leave the cottage at once so that he could perfect his work before he was interrupted.

Surely he could find dogs? Not in Shrewsbury, but if he went a different way back and found some villages which he hadn't visited for some time, surely he could find three? They must be fed properly, too, and that reminded him that there was a horsemeat shop down a side street by the post office.

He was in heavy traffic now, but he knew his way about this old town. Just as he slowed down and put out his hand to show that he was turning to the right he had that curious feeling that somebody had recognized him. He glanced over to the pavement and saw a pretty little red-haired schoolgirl staring at him. Her face was familiar, but even as he tried to remember her she turned her back and spoke to a bare-headed boy. A bus-driver behind him sounded his horn and as he swung the car round into the narrow street he realized that they were the two children who had brought the telegram this morning, and that they had recognized him.

First two children, twins, who seemed vaguely familiar, calling at The Limes, and now another two. He pulled up outside the horsemeat butcher's and looked back through the driving mirror. The narrow street was crowded, but he thought he saw the boy slip into a radio shop a few doors away.

He bought a good supply of meat, flung the soggy parcel on the front seat and drove off as quickly as he dare. There was no sign of the boy or the girl when he came out of the shop.

As he drove on he tried to remember where he had seen those twins before, but it was not until he overtook a woman with a Scottie dog on a lead that he remembered. They were the two who had refused a lift to Bishop's Castle only yesterday. He had been particularly impressed by their black Scottie, who looked to be a dog full of spirit and suitable for an experiment. That was certainly a very curious coincidence. How could they possibly have known that he was in The Limes? Or did they know? Were they just interested in the "Doctor," and if so, why? Why were all these children mixed up in their plans?

Suddenly Robens made up his mind. He would leave the cottage at once. He had found a secret place where he could stay, at least for a day or two, if he could get enough dogs to finish his experiment. That was all that mattered now. He was so near success. If only he could know what had happened to that puppy which the small boy had taken! If the dog had not gone blind he had almost certainly succeeded. Perhaps he could find the puppy again in Barton Beach? He was sure that the "Doctor" would never find him in his hiding-place, and he could keep his part of the bargain by passing over the formula when he had it. Once he had kept his promise he would be free of the "Doctor" for always and could make a fresh start.

Soon afterwards he stole his first dog—a mongrel, wandering on the outskirts of a village. It was ridiculously easy. Before he got out of the car he lightly sprayed his clothes from a sprayer with a rubber bulb which he took from his pocket, and then walked towards the dog whistling gently. The dog looked up, sniffed and came towards him without suspicion. Robens stooped, patted him and then picked him up and slipped him under the waterproof sheet covering the back seats of the car. Ten minutes later he picked up another in the same way, but the two dogs fought and made such a noise that he drove for Greystone as fast as he could and dared not stop in Barton Beach.

When he reached the cottage he took off the waterproof sheet, tied the dogs to one of the wheels of the car and hurried into the cottage. Now that he had made up his mind he was no longer nervous and worked quickly and methodically. From the upstairs landing he brought down two suit-cases and into the biggest packed a length of rope, candles and matches, two large electric torches, as many tins of food as he could cram in and some notebooks full of calculations. He dumped this into the back of the car and then went back for a pair of rubber boots.

The dogs, who had now stopped fighting, greeted him rapturously, but he pushed them into the car with the luggage and drove off back along the track until he reached the road.

As soon as he was sure that nobody was approaching he drove fast along the road towards Barton Beach for about two hundred yards and then turned cautiously into the wood again, where there were signs of a rough track. The undergrowth here was not so thick and within a few minutes he found himself in an open space at the foot of Greystone Dingle. Here the valley was wide enough for him to drive slowly up by the side of the track and stream. The old car lurched and swayed over the rough ground and the dogs began to fight again. He turned and shouted at them as they struggled under the cover of the waterproof sheet, and his voice and their barking echoed eerily back from the rocky hillsides; but he did not stop until he passed the place where Tom and Jenny had once found the Greystone treasure. Then he realized that the track had become too narrow for him to go further.

He jumped out and looked round anxiously. The dogs stopped snarling and all was very still. A great black crow flapped lazily up from a hawthorn tree, a rabbit scuttled through the bracken and a cloud of black flies, appearing as if by magic, buzzed above the parcel of horsemeat on the seat of the car.

That was all. He was alone.

Now that he had made up his mind he acted quickly. First he cut two short lengths of the rope to act as leads for the dogs and secured them firmly, and then with one of the suit-cases he hurried up the dingle. He was not unkind to the dogs, but quite indifferent to them. His only interest in them was for experimental purposes, and when they tried to fawn upon him he cursed them for getting under his feet. The suit-case was heavy, and because he was out of condition he was tired and out of breath when he reached the little grassy plateau outside the cave where David and Peter had been only yesterday. He rested only long enough to light a cigarette and to take the biggest electric torch from the suit-case, and then, dragging the dogs after him, he entered the cave.

At the beginning of the passage he hesitated, wondering whether to take the dogs or the suit-case first, for he could not take both and use the torch as well. Eventually he left the dogs tied to a spur of rock and slipped through the gash in the rock into a passage which ran uphill into the heart of the mountain. The loose stones were treacherous, and he cursed under his breath as he slipped and stumbled in his haste. He had only been here twice before, but he remembered, when he reached the place where the roof had collapsed, that he must turn sharply to the left round a jutting rock and drop two feet into another passage running steeply down. It was completely dark—so dark that he could almost feel the velvety blackness—but the air was fresh and cool. Soon he heard the sound of trickling water, turned sharply to the left again and found himself on a rocky platform some fifteen feet above a little beach of shingle, in the centre of which was a shallow pool.

He flashed the beam of the torch up and round the cave and noticed the trickle of water falling into the pool at the far end, and then, setting his torch in a crevice of the rock wall, he got out the rest of the rope and looped a length round a big boulder on the rock ledge. Then he dropped the suit-case and after picking up the torch and using the rope he lowered himself to the little beach. His feet scrunched in the loose stones as he walked unsteadily across to the pool, splashed through a few inches of water under the trickling waterfall on the far side and, slipping between two rocks, found himself in another cave, which sloped back and up like a narrow funnel. There was no glimmer of light, but a strong draught cooled his face as he put down the case, opened it and pulled out the bundle of candles.

The rock formation in this cave was very curious, for along one side, about four feet from the stony floor, was a ledge, perhaps two feet wide, rather like a workman's bench. It was this ledge which had intrigued Robens when he had first found this inner cave and given him the idea that, if the need arose, he could use this place as a secret laboratory. He lit a candle, set it on the ledge as far away from the draught as possible and unpacked the case, whistling under his breath as he did so.

"Tin-opener," he murmured; "Must remember that. Tins are no use without an opener," and then, with the empty suit-case, he crossed the pool again, hauled himself and then the case up to the rock ledge and went back to the outer cave.

The dogs greeted him joyfully, and he hesitated for a moment, wondering whether he should leave them here or take them to the secret cave. Then, remembering that he had still a great deal to carry in and had still to go back to the cottage for blankets and his chemical apparatus, he took them in, lowered them with the aid of the rope into the pool, dragged them across and then left them in the inner cave, howling with fear in the dark, and again tied to a rock.

He went back once again to the car for rubber boots and dogs' meat, which he left in the outer cave, and then, tired out, he drove back to his cottage.

Now was the most important task of all—the packing of his chemical apparatus and anything else he would need. He remembered the tin-opener, a saucepan, two loaves, a dozen boxes of matches, all the blankets he had and a warm sweater, and piled them in the narrow hall. He rummaged the house for old newspapers and then settled down to pack his bottles and test-tubes. He worked fast, and the first case was nearly full when something made him look out of the front window. He blinked with surprise and dropped a glass flask.

His greatest worry recently had been to get dogs, and certainly the two mongrels now howling in the darkness of the cave might not be enough for his purpose. Now one had called to visit him. Standing on the weed-grown path, just inside the gate, was a sturdy black Scottie with his head on one side and one paw lifted in polite inquiry. He was a king of Scotties. Alert, proud of mien and bearing, eyes bright, ears pricked and tail up.

Robens whistled softly, felt in his pocket to make sure that his special sprayer was still there, and ran for the back door. When he dodged quietly and quickly from behind the car the dog had walked a few steps up the path and was now sitting down watching the house. Robens spoke to him gently. The dog turned and growled, and then, catching his scent, wagged his tail and jumped up at the outstretched hand. At the same time the man sprayed a stream of vapour about his shaggy head. Nothing particular happened, except that his tail drooped and quite suddenly he looked as if there was no spirit left in him. Robens picked him up under one arm and took him into the house.

"Better in here than in the car, my lad," he said. "Finish your beauty sleep while I finish my packing. The only snag about you is that you'll probably fight and kill and eat the other two dogs before breakfast. I'll have to get to work on you first."

The dog sighed, rolled his eyes and flopped over on his side against the suit-case. Robens closed the front door, and then, before he could move, he heard the sound of a car stopping, and voices. Not daring to show himself at a window, he ran into the kitchen, locked the back door, and then, realizing that he could not be seen in the hall and that from there he would probably be able to hear all that was going on, he crouched down on the bundle of blankets with one hand on the dog's collar.

"Leave this to me, Peter," he heard a man's voice say as steps came up the path. "He must be here, as the car is outside."

"It's Mackie I'm worried about, Charles," a girl said. "I don't know what we shall do with Mary if we don't find him. This is the most terrible thing that has ever happened to us. We dare not go back without him."

"Let's have a word with this elusive gentleman first, Pete. Try not to fuss too much, my dear," and he knocked firmly on the door.

Under Robens' hand the little dog stirred and shivered, and quietly he brought the sprayer from his pocket and held it ready. The man knocked again, only a few inches from his ear, as he crouched against the door.

"He *must* be here, Charles," the girl whispered. "He wouldn't leave his car outside like that and have walked off somewhere."

"Go back and look at the car, Pete. Feel the radiator and see if it's warm," and he knocked again while Robens muttered under his breath. He had no idea who the strangers were and dared not move to a window, but it seemed as if they were something to do with this crowd of children who, for one reason or another, kept interfering with his plans.

The man knocked again, and then he heard the girl's footsteps running up the path.

"The radiator's hot, Charles, and I'm sure that dogs have been in the back of the car. It smells doggy and there are hairs on the seats. The car is absolutely filthy … Charles, darling, do you think he's hiding in the house with Mackie and is doing some beastly experiment on him? … Did I tell you that Jenny spoke to Johnny Ellis in the village and that his puppy has gone blind? We must break in, Charles. We've *got* to find Mackie."

"You can't break into people's houses just as you think you will, Peter—not even if we think Mackie is inside … I'll wait here in the front while you go round the house whistling and calling Mackie."

Peter's footsteps died away, but Robens knew she had stopped outside the window and was peering into his room. He could hear her calling the dog, who did not stir under his hand. Close to him Charles Sterling was whistling softly.

Peter was soon back again and sounded very excited.

"He's been inside the house, Charles, even if he's not there now. The living-room is in a terrible muddle. I'm sure that a lot of chemistry apparatus has been moved from the table under the window. Do you think he's run away, Charles? And if he has, where is he hiding? And why is his car still there?"

"I don't know, Peter, but I'm sure there's something very odd going on here, and I'm sorry now we didn't try to get hold of Cantor in Shrewsbury. I ought to have done what you all suggested. We haven't very much evidence for the police, but I think we ought to tell them just the same … Come on. We'll go home and telephone from there."

Peter hesitated.

"Yes. Let's do that … All the same, Charles, I've got the feeling that he must be hiding quite near. He may be in the wood, or even hiding inside and listening to everything we're saying. He may be listening to us now."

"I know!" Charles agreed. "That's what I'm afraid of. This is no place for you, Peter."

CHAPTER XI

THE CAVE

IT was barely light when Peter woke in the granary at HQ2 at Seven Gates the next morning. She was not aware, at first, of what had awakened her, but turned over in her sleeping-bag and saw through her little window that although the sky was grey a few brave stars still struggled with the dawn.

She sighed as remembrance of all that happened last evening came rushing back. They had met Charles in Shrewsbury as arranged and told him of their adventure at The Limes and of how Tom and Jenny had seen Robens drive off after buying his horse-meat. They had begged him to come with them to the police station and try to find Mr. Cantor, but even while they were telling him it was obvious that he had something else on his mind.

"One thing at a time," he had said. "We'll do something about all this as soon as we can, but just now I must go home and talk over something important with Father. I'm sorry, but this is business, and as soon as I've got his agreement all I've got to do is to telephone the man I've just seen, and then I'll do anything reasonable to help you solve your mystery."

They had soon realized that it was no use trying to make him change his mind, so, with some grumbling, they were driven back to Seven Gates, and while Charles was with Uncle Micah they went into the barn, lit their primus stove and began to get their tea. Peter remembered how she had asked Dickie to run round to the kitchen and ask Aunt Carol for some milk and Mary had said, "I'll come with you, twin, and we'll fetch Mackie, too. He's lazy when he stays by the kitchen range. It's horrid of him not to welcome us home."

A few minutes later they were back with the milk, but furiously angry.

"I know I ought not to say it," Mary said, "but Aunt Carol is jolly selfish and cruel. She doesn't know where Mackie is, but remembers seeing him at lunch time. He's not indoors, and now we'll have to search for him ... Don't wait tea for us."

Peter knew very well that they were all worried at Seven Gates and believed that Charles was either trying to sell some of their land or to take some big step which would affect them all. Uncle Micah was getting older, and she could understand that Aunt Carol might well have been so busy that she had not been able to watch Macbeth all the time. Mackie, upset because he had not gone with them, had probably wandered off somewhere on his own. They all knew that if Mackie had gone into the wood and started a rabbit he might well follow it up to the Devil's Chair if he was in one of his hunting moods. He was a very intelligent little dog, and he always did come home eventually, but with all this talk of missing dogs and their certainty that Robens was experimenting on them, Peter understood how Mary was feeling.

David, who was cutting bread, looked up and said, "Don't be such a baby, Mary. He won't go far and he'll soon come back. He always does when he's hungry. Let's have tea, and by that time I should think we can persuade Charles to telephone the police, and then we'll all look for Mackie."

At that Dickie had turned on his brother and stormed at him for being selfish, unfair and a heartless bully who liked to torture little helpless animals.

"All do what you like," he yelled with tears in his eyes. "Jus' sit there and guzzle your tea and fill your BELLIES, but Mary an' me are going to find Mackie," and they had run out into the wood whistling and calling.

Tom had shrugged his shoulders and glanced at Jenny as if to ask, "Shall we go, too?" but Jenny had said, "I'm sure he can't be far away, and, anyway, Robens can't have captured him for those awful things he does because we saw him in Shrewsbury at dinner time. Let's see Charles first and tell him all about it, and then go and hunt for the twins and Mackie, 'cos I'm sure they'll all come back together."

None of them had much to say as the sound of the twins' whistling died away and the kettle boiled over before anyone spoke.

"I didn't mean to upset them," David muttered into his mug. "I'm as fond of Macbeth as they are, but he can't come to any harm. He knows these woods as well as he knows Witchend, and he'll come back."

But he did not, and neither had the twins appeared when Charles came into the yard smiling broadly.

"That's O.K.," he told them. "I reckon we've done the right thing, but I can't tell you about it just yet. What's all this I hear about the dog? Carol seems upset and says the twins were very rude to her. Where are they?"

David had handed him a cup of tea and told him what had happened. "They didn't mean to be rude," he finished, "but I'd better go and apologize to Aunt Carol for them, although they'll be back soon. Will you try and get hold of Mr. Cantor now, Charles? We would like to tell him everything we found out to-day. I'm sure he'd like to know. Or if you're too busy p'raps I could do it?"

Peter remembered Charles putting down his mug, walking into the farmyard and looking up at the bulk of the mountain above them.

"I'll telephone presently, David," he said quietly. "I'd like you and Jenny and Tom to go out in different directions, looking for Mackie and the twins. Be back here in an hour. I should think the twins will stick together, and it's more important for you to find them than the dog. Try and keep in touch with each other. Peter is coming with me in the van to the cottage in the wood. I promised her we'd go together. After I've had a look at that place for myself I promise I'll telephone the police."

David had protested about this and said that he ought to go instead of her, but Charles had been stubborn and told him to go after the twins.

She remembered her excitement at finding Robens' old car outside the cottage, of her discovery that the engine was still warm and of evidence of dogs in the back. She remembered the signs of packing which she had seen through the window and the sudden fear which had made her voice shake as they had stood in the porch feeling that they were being watched and overheard. As they drove back Charles had looked very grim, but had done his best to comfort the white-faced twins who had been found by David and dragged back protesting to Seven Gates in the hope that Macbeth had come home.

He had not.

Then it had begun to rain and they had all gone indoors and been fussed over by Aunt Carol and boomed at by Uncle Micah, while Charles telephoned the police at Shrewsbury. He had been very annoyed during this long conversation because nobody at the other end seemed to know about Mr. Cantor, but at last, after describing him carefully, he was promised that the detective should be found and would telephone him.

"They say his real name is Green," Charles said as he replaced the receiver. "All we can do now is to wait for him to ring."

But the twins would not be comforted, and as darkness came down so the rain increased. The top of the mountain was shrouded in mist, the rain beat on the windows, the gutters gurgled and

the farmyard—as it always did when it rained—turned into a
large pool. Again and again Mary, who had now forgiven Aunt
Carol, pulled on her gumboots, put on her mack and ran out into
the yard calling and whistling, but no little black dog came in
out of the night and shook himself in the hall.

"He's dead—or worse than dead," Mary sobbed in Aunt
Carol's lap after the fifth excursion. "He's been captured by that
brute and is being tortured. I never ought to have left him—I
know he was happy with you, Aunt Carol, but, you see, he's just
so *used* to us, and I 'spect he fretted and came out to find us."

And then the telephone had shrilled and Charles went off to
answer it and closed the door so that they could not overhear his
conversation. When he came back she thought he had looked
rather annoyed, but all he said was, "That was your precious
Mr. Cantor, and I'm not sure where he was speaking from. He
says he can't do much to-night, but that he'll come along in the
morning and see us after he's called at the cottage."

"Did you tell him about Mackie?" Tom had asked.

"Of course. He can't do anything to-night."

"Yes, he can," Dickie had said. "O' course he can. He can
get lots of policemen with Tommy-guns and that sort o' thing,
and he can raid that cottage and tell that man to surrender and
rescue our Mackie, and then he can set the place on fire. That's
what I'd like to do. That's what we jolly well would do—Mary
an' me would—if you didn't keep us prisoners here against our
wills. You'll be sorry, all of you, one day," and he had turned his
back on them all so that they shouldn't see his face and David
had gone over and passed him a handkerchief, which incident
only she, Peter, had noticed.

She remembered how furious she had felt over this casual
message from the detective and how, when at last they had
persuaded the twins that nothing more could be done that night

and that the best thing to do was to go to bed so as to be fresh in the morning, she had turned on Charles.

In the dim light of the dawn she blushed now when she remembered that she had told him that if only they had done what they thought was right instead of putting off going to the police when they were in Shrewsbury they would not be in this trouble. She had even turned on David next and told him that he was always too quick to do what grown-ups suggested. She didn't really mean these things, but she loved Mary and she knew how she was feeling about Macbeth. But at last, very reluctantly, the twins had promised Charles that they would not go out during the night and they had all gone over to the barn through the rain, lit the lanterns and hung their macks on the nails just inside the big doors, which David had promised to leave ajar in case the wanderer came home. Then, unexpectedly, he had bent and kissed his sister.

"He'll be home in the morning," he had said gruffly. "And if he comes in the night and I hear him I'll wake you up—or Dickie will."

Then she and Jenny had taken Mary upstairs, fussed over her while she undressed, kept quiet while she said her prayers and then tucked her into her sleeping-bag. Long after the lantern was out and the boys down below had stopped talking she had heard Mary sobbing until, exhausted and unhappy, she must have forgotten her miseries in sleep. At last the only sound was the wind in the trees of the whispering wood and the song of water gurgling in the gutters.

Peter stirred again and realized that it was no longer raining. But this was not what had wakened her so early. She rolled over on her back and in the dim light saw Mary, standing like a little statue in her knickers and vest with her shorts in her hand, not daring to move.

Peter sat up.

"Mary! You promised not to go out."

"I'm not breaking my solemn swear," she whispered. "It's not night any more. It's getting light. I'm just going to see whether my darling is sitting outside in the cold waiting to come in."

Peter scrambled out of her sleeping-bag, stepped across the sleeping Jenny and put her arms round Mary.

"David left the doors open. We should have heard Mackie, Mary. He would have barked if he'd come home, and, anyway, David promised to wake us."

"He wouldn't wake up. He's *awful* about getting up, Peter. He may not have heard Mackie come in. Let me go. I want to see if he's there."

"All right, Mary. Be very quiet, and if he's not outside promise to come back at once. I'll be dressing, and I'll get Jenny up, too. I've got an idea about all this, Mary. This Club is getting lazy, and I've made up my mind it's going to do something to-day … Don't you worry. I'm going to see that every single member of this Club has only one job to-day, and that is to find our Mackie."

Mary wriggled herself free, pulled on her shorts and fumbled for her sandals.

"If you say that, Peter, then everything is *all right*, and I know we'll find him. It was so terrible last night 'cos nobody wanted to do anything. Everybody was so *feeble* … I don't think I've ever said so before, Peter, but Dickie an' me—specially me—love you very much." She pulled a sweater over her head, swung herself through the trap-door to the ladder and as Peter shook Jenny into wakefulness she told herself that what she had just promised Mary should come true. To-day there was to be no waiting to see what the grown-ups told them to do.

"You've got to get up, Jenny. We're going to have a Club

meeting right now before breakfast. Mackie hasn't come back
… Time? Just on six … Buck up. Get some clothes on."

Jenny sat up.

"Beast! Why can't you leave me alone? It's still night."

"No, it isn't. It's day-time, and we're going to find Mackie,
and we're going to be away before they're up in the house. I've
made up my mind and I've promised Mary, too. *Please* get
dressed, Jenny … I'm going to wake the boys, and we'll have a
meeting before breakfast."

"Oh, all right," Jenny sighed as she wriggled out of her bag
and shivered as she stepped on the bare boards. "I'll do anything
for you, Peter—or Mary, or any of the others for that matter, but
it's too early *even to think*!"

Then Mary came to the foot of the ladder and whispered,
"He's not there, Peter. He's not come back. What shall we
do?"

"Wake the boys," Peter called. "Don't have any mercy on
them, Mary. Tell them to get dressed right away."

Mary did her work thoroughly. She shook and pommelled
them and yelled at them, and within five minutes they were
more or less dressed.

"What's all this about, Pete?" Tom yawned. "Any news of
Mackie?"

"No. That's what I want us to discuss. David, you're the
captain of this Club, so please will you call an extra special
meeting? I know we're really having a meeting already, but I
s'pose it's proper for you to announce it formally."

David looked surprised.

"All right, then. This is an extra special emergency meeting
of the Lone Pine Club held at HQ2 on August 10th. The only
absent members are Jon and Penny, and they can't help it, so
will you please tell us what's happened, Peter, and why we can't

have breakfast first? And let's all sit on my mattress, although the straw seems to be working up to one end."

All except the twins accepted this invitation. Mary was leaning against the great wooden pillar at the end of the cubicle while he was speaking, and Dickie walked over and joined her. Peter noticed that they were watching the open door of the barn and caught her breath at the misery in their eyes.

"Mary and me talked this over just now," she began, "and we're sure that we're right ... Yesterday, except for The Limes, I think that as a club we were feeble. Instead of making up our minds what we were going to do and sticking to it, we kept on being influenced by Charles, who wasn't interested in us or our problems until we got back here and he had fixed up the business which has been worrying him for some time. He persuaded us not to try and find Mr. Cantor, and so we wasted a lot of time, and then we realized that Mackie had gone, but were persuaded to stay where we were just because it was raining ... I think it's *awful* of us to be so—so futile."

"It was rather feeble of us," David agreed. "I think I realized that Charles was worried, and, to be honest, I don't like what's going on at that cottage in the wood. I wasn't keen for any of us, the twins especially, to get caught by that chap Robens. I think that's why I wanted Charles to come in with us. There's something beastly about this business with dogs that I don't understand. And I don't like that cottage either, but if you and Mary have got a good idea about Mackie let's hear it."

Peter smiled at David.

"I know you're not nearly as scared of those two men as I am, David, but it's just that I feel we weren't doing anything on our own. I propose that we all make a solemn Club promise that to-day we won't wait for Charles or Mr. Cantor or anyone else, but make plans now and search for Mackie until we find him.

Nothing else is to be so important. Would we all swear to do that? We needn't sign in blood, but we do all promise?"

They all nodded their agreement except Mary, who, still looking across at the empty farmyard, said, "This will be the most terrific thing the Club has ever done. It's one of our rules to be kind to animals, isn't it, and Mackie really does belong to the Club."

"Mary and me don't want to be in it if Mackie isn't a member, too," Dickie interrupted. "We don't care what any of you say. That's just how it is."

"It's a good scheme," Tom said. "Let's do that. We all want to find Mackie, and nobody is suggesting that we don't, only you twins will have to work in with everybody else, and don't dash off on your own. Whatever we do, though, I reckon we ought to keep an eye on that chap at Greystone. He's the chap who's pinching dogs, and old Cantor will have to be told what we know about him. He wasn't buying horse-meat to eat himself. He wants it for the dogs he's playing tricks with."

Mary opened her mouth for another outburst, but Peter spoke first.

"That may be true, Tom, but there weren't any dogs at his cottage last night when I went with Charles. I'm sure of it."

"But you said that he'd had dogs in the car," David remarked.

"Yes, I know, but I'm not sure when. It smelt doggy, and there were dogs' hairs all over the place."

Then Jenny, who had been looking sleepy and rather bewildered, spoke up.

"I don't see that the man who lives in that cottage has got anything to do with Mackie. How could he have? He was in Shrewsbury till after dinner time 'cos we saw him, and he can't have come here specially to steal Mackie 'cos somebody would have seen him. Mackie disappeared when that man was somewhere else."

Tom got up, stretched and yawned.

"Sorry, Jen, but I reckon you're wrong. Find that nasty bit of work, and I believe he'll lead us to Mackie. He knows all about the disappearing dogs. Let's borrow some food from the house, have a quick breakfast and get cracking … I suppose we shall have to split up again to save time?"

"And you swear we'll none of us meet again until Mackie is found?" Mary pleaded.

"Of course we won't do anything so silly," Tom said. "You're getting too old for remarks like that, Mary," but all the same he went over to her, rumpled her hair and whispered something which brought a shadow of a smile to her face.

"Let's move, then," David said. "Peter and Jenny, slip into the house—they never lock the back door—and borrow something for sandwiches and make them up rough. Leave a note for Aunt Carol, Peter, and explain about what we've borrowed, but I know she won't mind."

"Yes, I'll do that. I'll write to Charles, too, and let him know that we don't care what he tells Mr. Cantor and that he's not to worry about us, but we won't be home until we've found Mackie … You come, too, Mary, and help us. The boys can make us some tea now on the Primus stove. Boil some eggs in the kettle, David—*before* you make the tea."

The girls were back in twenty minutes with some untidy parcels of very untidy sandwiches.

"Nobody up yet," Peter whispered. "I've left the notes on the kitchen table … Now give me my tea and we'll go as soon as we can. How do we split up, David?"

Dickie answered first.

"We think—Mary an' me think—that Mackie has gone up

the Dingle and got lost after hunting rabbits. He may have got inside the mountain again like he did before, and if you like Mary and me will go up the Dingle to the Chair, along the top and down Greystone until we come to our cave where the river came rushing out and where I punched Powerless Percy in the nose—"

"It wasn't his nose, twin—it was his eye. Anyway, David, we would do that if you like and meet you an' Peter and Tom and Jenny at the cave if you go round the other way and *up* Greystone."

They talked it over while munching eggs and bread and marmalade, and Tom held to his point that if they could find Robens again, or discover what he was doing, he would lead them to Mackie.

"If Jen will come with me we'll hide in the wood and watch the cottage, and if something happens one of us can always act as messenger and come back here or to the cave to report."

"Now that you've all had plenty to say," David remarked as he drained his mug, "I'll tell you what we'll do. I told you before that I don't like this chap Robens. We don't know where he is, and until we know I'm not going to let the twins wander about by themselves. I think Tom has got something about the cottage, so he can take Jenny and Dickie and search that area, and as long as one stays hidden as a spy near the cottage the other two can explore anywhere they like *up* the Dingle as far as the cave … And it's no use looking like that, twins, and opening your mouths to scream as if you were babies. You're not going together by yourselves, whatever fuss you make. You agree, don't you, Peter? Good! Captain and Vice-Captain's orders, and no more argument. You come with Peter and me, Mary, and we'll do what you suggested—up Black Dingle and down Greystone to the entrance to the mine. If the cottage party have anything to report they can come up to meet us, and if we find anything we'll send a messenger down Greystone to you … Divide the food up into two lots, Peter, and stuff ours in a haversack with our torches. We shall want those to search the caves, but somehow I don't think Mackie would go inside the mountain again."

"He might have been kidnapped and *thrust* inside and imprisoned," Mary gulped. "*Please* let us start now … Good luck, twin."

Dickie nodded. "It's ridickerlus us not going together, Mary, but p'raps we'll be able to help the others more if they have one each of us. I wish I had a weapon … Good luck, twin."

Jenny pushed the dirty crocks in a bucket of water, feeling very ashamed not to have washed them up, and then they closed the doors of the barn gently and parted in the farmyard. Tom, Jenny and Dickie went down through the wood to Barton, while the others used the little white gate on the opposite side of the yard which led to a short cut into Black Dingle. They walked for five minutes in silence—David in front with the haversack on his back, and then the two girls with Mary holding Peter's hand.

Mary spoke first. "I can't remember ever feeling like this before. Not quite like it. I feel sick, Peter. Really sick inside when I wonder what's happened to him and why he doesn't come home to us … I hope I'm going to be brave, Peter, if he doesn't come, but I don't think I am."

"Of course you'll be brave, Mary, but I don't think you'll have to be. We shall find him to-day, shan't we, David?"

"We've got to. We'll start calling and whistling soon. We'd better take it in turns to whistle about every hundred yards."

They reached the old signpost and, turning to the right, began to climb the track by the side of the stream. The Devil's Chair was still shrouded in the mists of early morning. Greystone Dingle was wild and lonely, but Black Dingle had an unpleasant atmosphere about it which had been recognized by generations of those who had lived near it. The mountain dividing the two dingles was well named by Jenny—neglected, hated and forbidding.

They stopped and Peter whistled, but although they strained their ears there was no answering bark. No sound but the flapping of the wings of an old crow which cluttered up from a hawthorn tree. When they came to a track leading off to the left towards the steep side of the mountain Mary reminded them that they ought to walk over to the old entrance to the mine.

"I know we can't get in there 'cos that rocking stone fell and blocked the entrance, but once there was a little space which Mackie used. P'raps he's gone that way, and if we call to him he'll squeeze through again."

"We've got to try everything," David agreed. "But I don't see why Mackie should want to go in that way, and if he did I should think he'd want to come out again as soon as possible. We'll go over and call him."

It took them twenty minutes to reach the side of the cliff, and Mary went on her knees and called through the hole which she had remembered from a previous adventure.

"Let's get to the top as soon as we can," Peter said sharply. "I hate this dingle. It give me the creeps, and always has. All right, David. I know what you said about it, and I know what I said, but I still hate it. I don't like the Chair either, but at least the air will be fresher up there."

Mary took Peter's hand and called again and again for Macbeth in her clear little voice as they went back to the main track.

They reached the top half an hour later, and rested for a few minutes in the heather not far from the tumbled black rocks of the Chair.

David was thinking, although he dare not say so, that this was a hopeless search. How could they find a little dog, who might even now be dead, in all this wild solitude? He might have been chasing a rabbit along the top here and fallen over one of the cliffs. He might not even have come this way at all and got caught in the trap of a rabbit poacher. He might even have got run over, and then David remembered thankfully that the Witchend address was on his collar. Perhaps he had returned there and because Witchend was not on the telephone they could not ring Seven Gates until someone walked down to Onnybrook? David wondered whether this was worth mentioning and looked across at Peter, who was sitting upright in the heather with hands clasped round her knees, looking out over the countryside below them across to their own Long Mynd in the east.

Mary was sitting beside her fidgeting with the strap of her sandal.

David's thoughts wandered. He remembered the long letter Peter had sent to him at the beginning of the term telling him about her adventure with Robens and the "Doctor," and of how he hadn't done very much about answering it. Not as much as he ought to have done, anyway. What a good friend she was—to him especially, but to everyone who got to know her and was accepted by her. He had known her long enough now to realize that she set a very high standard for her friends—and also for herself. She was nearly always the same, too—not up in the air more often than not, like Penny Warrender, who led her cousin Jonathan a pretty dance. There was certainly something about Penny, though. Never a dull moment with her! There was something about Peter, too. Dependable? Certainly. Loyal? Of course. Unselfish? More than most.

What else? David wondered. She was certainly very pretty with her fair hair, brown skin and steady blue eyes, and he had never been so aware of this before, but even as he looked at her he suddenly knew that the best thing about Peter was that she was entirely natural. She was always herself and never put on an act. You knew where you were with her. If she was angry you soon knew it because she never sulked. If she was as sure of herself as she had been this morning she didn't waste time, but said and did what she thought was right. If she made a mistake she admitted it. She was grand!

"Why are you staring at me, David?" the subject of his thoughts said suddenly. "Isn't it time we went on?"

He noticed a faint pink under the tan of her cheeks and felt himself colouring, too.

As they walked along the ridge towards the top of Greystone Dingle the sun broke through the low clouds and their shadows marched before them. After a little they stopped whistling and calling for Mackie, for there seemed no sense in it; but it was Mary who said, "I don't think he'll be up here. I'm sure he's inside the mountain, David. Let's go to the cave as quickly as we can," and then she dropped behind and said to Peter, "I don't think I've ever been as miserable before. I can't think what Mummy and Daddy will say when we tell them that Mackie has gone for ever … They loved him, too, Peter. … We all loved him, didn't we? You used to tease me about him, but you do know that he was something very special to Dickie and me, don't you? Did you know why Daddy called him Macbeth, Peter?"

Peter couldn't quite trust her own voice, but she nodded, "Yes."

"I'll tell you, Peter. Daddy has told us lots of times. When he was a very little puppy and quite new with us he made a terrible noise in his basket at night. I s'pect it was just because he wasn't used to us yet. We hadn't quite made up our minds what to call him, but Daddy thought of it. He called him Macbeth because in a very grown-up and famous play by Shakespeare a man called Macbeth murdered sleep. Wasn't it clever of Daddy? We've never heard of another dog called that, have we?"

Talking seemed to help Mary and she didn't mind very much if nobody answered her. Peter was scared. She would have found it easier to understand Mary if she had been crying.

Soon they came to the track leading down into Greystone Dingle, and now the mountain was almost sheer on their left-hand side. Far below them, perhaps two miles away, they could see a green smudge which was the wood in which Tom, Jenny and Dickie were spying on the little stone house. David hoped they were having more luck than his party were. As soon as they left the top Mary began calling Mackie again, and her clear voice echoed back weirdly from the rocky hillside. But there was no sign of the little black dog, and Peter felt more and more depressed as the sides of the dingle closed in round them. Once again she had that horrible feeling of impending disaster—she *knew* that something was going to happen and, strangely enough, wanted to get it over.

"Let's hurry," she said unreasonably and sharply to David. "If we're going to explore the cave the sooner we get in there the better."

He looked at her in surprise.

"We're nearly there, surely. Just round the next bend, but running that distance won't save us much time, and, anyway, Mary can't go much faster."

"Sorry!" Peter said almost humbly, but all the same she ran on ahead and was scrambling up to the plateau outside the cave before the others were round the corner.

Something was gleaming in the sunshine. She bent and picked up a fragment of curved glass—and then another. The glass was thin and curved much more than a watch glass. She looked round carefully and found some more splinters and then a metal ring about an inch in diameter, with a break in it which was forced wide open.

"What have you found, Peter?" David called as he gave Mary a hand and pulled her up the steep slope.

"I'm not sure. It's broken glass. Look!"

David laughed triumphantly.

"What a clue! That's part of a bust test-tube, Peter, but maybe you don't do science at the Castle School? Surely nobody round here but Robens would have a test-tube? What's that ring?"

"I'll have a guess now. That's the sort of ring which holds the handle on a cheap suit-case. I had one like that, and it was always being forced open by the weight and the handle comes away from the case ... David! I think we've found his hideout. He's in our cave and he came here with a heavy suit-case full of chemistry things, and he heaved it up here and the handle broke and the case fell and bust open and smashed up some of his things ... Do you think he's inside now? What shall we do?"

David looked at them both carefully before he answered. He was wondering whether he dare suggest that before they went into the cave they should fetch the others and make up a proper search party. He was not a coward and he certainly was not a fool, and he did not want Peter to think that he was either. He would not have known quite how to put it into words, but he valued Peter's opinion of him very much, and she had already reminded him once to-day that he had been too careful and cautious. Even so, he reasoned, he was the eldest and was responsible for them.

"Well," Peter said again, "what shall we do?"

Mary was looking at her brother. She seemed to know what he was thinking.

"I'm not scared, David. I'm not afraid to go in there with Peter and you. Even if he's in there he'll be more afraid of us. He can't do anything. If he's got Mackie he knows he's in the wrong, and we'll just take him away and then go and tell Mr. Cantor and Charles. He can't hurt us, David."

"I don't think he can, Mary. All the same, Peter, there's something very odd about that chap Robens, and maybe if you'd stay out here with Mary just for a few minutes I could go in with the torch and—"

"And what?" Peter said ominously.

"And—well, I wouldn't make as much row as three of us, and I'm not very keen on Mary—"

"It's no good you saying that, David. I think Mackie is in there, and I'm going to fetch him, and I want Peter and you to come too because, although I'm not afraid, I'm not very big."

"Don't bother to think of any more excuses, David," Peter said. "I know what's worrying you, but you're not going in the cave alone, and although I believe it would be better if Mary ran down to fetch the others as soon as we've gone in there, I know she wouldn't go … Let's go in with the torches and see what we can find. I believe he's taken some dogs in here and all his chemistry stuff, and I dare say Mackie was wandering up the dingle, smelt these dogs and has followed them in … Come on, David. Please don't argue."

"All right—but we've got to be careful, and you will do as you're told, won't you, Mary? We don't want you falling into that pool again. Do you think we ought to leave a note outside here in case one of the others comes up to find us?"

"Suppose Robens is not inside," Peter remarked very sensibly. "If he comes back here presently he's as likely to find a note we leave as Dickie is. We should have to put it under a stone or where it can be seen easily. All that we should do is to warn him that we're inside."

David nodded, opened the haversack and brought out two torches.

"I'll go first," he said. "Mary behind me and Peter at the back. Don't use your torch unless you have to, Pete. Save the battery. And don't talk. All right, Mary? Hang hold of my jacket—or my hand if you'd rather."

"Hand, please," she said, trying hard to keep her voice from shaking.

David hoisted the haversack on to his back again and without another word led the way into the cave. The sand was soft underfoot until they reached the old entrance to the mine. David swung his torch up and they saw water dripping from the roof and down the walls and, with daylight now behind them, the air struck dank and cold as they edged forward. After about fifteen yards the passage ran sharply uphill, and then they came to the place where the roof had fallen.

"All right behind, Pete?" David whispered. "We go down to the left here if you remember. Use your torch and don't slip."

He stepped down into the lower passage and then held up his free hand to help Mary. Her hand was cold and she was trying to stop her teeth from chattering.

"Hold the torch," he said, and turned to help Peter, who gave him a quick smile as she slithered down.

This passage was dry and the air blew strongly towards them as they stood still for a moment listening.

"I can't hear the waterfall," Peter whispered. "It's horribly quiet."

Last time they had been here the underground lake was being fed by a waterfall following weeks of rain, and they had heard its roar as soon as they reached the second passage, but before David could remind them that this had been a dry summer Mary gripped his hand hard and said, "It's very quiet and lonely, isn't it? I don't think Mackie would come here by himself, but let's go as far as the pool in the big cave."

David and Peter were both sure that Macbeth would never come as far as this by himself, but they did not remind Mary of the test-tube clue and that Robens might be only twenty or thirty yards away. David was liking this expedition less and less, and was already regretting that they had brought Mary with them. So far as he could remember this passage ran straight for about twenty yards and then turned sharply to the left on to the platform above the pool, and he was thinking that if Robens was in the pool cave he would probably see the light reflected from the torch. But if he was down there he would surely have some light himself which they would be able to see?

"Hold tight, girls," he whispered. "I'm going to put the light out."

Suddenly they were in thick darkness—a blackness which closed down on them with horrible abruptness. He heard Peter draw in her breath sharply and sensed that she had put her arm round Mary. There was no glimmer of reflected light at the end of the passage, and David had his finger on the switch of his torch when the thick silence was broken by a long, inhuman wail that made their scalps tingle. Mary cried out in surprise and fear and Peter's sharp, whispered, "Oh, David!" steadied his own nerves.

The cry came again—quivering through the darkness.

"It's a dog," Mary sobbed. "It's Mackie! It must be!"

David switched on the torch. The yellow cone of light stabbed through the darkness.

"Come on," he said through clenched teeth. "We'll see this through. Be as quiet as you can."

He counted twenty-two steps before turning to the left.

"Careful," he whispered. "Keep your backs to the wall. We don't want to fall down here again. Now use your torch as well, Peter, and let's look at the water."

He swung his beam round purposely so that he could see her face. He wanted to see if she showed any fear, because *he* could not remember ever feeling so frightened before. Her left arm was round Mary's shoulders, but when Peter felt the light on her face she turned towards him, blinked and then gave him a shaky smile. And then the cry, much nearer now, came again.

"Down," David whispered. "Shine yours down, too, Pete."

The lake which they had seen there before and in which the twins were trapped as the waters rose had now shrunk to a shallow pool surrounded by a beach of shingle. Away to their right, where the waterfall had crashed over its lip of rock, there was now only a trickle of tinkling water. The surface of the pool was still and dark.

Suddenly Mary screamed and flung her arms round David's legs.

"Something touched my ankle. It did. *It did!*"

Peter turned her torch to their feet.

"It's a rope," she said. "It goes over the edge. Look! It's tied round this lump of stone."

"We're getting hot," David whispered. "P'raps he lets himself down by the rope. Now that the water is so much lower we may find the entrance to another cave."

The beam of his torch swung round again.

"Look at the shingle over at the end. Those marks are footsteps. They run right across to the edge of the pool ... Will you stay with Mary, Peter, while I go down and explore?"

"No," Mary whispered. "That dog may be Mackie. I've got to be the first to find him. Let me come with you both, *please* ... PLEASE don't leave me behind, David. Let us both come."

"Yes, David. Let's stick together now. I'd rather be with you whatever we do."

"I'll go down first, then," David whispered. "If the rope takes me it will take you. Your light, please, Peter. You can throw my torch down to me," and not until he had dropped two feet to the shingle did he realize what Peter had said to him!

Mary was used to a rope and came down like a little monkey, and then Peter dropped the torches, one at a time, for David to catch safely, and followed. As they scrunched across the shingle following the footsteps the dog howled again, and now there was no doubt that the sound came from the other side of the pool. They splashed through a few inches of shallow water under the trickling waterfall and saw that the footsteps on the other side led up to a narrow opening between two jutting rocks.

"That's it," David whispered as he felt Peter's hand on his arm. "There's another cave. We've never looked the other side of the pool before, and when it was full nobody would be able to get across, anyway ... He can't be there. There's no light."

"Maybe not, but there's a dog there," Peter said. "Let's go."

"*Please* may I call him, David?" Mary sobbed. "I just want to let him know we're here."

"Yes, Mary. But don't go ahead without us."

She called and whistled, and there came at once an excited whining and howling.

"Doesn't sound like Mackie," David said. "Let's go and see."

He slipped between the rocks and so discovered Robens' secret laboratory, with a level ledge of rock on the left-hand side covered with chemical apparatus. Tied together to a rock were two struggling mongrel dogs. A few feet away, higher up the cave in the shadows, lying stretched out on the ground, was a little black shaggy body.

With a cry Mary flung herself on him.

"He's not dead, is he? *Mackie*, Mackie darling! It's me. It's Mary. We've rescued you, Mackie."

The Scottie's body was limp—but it was also warm when Peter gently pushed Mary aside and lifted the dog in her arms.

"It's all right," she said. "He's not dead. He's doped. He's trying to wag his tail."

Mary was now sobbing quietly into his rough coat, and in a brief moment of silence David heard, above the scuffling and whining of the mongrels, something that sounded like a human whistle.

"Be quiet," he whispered as he switched out the torch. "He's coming back."

He felt Peter's hand on his arm in the thick darkness, and then she whispered, "Take Mackie, Mary," and then, in his ear, "Robens mustn't catch us here, David. We must be certain who it is first, and I'm sure we can hide at the back of the cave. It slopes back like a funnel … Look, there's a light coming now! Hurry!"

Above the whimpering of the two mongrels they could hear now the crash of boots in the loose shingle and then the sound of a splash. As they faced towards the main cave they saw the reflected light of a torch on the rocky walls.

David often asked himself later why it was that he allowed Peter to take the lead in their scramble up the funnel of the second cave. It may have been because they had so little time as the man's footsteps came nearer, but he did realize that if they did not give themselves away Robens was unlikely to suspect that they were there and that they could escape with Mackie when he went out again. As Peter reached back and passed him her torch, and then took his hand and dragged him forward, he also realized that they might well be trapping themselves for some hours if Robens made this place his new home.

"Mind your head," Peter whispered as she scrambled upwards. "The roof is low. I believe this tunnel leads somewhere. Can you feel the draught?" But David was more worried about Mary, scrambling behind him with Mackie in her arms.

"I'm all right, David," she puffed. "Mackie is struggling a bit. I think he knows us now."

"Can he walk?" David gasped as, twenty or thirty feet below them, he saw the light from Robens' torch swing across and gleam on the glass of test-tubes and flasks on the shelf of rock just inside the entrance. Then a lot of things happened.

First Robens entered the cave and the three fugitives froze into silence. David realized that Peter was apparently crouched on a pile of loose stones and rocks about two feet above him. His back was pressed against her leg, and when she leaned forward to whisper to him that the roof was only just above them one of her plaits tickled his cheek. He was aware, too, of a very strong draught and that Mary, on her knees on the steep slope below him, was doing her best to quieten her breathing and to stifle a sob. He leaned forward and with one hand grasped her shoulder.

"Mackie," she breathed. "Take him, David. The stones are slipping."

He moved his hand until it touched the dog's shaggy coat, and then, to his horror, felt the pile of stones at his back begin to move. He heard Peter draw in her breath sharply and then suddenly her arm slipped round his neck and he felt her weight dragging him backwards. Pandemonium broke loose. Mary began to slide backwards as stones cluttered down into the cave, and she only saved herself by clutching her brother's ankle.

The beam of Robens' torch swung up and discovered them. David, with Mary holding his foot and Peter dragging at him from behind, struggled for some sort of foothold in vain as the mass of stones and rocks on which they were clinging precariously broke up and slid—not only towards Robens shouting below them, *but backwards into another pit or cave the presence of which they had not suspected.*

As for Peter, perched on the top of this shifting pile, she had realized as soon as Robens had entered the cave that she had led the others into a trap, for when she had put one hand behind her she had felt nothing at all. In the darkness she had no idea whether the drop behind her was of two feet or two hundred, but the air blew strongly round her head and she had an awful feeling that, as in a nightmare, she was suspended over a bottomless pit. Instinctively she put one arm round David's neck as Robens shouted and stones began to clatter down *behind* her. In the brief flashes of light from Robens' torch she saw Mary's anguished face as she clutched at David's foot. She felt the muscles in David's arm tense and saw a trickle of perspiration on his cheek.

Then with a stab of terror she knew that most of the moving stones were slipping into the black, empty space behind her and that she would fall that way, too, unless David's strength could hold her and Mary, too. But David's job was Mary ... his sister; the brave little girl who would never have hesitated to do anything for any of them. He could never hold them both, and even now she knew that her weight was dragging him back, too.

"Hold Mary," she gasped and let go.

All that she realized in the next few seconds was the roar of falling stones, bright-coloured stars in the blackness as something struck her head and then a terrible searing pain

"HOLD MARY!" CRIED PETER AS SHE LET GO AND DROPPED BACK
AMIDST A ROAR OF FALLING STONES.

in her ankle as her fall was checked before she slipped into unconsciousness.

She was at the end of a long, long tunnel. There was a roaring in her ears. She felt sick. Horribly sick. There was a speck of light at the end of the tunnel. Her cheeks were wet and her forehead cold with perspiration. She could feel her heart thudding and keeping time with the rhythm of pain beating from her ankle up her leg. She was sitting up and leaning, not against rocks, but against something warmer and softer. Somebody, in a strange but vaguely familiar voice, kept repeating her name, and as more feeling came back to her bruised body she realized that a hand was stroking her hair and that a firm arm round her waist was holding her upright.

"Peter! Say something, Peter. Say you're all right, Peter. You must hear me. Speak to me, Peter. Nothing matters if you're all right. You've got to know that, Peter. I don't care if you can't hear me, but I've got to say it ... Just say you're all right and we'll soon get you out of here."

She opened her eyes and saw the orange glow of an expiring torch near her. There was just enough light for her to see a bare brown knee which was not her own at her side, and that her own fingers were clutching the hand that was holding her up. Then another wave of pain forced a cry to her lips and her head slipped sideways.

"Pete, are you all right now? It's me, David."

David, of course. It would be. Whatever happened to her David would be there. She felt the blood rush into her cheeks and then closed her eyes with a sigh that changed into a sob, and then once again she fainted—but only for about half a minute.

The next sound of which she was conscious was Mackie's bark and then David's voice, close to her head.

"Pay attention, Mary, and listen to what I say. Are you all right?"

"Yes, David. I'm not hurt. Mackie is all right now and the stones have stopped slipping. That brute who stole Mackie is here."

Then Robens' voice.

"How many of you are down there? What's happened?"

David's voice was firm and strong as he answered:

"We were looking for our dog that you stole, Mr. Robens, and when we heard you coming we climbed up to the top of the cave. Our weight moved the loose stones, and one of us, Peter, fell over the edge. She's badly hurt, and I think her ankle is broken. You've got to get help quickly—plenty of ropes, and maybe a stretcher. If you go back to your cottage you'll find somebody there who will take a message to the village and telephone to Mr. Charles Sterling at Seven Gates ... My torch is smashed and this other one won't last much longer. Shine yours down so that we can see if we dare move."

Robens made no answer until he had picked them out with his torch, and then swung the beam round their prison.

"You're all right," he said at last, "but the rope I've got in the other cave won't reach you. You're at the bottom, and although I can't see far beyond, I wouldn't move far ... What about this kid here? Is she safe to leave?"

"Of course, I'm going to stay here and guard David and Peter. Mackie will help me, too, unless you've done something so beastly and foul to him that he'll go to sleep again."

David, gazing up to the rocky platform high above them, saw Robens swing the torch round until it lighted up Mary's face.

"He won't do that," he said quietly. "I haven't hurt him. I haven't hurt any of them."

"What about sending them blind?" Mary flashed. "Don't you call that hurting them, you great beastly bully? Jus' because we're stuck inside this old mountain with you and Peter's hurt, don't you think we're afraid of you. We're not. We've never been afraid of you, and if you won't go and get some help *right away* I'll jolly well go myself with Mackie. Are you going?"

Robens laughed. Laughed almost as if he'd suddenly made up his mind about something and was pleased with his decision.

"Yes, I'm going, and I'll be back soon. You kids have got plenty of pluck, anyway … Come down a little way with me, Mary, and I'll give you some candles and matches."

He leaned over the ledge and shone the torch down again.

"What's your name down there?"

"David Morton, and the girl who's hurt is Peter Sterling—Petronella. And for God's sake be quick. We've got to trust you, Mr. Robens."

Mary's clear little voice came down to them next.

"Don't worry, David. I'll be back in a sec. with some candles, and now that Mackie is all right I'm not afraid of anything … Give Peter my love."

The darkness closed again round the two huddled together on the loose stones in the unexplored cave as the echoes of Mary's voice died away.

"Did you hear all that, Pete?" David whispered. "Mary will soon be back with a light and then it can't be more than half an hour or so before we have you out of this. Is the pain very bad?"

She moved her head against his chest, not daring to trust her voice. The pain was bad, but somehow it didn't seem to matter quite as much as it had.

"Can you bear it if I move a little?" David went on. "I'm kneeling on some sharp rocks, and I'd like to make you a bit more comfortable. Maybe you could lie down if I got my jacket off and rolled it up?"

She didn't want that at all. She knew that when she moved the pain would be so sharp that she would just have to cry out. But David was already moving. The hand that had been on her hair was on the ground and he was trying to sit instead of kneel. She heard the breath whistle through his clenched teeth, and this roused her.

"David! Are you hurt, too?"

"Only uncomfortable. I've got a scrape on my leg and a bruise on the knee, and I want to stretch it a bit ... That's better. Would you like to try and lie down?"

"No," she whispered. "Stay like this if you can stick it, please."

He didn't seem to mind and his arm tightened round her comfortingly.

Then Mary's voice came to them eerily from above.

"I'm coming, David. I've got the candles, but I must be careful, else I shall drop the lighted one."

Peter moved her head and looked up to where a flicker of yellow light showed the ledge from which she had fallen. It seemed a long way off.

"David," she whispered suddenly, "how did you get down here? When I fell I was by myself. I mean—"

"You mean you deliberately let go of me when you thought you might drag us both over. That's what you mean, isn't it?"

She was glad he couldn't see that she was crying. She felt weak and rather silly, but it was clear enough that he must have scrambled or dropped down after her when he had seen where she had fallen. There didn't seem anything else to say.

David was quiet, too. He could not have put into words his feelings as, with Mary clinging to him and with Robens climbing up behind them, he had shone his torch down and seen Peter lying in a crumpled heap at the foot of a scree of loose stones—lying as if she would never move again. He could not even remember how he did get down to her after yelling to Mary to stay where she was, but dimly he realized that never in all his sixteen years had he felt more grown-up than in that second when he had seen her lying there so pale and still.

Mary's voice came down to them clearly.

"I'm here, David. I can't see you properly, but I'll throw down some candles and matches … How is Peter, David?"

"It's only my stupid old ankle, Mary," Peter called. "I'll be all right when we can tie it up. David is looking after me. Did Robens say how long he would be?"

"No, but I'm sure he'll hurry."

Peter's fingers tightened over David's hand. Perhaps she was wondering, as he was, whether Robens was to be trusted or whether, now that he had been discovered, he would hurry out into Greystone Dingle and never come back.

CHAPTER XII

THE END OF THE ADVENTURE

THREE days later, at four o'clock in the afternoon, a large party began to assemble at Seven Gates. Once again the Lone Piners' HQ2 was transformed into a banqueting hall with a long trestle-table set down the centre, and with forms and chairs borrowed from the house ready for the guests. The table was laid for fourteen.

Uncle Micah and Aunt Carol were in the house getting ready; but the Lone Piners, except Peter, had been waiting on the top gate for half an hour.

"You're sure she's all right now, David?" Jenny asked for the third time. "I mean, it is safe for her to come home?"

"Of course it is. They wouldn't let her come if it wasn't. Charles saw her this morning and said on the 'phone that her ankle and leg is in plaster and she can hobble with a stick. He says she's fine and can't think why they kept her in bed for two days ... But I know why."

"Why?" Tom asked.

"I asked my father when I saw him yesterday, and he said because of shock."

"I had shock, too," Mary explained. "Aunt Carol put me to bed in the spare room as soon as we got home. I don't suppose any of you have ever seen her spare room, and I would like to tell you that it's most peculiar with very old, *frightening* sort of furniture and a bed with iron bars and brass knobs, and a wallpaper that makes you blink ... She gave me some aspirins, and I slept a very long time, and now I haven't got any shock at all—just like our darling Mackie here," and she jumped off the gate and flung herself on the Scottie, who was sitting with his head on one side watching the track between the pine trees.

Dickie looked at his twin admiringly. He was very proud of the part she had played in the adventure—and so was David, which was why he did not blame her now for boasting a little.

"I don't know what we shall say to Peter when she does come," Jenny went on. "I think she's the bravest and most wonderful girl I've ever known. I'm sure we all do, and I think we ought—"

David looked horrified. "We can't do or say anything now, Jenny. Peter would never forgive us. We've just got to be what we always are ... I can hear a car coming."

They climbed off the gate and ran down the track to greet Mr. and Mrs. Morton from Witchend.

"Is she back yet, David?" his mother said as she disentangled herself from her twins.

"Not yet. We're expecting them now. Charles has got Mr. Sterling with him, of course, and they're going to Bishop's Castle on the way to pick up Trudie. He telephoned this morning after he'd been to the hospital and before he went to the police station. He says she's fine, considering everything."

Then they heard the sound of the estate van's horn from the bottom of the hill.

"I'll get the car into the farmyard out of the way," Mr. Morton said. "We mustn't interfere with a triumphant home-coming. I suppose we shan't be allowed to say it to her face, but we all say 'God bless Peter', don't we?"

Nobody found the words to answer this question, and as the car drove into the yard Mr. and Mrs. Sterling came out to meet them. Then, almost before they were ready, Charles, with his Uncle Jasper Sterling beside him, brought Peter back to all those who loved her.

The twins, with Mackie barking wildly with excitement, rushed to the door at the back of the van.

Peter was sitting, propped up with cushions, on a camp-bed with her left leg, stiff in plaster, stretched out before her. Trudie, all smiles, was sitting beside her.

Mary was first in and smothered Peter's rather breathless "Hullo" with a hug. Jenny took a quick look at her and saw with a shock that she was very pale. Perhaps they hadn't realized what an ordeal she had been through? But David must have known. Jenny looked round for him, wondering how he would greet Peter. Jenny was interested in things like that! But David was with Peter's father, who had just got out and was raising his hat to Aunt Carol. When he had shaken hands with her and with his brother Micah, he turned to David.

"Petronella has not told me much about your escapade," he said, "but I gather that you followed her down into an unknown cave after her fall and did everything you could for her and helped her to keep her courage up. I am sure you kept your head, my boy, and I am sure you helped my girl. I am grateful."

David flushed. "She's got more courage than all the rest of us put together, sir. Did she tell you that she deliberately let go of me when she was slipping because she thought she might drag Mary and me down with her? Did she tell you that, Mr. Sterling?"

The old man looked back at his only daughter laughing up at Jenny and Tom, and then shook his head slowly.

"No," he whispered. "No. Of course she would not tell me that, but now that I know I am not surprised … Thank you, my boy." His eyes—and they looked suspiciously moist—twinkled behind his old-fashioned spectacles. "You had better go and pay your respects, David."

Then Charles pushed him aside and went to the back of the van.

"I'm going to hire myself out as an ambulance," he said. "You've got to walk with your stick in a sec, Peter, but I must haul the bed out first so that we can slide you out ... I don't think much of your nurse. She seems to allow you too many visitors."

David and Peter looked at each other and then laughed rather loudly, and Trudie, breaking an awkward silence, said, "Hullo, David. I hear you've been up to some odd games since I last saw you ... Let me out first and then you and Charles can play at nurse while I help to get the tea. He'll tell you the whole story soon."

Peter managed very well with her stick and hobbled across to the barn with David on one side and Tom on the other.

"Isn't this ridiculous?" she said. "I feel an old, old woman. You'll have to get a wheeled chair and push me up the dingle."

"Does it still hurt?" David said. "Sure you're all right?"

"I'd love to say I was in agony so that you would all make a terrific fuss of me, but I must tell the truth. It doesn't hurt much now, but I feel very excited and peculiar inside, and as if I'd been away for *months* instead of two days ... I think you all might have come to see me in hospital," she added with a twinkle which was not noticed by either of the boys.

"They wouldn't let us," Tom replied indignantly. "Of course we wanted to come. We all did—even David!"

"We knew your father was staying in Shrewsbury," David added, "and we did ring up, and they said it would be better if we didn't come ... We all went back to Witchend to tell them about it yesterday. Mother and Dad are here now. They wouldn't be left out of your party. Here they are."

Neither Mr. nor Mrs. Morton found it difficult to make a fuss of Peter, for they were very fond of her.

"Mary says you saved her life, darling," Mrs. Morton said as she kissed her. "I'm not sure how true that is, but we do want you to know that it's exactly what we should expect of you … Apart from that, we don't think any of you have been behaving very well—you seem to have got mixed up in some trouble."

Peter blushed. "*Please* don't say anything more about that, Mrs. Morton. I don't think the three of us want to remember that cave if we can help it, but I do think you ought to know how brave Mary was and how she never lost her head. She was wonderful … My knees are wobbly and I'd like to sit down."

Then Aunt Carol called for volunteers to help with the teapots and hot water, and Mr. Sterling came and sat down next to his daughter in the centre of the long table and patted her hand rather vaguely. Uncle Micah sat next to her on the other side and upset the plans of the Lone Piners, who all felt that she belonged to them and wanted to sit next to her.

During a short lull in the chatter during tea Tom managed to say to Charles, "S'pose you've told Peter everything on the way here. We want to hear the end of the story and what they said to you at the police station. What's happened to Robens, anyway? We ought to know that."

"I'll tell you as soon as we've finished. I offered to tell Peter, but she asked me to wait until we were together."

Jenny sighed. "Peter's inhuman over things like that. She's too good to last. I should have been so *utterly consumed* with curiosity that I wouldn't even have let Charles drive on until he'd told me everything … And before you do tell what you've found out to-day, Charles, Tom and Dickie and me think we ought to explain exactly what happened before you arrived at Greystone End that awful afternoon."

"That's a good idea," Peter said. "I'm the only one who doesn't know anything at all. I want to know what's happened to Mr. Cantor and to the Doctor and—oh! I want to know everything, and then I'd like to forget it for the rest of the holidays. Anyhow,

I don't want to remember that cave and I never want to go inside Jenny's neglected mountain again."

"Jenny's what?" Mr. Morton said as he passed his cigarette-case to Trudie.

Jenny went rather pink.

"It's just a name I made up for it, Mr. Morton. I hate it more than ever now. It doesn't like being interfered with, and now it's hurt Peter and David."

"It's a good name, Jenny, and perhaps you're right about leaving it alone. There's generally a reason for superstition. I'm going to forbid you all to go into any of those caves again, and I'm sure I shan't change my mind when I've heard the whole story … Who's going to begin?"

Charles looked at Jenny, who nodded brightly to Tom.

"You begin, Tom. I'll help you if you forget, but you were really in charge of us, so you ought to tell the story."

Tom hated this sort of limelight and looked down at his plate as he began to speak.

"We had a jolly boring morning, really. We just called in at Mr. Ellis's baker's shop on our way down and heard that Johnny's puppy could see again and was none the worse, and then, when we got to the wood, Jenny and Dickie went one way and I went the other, so that we came up to the cottage from different directions. I went round so that I could spy on the back of the house and the other two hid in the bracken near the track which leads down to it."

He looked up then and grinned at the grown-ups.

"We've got a secret signal for each other," he went on, "and we planned that if there wasn't anything to spy on I'd give the signal and they would answer, and then we'd join up and make some plans. That's what happened. I crept up to the back and had a good nose round, but there wasn't a sight or a sound of anybody, except that Robens' car was still standing at the side of the house, which seemed rather rum to me. I tried both doors, but they were locked. I could see through the window that the downstair room was in a muddle like Peter said, but I was sure that Mackie wasn't there … Seems funny when I think of it again, but I couldn't get rid of the idea that Robens wasn't very far away, else why should he leave his car?"

"I don't think he knew what to do with it," Charles interrupted. "If he'd left it up the dingle nearer the cave it might have given the game away. Perhaps he thought that if he wanted to escape in a hurry the car would be useful … But go on, Tom. Or what about you, Jenny?"

"Well," Jenny said as she sat up very straight and serious, "I don't mind telling you what happened next, although it isn't at all dramatic or romantic … Nothing happened except that Dickie and me found a fine hideout and nearly got eaten by flies and skeeters and all the terrible insects which lurk in bracken. We swore we'd never hide in bracken again … Tom was very quiet, and we didn't hear him until he gave the signal, and then we all hid in the same place where we could see anyone coming down the track, and got bitten worse than ever. The time went slowly, but soon Tom made us split up and keep on walking round the cottage through the wood while one stayed on guard in the bracken. It was hot and we got tired and a bit snappy, but all the time Tom said that if Robens didn't come back somebody else might, and that, anyway, we'd promised to stay round about here until David or Peter or Mary came down to meet us."

"I ought to go on now," Tom said, while Dickie looked as if he was going to explode because he had not been invited to speak. "I may as well own up, that I did an awful thing in the afternoon, although I don't believe that it made any difference to what had happened."

They all looked at him in astonishment.

"After we'd had our grub," he went on, "we got jolly thirsty. We were fools not to bring something to drink, but we went off in a hurry and never thought of it. You know how it is when you're thirsty and haven't got a drink? You think of cold ginger beer and iced coca-cola, and it just gets worse and worse. I told Jenny and Dickie to go back to Barton and have a drink and bring back three or four more bottles. They promised to go very carefully and keep off the track just in case Robens came back that way, and I don't think they were more than an hour. I just sat in our hideout and watched the front of the house, and I think I went to sleep. I don't remember going off and I don't remember waking up. I was awake when they came back with the bottles of pop, but I've thought since that I must have dropped off, because I'm as certain as I can be that when we had our sandwiches the garden gate was closed, and when I looked at it again while I was drinking it was wide open. It didn't dawn on me then, but I was sure when David told me that Robens wasn't in the cave when they first went in that he had been back to the cottage for something and that I'd been a feeble flop and missed him. I don't feel too good about it, but you *can* go off to sleep and not realize it, can't you?"

"Of course you can, Tom," Peter said quickly. "We all do it sometimes. I've often been to sleep on Sally's back. Don't you worry, Tom. You had the most boring part of the job, and we all think you were wonderful about it."

"It didn't matter, Tom," Charles put in. "Robens did come back for some chemicals he'd forgotten. He told me that he wasn't in the house three minutes, so I don't expect you did more than doze off. He didn't come down the track you were guarding, you see—he came down the dingle."

"I was a bigger fool than I thought, then," Tom said glumly.

"I ought to have kept a sentry down there, but I knew Jenny and Dickie were fed up."

"I was *not*, Tom," Jenny said indignantly. "You kept on telling us that we were doing a jolly important job. I got bitten worse than you, and I was jolly thirsty, but I wasn't fed up."

"I was," Dickie said morosely. "It was the most stupid thing I've ever had to do. Mary and me never ought to have gone separate."

"Richard!" his mother protested. "What grammar!"

"Well, we never ought," he persisted, "but it did get more exciting soon after we got back with the drinks. Shall I tell it? Good ... After a bit Tom said we would go down nearer the house, and we found another hiding-place behind a bank under some pine trees. And then do you know what happened?"

"Yes," David said. "Buck up!"

"You don't. Two things happened. The first thing was that man Robens came running through the trees from the dingle and rushed up and opened the front door with a key, and while we were all wondering what to do there was a fut-fut-fut behind us and down the track came that fat chap who said he was a doctor. He was on a bike which looked too small for him and which has one of those little motor things on the back wheel ... That's just what I want, Dad. I know how worried you and Mummy get about our birthday time. Mary would like one of those, too, so you don't have to worry any more 'bout our birthday presents."

"Thank you, Richard," his father said politely. "Please go on."

"*Well.* We weren't close enough to hear everything they said, but we saw Robens come out of the house with a coil of rope and wave his hands at the doctor chap as if he didn't want to see him, and we thought we heard him say something like, 'One of those kids has had an accident in the mine'."

"It did sound like that," Tom interrupted. "I think Dickie thought it might be Mary and he dashed out of our hiding-place and we just had to follow him. When we got down there he was dancing round both men, shouting, 'Who's hurt in the mine? What's happened?' I must say the Doctor is a very poor type. His language was disgusting and he didn't like Dickie a bit. Robens looked queer, and he was very rude to the other man. 'Do what you like,' he said. 'Go and live in there. I can't leave that girl at the bottom of that hole. I think she may have broken her leg.' Then he looked at us and said, 'I expected to find you about. One of you go and tell Mr. Charles Sterling,' and before I had time to be surprised there was Charles coming down the track in a car with old Cantor and a bobby beside him … You could have knocked me down with a fevver," Tom finished unexpectedly.

"You ought not to allow these children to get mixed up in this sort of thing, Charles," Aunt Carol said, and Peter hobbled round the table and kissed her.

"Now I'd better take over," Charles said. "I suppose you know that we weren't very pleased when we found Peter's note in the kitchen telling us that you weren't coming back without the dog, but I had promised to wait in until Cantor telephoned or called for me. Detective-Sergeant Green is his real name, and he's a very annoying little man, although he's a very cute one. He 'phoned from Shrewsbury, I imagine, about ten o'clock and asked for Peter because he wanted a first-hand description of the Doctor. He was annoyed when I told him I didn't know where any of you were, but I repeated what you told me about him. He didn't say much, but I thought he was interested and then, for the life of me, I couldn't remember the name of the road where we followed Robens, but I thought the house was called The Oaks."

"You're hopeless, Charles," Peter laughed. "We shall have to give you some lessons in detecting."

"True enough, Peter. I asked him whether he wanted me to go and watch Greystone End, and he said no need to bother, but that he'd call for me later, and rang off. We weren't really worried about you kids—Carol was, I suppose—but I didn't like hanging about the farm all day waiting for Cantor, but I promised to do so. When he did turn up with the policeman he told me that the Doctor was the man he wanted and that the police had been looking for him for a long time for something much more serious, and that they had followed him as far as Barton on his motor-bike thing just to see what he was up to. The Doctor was certainly surprised and angry when he saw the policeman and Cantor—we shall always call him by that name, shan't we?—outside the cottage. He turned on Robens, as Tom and the others know, but Robens just didn't seem to care and looked mildly exasperated because we wouldn't pay immediate attention to him. I was astonished when he asked me if I was Charles Sterling and told me about Peter, although you others had all been trying to tell me for five minutes. I've seen Cantor in Shrewsbury this morning and he's told me a lot. What would you like to know?"

"I'd like to know first how you rescued me so quickly, although it seemed an awful long time waiting at the bottom of that hole," Peter said. "I don't know what we should have done without those candles and Mary being so brave up above there with Mackie. She sang to us most of the time, and then we talked to each other about our other adventures, and particularly about Jon and Penny … I didn't talk much, though. I didn't feel like it."

"What did you sing, twin?"

"It's quite 'straordinary the things I forgot," Mary said. "I remembered 'My boy, Billy' and 'Onward Christian Soldiers,' and some of the silly things they sing on the radio, and I recited most of 'John Gilpin was a citizen of credit an' renown,' and I wish I knew where Edmonton is, although David once saw it on a bus in London."

"Yes, I remember John Gilpin, Mary. What else happened, Charles?"

"Cantor and the bobby took off the Doctor after the detective had spoken to Robens—I didn't hear what he said—promising to send back another car and help from the village after I'd explained where you were and what had happened. Then Robens and I scrounged round the house, but we didn't bring much more because that extraordinary chap said he'd got blankets in the cave. We were short of torches, as you know, but it was Jenny who ran back here to warn Carol and bring the brandy flask. Anyway, Peter, with David's help we got you up, and although I don't think you remember much about it, you came out of the mine mostly on my back, and when there was room for two abreast Robens or David helped. The car from the village was up the dingle ready for you, and within half an hour you'd seen a real doctor, and not so very much later you were tucked up in hospital. I expect your father told you that David, after all he'd been through—and he was feeling fairly groggy—tried to persuade us to let him walk up to Hatchholt to tell him all about it?"

"I knew," Peter whispered. "I don't know why everyone is so wonderful to me. I can't tell you how happy I'm feeling at this minute. Now tell us about Robens and whether what we guessed about him and the Doctor is true. What's the Doctor's real name, anyway?"

"I forget what Cantor called him. William Harris, I think. So far as I can find out, there isn't much harm in Robens and the police haven't anything against him except the stealing of dogs. There's no doubt that he's a very odd, highly-strung sort of chap, with dreams of being a famous scientist some day. I think he'd done something wrong or foolish when this man Harris got hold of him and offered him money if he could work on this idea. As soon as he was arrested Harris tried to put the blame on Robens, and then the latter volunteered to tell the police everything. I don't know all the story, but apparently Harris was so sure that there was a lot of money in the sale of this formula for making watchdogs helpless that he was prepared to spend a lot to get it. The original scheme was to find a quiet place for Robens to work in Ireland, and Harris, who had been trying hard for some weeks to get up Robens' enthusiasm, chartered the private plane which got into trouble and came down on the Long Mynd. Robens admits that he was very tired and overworked and that just before the final crash he got out of his safety strap and then banged his head as the plane came down, and after that, as he told Peter, he just couldn't remember who he was for a bit, although he realized he mustn't give anything away."

"Now I understand why they were both so curious about where we lived," Peter interrupted. "I s'pose that after they saw the Mynd and this country they felt there was no need to go to Ireland to find a lonely place to work ... What else do you know, Charles? I don't think Robens is too bad except for his beastly habit of experimenting on dogs. P'raps he'll be all right now he's got rid of Harris. I wonder if he completed the experiment? Mackie seemed doped, didn't he?"

"He said he's going to tear up everything he's discovered. I dare say he'll keep his word. I think he will. He was decent enough to you in the cave, wasn't he?"

"He was terrified of Mary, I think," David said. "He wouldn't have dared do anything else but help us. I still think he was a bit crazy, and I can't understand why a young, clever chap like that should be so short of money that he has to join up with a crook, because that's what Harris was. At one time we thought he was scared of him."

"There was something else, as I said just now," Charles admitted. "It's not our business, and I know he's told the police everything. He may have been scared of Harris once, but he wasn't at the end. He was weak, but he always despised him, and I'm sure he's thankful to be free of him."

"So are we," Jenny said. "We all hated him, but the twins got the better of him at his house. I wish I'd been there."

"It was a good performance," Peter admitted. "I had a front seat ... Daddy darling, I'll come home with you to-night if some of the strong men can carry me up Hatchholt."

"She'll do no such thing, Jasper," Aunt Carol said indignantly. "She'll stay under this roof until that ankle is well enough to carry her up that rough track to Hatchholt without the risk of a tumble."

"We'll fit her in somewhere at Witchend if that would be more convenient," Mrs. Morton said, and then caught a glimpse of Mr. Sterling's face. "Poor Mr. Sterling. He never seems to have his daughter with him. Everybody is so fond of her that they want to keep her. I'm sure you're very proud of her really."

"Very kind. Very proud," Mr. Sterling murmured, and managed not to look embarrassed when Peter kissed him.

"I've had enough adventure for a week or two," she said. "I want to come back to Hatchholt just as soon as I can—and thank you all for giving me such a lovely welcome to-day, and thank you, Aunt Carol and Uncle Micah, for being so kind to me and so generous to all us Lone Piners because we're always eating your food when we come here to camp."

Dickie, who had been silent far too long, jumped on to his

chair and called, "Three cheers for the grown-ups," and then the party began to break up.

Mr. and Mrs. Morton arranged to take Mr. Sterling back to Witchend and then Tom said, "Could you find room for Jenny's haversack, please? I'm cycling back to Ingles with her to-night because Uncle Alf starts on the harvest to-morrow, and she's going to help us."

"What about you three?" Mr. Morton asked his children.

"We'll stay to-night, Father," David said. "Peter has to sleep indoors, of course, but Mary can bring her sleeping-bag down and sleep in Tom's cubicle … Don't you worry about us, Tom and Jenny. We'll pack up in the morning, and if you want to get off soon we'll help Aunt Carol get the worst of this cleared up to-night."

"*Of* course," Dickie remarked. "Always call on us. Mary and me are just Old Faithfuls."

"*Never* complainin'," Mary added. "Just always working and willing like two little—two little—"

"Nuisances," Tom finished for her. "Let's all help get these tables cleared up, anyway. We haven't got to go yet … What are we going to do with Peter? We ought to build her a sort of throne out here so that she can be comfortable and yet see what's going on."

"You're going in to bed soon, my dear," Aunt Carol said. "You must be tired out, but you can stay here until the others have gone."

They cleared the tables and stacked them along one side of the barn, and then Mr. and Mrs. Morton and Mr. Sterling went. Peter sat at the scullery door and watched the rest of the Lone Piners deal with one of their very biggest washings-up and rather enjoyed herself. When that job was done Tom and Jenny said they must go.

"Take me over to the gate," Peter suggested. "I'll stay there for a bit and see you off, and then I s'pose I ought to go in. I'm tired."

Tom and David gave her a bandy chair across the rough farmyard and then found a bale of straw for her to sit on. The twins followed with Mackie and perched themselves, as usual, on the top bar of the gate and cheered when Jenny appeared with her bicycle and a green beret on the back of her head.

"Bet your tyres want blowing up," Dickie said. "And betcher I don't do them. You'll have to ask Tommy. He'll wear himself out blowing up your tyres."

"He *likes* doing them," Jenny protested, at which the twins jumped off the gate and rolled on the ground in helpless laughter while Mackie barked round them. But when Tom arrived with threatening gestures they fled, still laughing, into the wood.

"I want to say how wonderful it is to have you back safe again, Peter," Jenny said, while Tom got to work with the bicycle pump, "and you do understand about the harvest, don't you? Mr. Ingles says he'll never manage without me ... And—I nearly forgot—Dad and Mum said they're glad you're better and that we're all to keep away from the caves in future."

"Nobody else has to tell us that, do they, Peter?" David said. "We've had enough of your neglected mountain, Jenny ... Cheerio. We'll call in and see the farmers at work to-morrow or the next day. Maybe we'll come and give you a hand with the stooking, and Peter, in a lovely sunbonnet, can lounge in the shade and watch us ... See you soon."

As they disappeared down the track he came back and sat on the bale next to Peter.

"What a day! Sure you're all right, Peter?"

"Of course. The leg aches and so does my head a bit, but it's been so exciting. What a long time ago it all seems, David, and it's only three days."

"Let's forget it. It's all over now."

"I don't know that I do want to forget all of it ... David, this isn't the first adventure we've finished here at Seven Gates, is it? I remember the first day I came here and how scared I was. That was the day I met Jenny for the first time, and I never guessed what it would mean to all of us ... David. Before the twins come back I want you to know that I wouldn't have had any courage at all in that horrible pit if you hadn't been with me. You just made the difference. I knew it would be all right in the end."

Before he could answer, Charles and Trudie, arm in arm, came out into the farmyard, and the twins came out of the wood and climbed on to the gate again.

Trudie flashed them a smile and sat down next to Peter as David got up.

"I've come to offer you a job, Peter," she said as she put her arm round her shoulders. "It's a special job, and I hope you'll say yes. Next Christmas."

"A job? For me? What do you mean?"

"You're the nearest sister I've got, Peter. Will you please be my bridesmaid? I should love it if you would and Charles is so keen that I'm nearly jealous."

Peter blushed.

"But, Trudie! It's wonderful of you, but surely there's somebody more important? Someone you've known longer? And I'm only sixteen and—"

"And there's nobody I want more ... Don't be ridiculous, Peter! We'll have a grand wedding, won't we?"

David found himself shaking hands at the same time with Charles and Trudie, while Peter seemed to be crying. The twins took the news much more calmly.

"It will be the first Lone Pine wedding we've ever had," Mary said with a certain amount of relish, and later, after Charles and Trudie had gone out for their stroll and Peter and David were sitting on the bale of straw again, Dickie said,

"It's a funny thing how all us families seem to have got mixed up together. First there was Peter, and now these Seven Gates people, and Jenny's family a little, and Uncle Alf Ingles and now, because of Charles, there's Trudie. I quite like it, but it gets a bit confusin'. All the same, Peter really seems to belong to us now."

Mary paused before she answered.

"Yes," she said at last. "That's right, twin. When I was in that awful cave waiting for you all to come and rescue us I was sure that Peter will always belong to our family."

"What do you mean, Mary?"

She looked at him and then across to her elder brother.

"Sometimes little boys are very silly," she laughed.

THE END

Written at Toft House,
Downside Road, Guildford.
May-July, 1952.

The other books about
the Lone Pine Club are
MYSTERY AT WITCHEND
SEVEN WHITE GATES
THE GAY DOLPHIN ADVENTURE
THE SECRET OF GREY WALLS
LONE PINE FIVE
THE ELUSIVE GRASSHOPPER
The next book in this series will be about Jon and Penny.

APPENDIX I: ERRORS IN THE FIRST EDITION

The first edition contained a few typographical errors, and here we explain what we have done about them.

We have changed an occurrence of 'the the' to 'the', a single quotation mark to a double one, the first full stop to a comma in 'hurry up. Tom.' on page 193, a single instance of 'Robins' to the usual 'Robens', and 'the Lone Piner's job' to 'the Lone Piners' job' on page 219 (where it was clear that the plural was meant). We have deleted 'a' in 'there was a no spirit' (p227) and the apostrophe in 'he let's himself down' (p251).

In two places 'the top of Mynd' occurred, and we have inserted 'the' to match the normal style. We have inserted ', who' after 'Jenny' in the sentence beginning 'They all had bicycles' on page 70, and 'of' in 'one them insisted' on page 132.

We have standardised the spellings of 'hols', 'HQ2' and 'to wash-up'. Interestingly, 'hols.', 'H.Q.2' and 'to wash up' occurred only in Chapter I—if the inconsistencies were the author's, it might suggest that he paused in writing the book.

We were unable to standardise 'horse(-)meat' and 'pipe(-)line' because each variant occurred the same number of times.

The word 'cluttered' on pages 162, 243 and 254 might be a mistake for 'clattered', but we could not be sure of this, so we have left it as it was. Similarly, we have left the apostrophe in 'clothes' pegs', we have not corrected the grammar of the sentence beginning 'They rode on down' on page 134, we have not changed 'curb' to 'kerb' on page 200, or 'dare' to 'dared' in 'as quickly as he dare' (p222), and we have not altered '"Let's go Greystone"' on page 159.

Sarah Woodall
2009

APPENDIX II: MATERIAL FROM THE SECOND ARMADA EDITION

FOREWORD

EVEN if you've never read any of the other adventures of the boys and girls who founded the Lone Pine Club, and who are now known in many parts of the world as the Lone Piners, you will find this story complete in itself.

All the Lone Piners' adventures are set in parts of Britain which you can visit yourself. The scene of this story is in the wild and lonely border country between Wales and Shropshire, hard by a mountain known as the Stiperstones. It is said that the curious outcrop of black quartzite rocks on the summit, known as the Devil's Chair, is one of the oldest parts of England—older even than the ice age—and it is little wonder that this desolate, neglected country is rich in folk-lore and legend.

You will find the Stiperstones and the Long Mynd, with its Gliding Station, on the map and you can go to Shrewsbury, to Clun, Craven Arms and Bishop's Castle and explore them for yourself. But you will not find Black Dingle or Greystone Dingle or Barton Beach for these places are as imaginary as are all the characters in this adventure, which I hope you will enjoy.

M.S.

THE LONE PINE CLUB

The Lone Pine Club was founded as a secret society at a lonely house called Witchend in a hidden valley of the Long Mynd in Shropshire. The first headquarters of the Club was a clearing, marked by a solitary pine tree, on the slopes of this valley. The original rules of the Club are very simple and are set out in full in *Mystery at Witchend*, which is the first story about the Lone Piners and was written over twenty years ago.

There are now nine members of the Lone Pine Club, but it is not usual for them all to appear in one story. The following appear in this one:

David Morton: .Age 16. Is captain and co-founder of the Lone Pine Club. He goes to a boarding school and his home is in London.

Richard (Dickie) and Mary Morton: David's ten-year-old brother and sister who are 'look alike' twins. They are inseparable except when at their separate boarding schools.

Petronella (Peter) Sterling: Just 16. Really the founder of the Club. Has lived in the Shropshire hills all her life and goes to boarding school in Shrewsbury. She has no mother and in the holidays lives with her father who is in charge of a reservoir called Hatchholt, not very far from Witchend. She is David's special friend.

Tom Ingles: A sixteen-year-old Londoner who now lives and works on his uncle's farm near Witchend.

Jenny Harman: 15. Tom's special friend who lives with her father and stepmother at Barton Beach where they keep the local general store and post office. Jenny has lived in Shropshire all her life.

Macbeth: The Mortons' Scottie dog who long ago was made an honorary member of the Club.

The other members are: Jonathan (Jon) Warrender, only son of Mrs. Warrender who owns the *Gay Dolphin* in Rye, Penelope (Penny) Warrender, Jon's cousin who is living at the *Gay Dolphin* while her parents are abroad; and Harriet Sparrow—a special friend of the twins—who lives in London.

COMPLETE BIBLIOGRAPHY

1. *Mystery at Witchend*, London, Newnes (1943)
2. *Seven White Gates*, London, Newnes (1944)
3. *Country Scrap-Book for Boys and Girls*, London, National Magazine Company (1944)
4. *Trouble at Townsend*, London, Transatlantic Arts/Hyperion (1945)
5. *Open Air Scrap-Book for Boys and Girls*, London, Gramol (1945)
6. *The Gay Dolphin Adventure*, London, Newnes (1945)
7. *Seaside Scrap-Book for Boys and Girls*, London & Chesham, Gramol (1946)
8. *Jane's Country Year*, London, Newnes (1946)
9. *The Riddle of the Painted Box*, London, Transatlantic Arts/Royle (1947)
10. *The Secret of Grey Walls*, London, Newnes (1947)
11. *Redshank's Warning*, London, Lutterworth Press (1948)
12. *Two Fair Plaits*, London, Lutterworth Press (1948)
13. *Strangers at Snowfell*, London, Lutterworth Press (1949)
14. *Lone Pine Five*, London, Newnes (1949)
15. *The Master of Maryknoll*, London, Evans Brothers (1950)
16. *The Flying Fish Adventure*, London, John Murray (1950)
17. *The Sign of the Alpine Rose*, London, Lutterworth Press (1950)
18. *The Adventure of the Life-Boat Service*, London, Macdonald (1950)
19. *The Elusive Grasshopper*, London, Newnes (1951)
20. *All Summer Through*, London, Hodder & Stoughton (1951)
21. *The Luck of Sallowby*, London, Lutterworth Press (1952)
22. *The Buckinghams at Ravenswyke*, London, Evans (1952)
23. *The Coronation Gift Book for Boys & Girls*, London, Daily Graphic/Pitkin Pictorials (1952)
24. *The Ambermere Treasure*, London, Lutterworth Press (1953)
25. *The Secret of the Hidden Pool*, London, John Murray (1953)
26. *The Neglected Mountain*, London, Newnes (1953)
27. *Christmas at Nettleford*, London, Hodder & Stoughton (1953)
28. *The Long Passage*, London, Evans (1954)

29. *Susan, Bill and the Wolf Dog*, London, Nelson (1954)
30. *Susan, Bill and the Ivy Clad Oak*, London, Nelson (1954)
31. *Spring Comes to Nettleford*, London, Hodder & Stoughton (1954)
32. *Susan, Bill and the Vanishing Boy*, London, Nelson (1955)
33. *Susan, Bill and the Golden Clock*, London, Nelson (1955)
34. *Saucers Over the Moor,* London, Newnes (1955)
35. *The Secret of Buzzard Scar*, London, Hodder & Stoughton (1955)
36. *Where the Bus Stopped*, Oxford, Blackwell (1956)
37. *Susan, Bill and the Dark Stranger*, London, Nelson (1956)
38. *Susan, Bill and the Saucy Kate*, London, Nelson (1956)
39. *Wings Over Witchend,* London, Newnes (1956)
40. *Young Johnnie Bimbo*, London, John Murray (1956)
41. *Treasure at the Mill*, London, Newnes (1957)
42. *Lone Pine London*, London, Newnes (1957)
43. *The Fourth Key*, London, John Murray (1957)
44. *The Secret of the Gorge*, London, Newnes (1958)
45. *King of Kings*, London, Nelson (1958)
46. *Four-and-Twenty Blackbirds*, London, Newnes (1959)
47. *Small Creatures*, London, Ward (1959)
48. *Mystery Mine,* London, Newnes (1959)
49. *Susan, Bill and the Bright Star Circus*, London, Nelson (1960)
50. *Sea Witch Comes Home*, London, Newnes (1960)
51. *Susan, Bill and the Pirates Bold*, London, Nelson (1961)
52. *Malcolm Saville's Country Book*, London, Cassell (1961)
53. *Malcolm Saville's Seaside Book*, London, Cassell (1962)
54. *Not Scarlet But Gold*, London, Newnes (1962)
55. *A Palace for the Buckinghams*, London, Evans (1963)
56. *Three Towers in Tuscany*, London, Heinemann (1963)
57. *Treasure at Amorys*, London, Newnes (1964)
58. *The Purple Valley*, London, Heinemann (1964)
59. *Dark Danger*, London, Heinemann (1965)
60. *The Thin Grey Man*, London, Macmillan (1966)
61. *Man With Three Fingers*, London, Newnes (1966)
62. *White Fire*, London, Heinemann (1966)

63. *Come to London*, London, Heinemann (1967)
64. *The Secret of Galleybird Pit*, London, Armada (1967)
65. *Strange Story*, London, Mowbrays (1967)
66. *Power of Three*, London, Heinemann (1968)
67. *Come to Devon*, London, Benn (1969)
68. *Come to Cornwall*, London, Benn (1969)
69. *Rye Royal*, London, Collins (1969)
70. *Come to Somerset*, London, Benn (1970)
71. *The Dagger and the Flame*, London, Heinemann (1970)
72. *Strangers at Witchend*, London, Collins (1970)
73. *Good Dog Dandy*, London, Armada (1971)
74. *See How It Grows*, London, Oxford University Press (1971)
75. *The Secret of the Villa Rosa*, London, Collins (1971)
76. *Where's My Girl?*, London, Collins (1972)
77. *The Roman Treasure Mystery*, London, Armada (1973)
78. *Diamond in the Sky*, London, Collins (1974)
79. *Eat What You Grow*, London, Carousel/Transworld (1975)
80. *Portrait of Rye*, East Grinstead, Henry Goulden (1976)
81. *The Story of Winchelsea Church*, Winchelsea, Winchelsea Church (1978)
82. *Marston—Master Spy*, London, Heinemann (1978)
83. *Wonder Why Book of Exploring a Wood*, London, Transworld (1978)
84. *The Countryside Quiz*, London, Carousel/Transworld (1978)
85. *Home to Witchend*, London, Armada (1978)
86. *Wonder Why Book of Exploring the Seashore*, London, Transworld (1979)
87. *Words For All Seasons*, Guildford, Lutterworth Press (1979)
88. *Wonder Why Book of Wild Flowers Through the Year*, London, Transworld (1980)
89. *The Seashore Quiz*, London, Carousel (1981)
90. *The Silent Hills of Shropshire*, Worcester, Mark O'Hanlon (1998)
91. *The Flower-show Hat* in *The Guide Gift Book*, Worcester (1950), Malcolm Saville Society (2001)

Girls Gone By Publishers

Girls Gone By Publishers republish some of the most popular children's fiction from the 20th century, concentrating on those titles which are most sought after and difficult to find on the second-hand market. We aim to make them available at affordable prices, thus making ownership possible for both existing collectors and new ones so that the books continue to survive. Authors on our list include Margaret Biggs, Elinor Brent-Dyer, Dorita Fairlie Bruce, Gwendoline Courtney, Monica Edwards, Antonia Forest, Lorna Hill, Clare Mallory, Violet Needham, Elsie Jeanette Oxenham, Malcolm Saville and Geoffrey Trease. We also publish some new titles which continue the traditions of this genre.

Our series **'Fun in the Fourth—Outstanding Girls' School Stories'** has enabled us to broaden our range of authors, allowing our readers to discover a fascinating range of books long unobtainable. It features authors who only wrote one or two such books, a few of the best examples from more prolific authors (such as Dorothea Moore), and some very rare titles by authors whose other books are generally easy to find second-hand (such as Josephine Elder).

We also have a growing range of non-fiction: more general works about the genre and books on particular authors. These include *Island to Abbey* by Stella Waring and Sheila Ray (about Elsie Oxenham), *The Marlows and their Maker* by Anne Heazlewood (about Antonia Forest) and *The Monica Edwards Romney Marsh Companion* by Brian Parks. These are in a larger format than the fiction, and are lavishly illustrated in colour and black and white.

For details of availability and ordering (please do not order until titles are actually listed) go to www.ggbp.co.uk or write for a catalogue to Clarissa Cridland or Ann Mackie-Hunter, GGBP, 4 Rock Terrace, Coleford, Bath, BA3 5NF, UK.